About the Author

*Martin Roy Mortimer is a Cultural Anthropologist, having graduated
with honours for field work
performed through the
University of Newcastle in Australia.
A former high school teacher, he now resides in
the NSW Riverina district and has plans
to continue writing and publishing
science fiction into the future.
Watch for his next book!*

Novels by this author:
Suspended Earth
Starlight
Dance of Nevermind
Shades of Farthrow
Armada's Disciple

The Cinder Chronicles:
Flame Rangers
Ice Rangers
Sand Rangers

Short story collection by this author:
When History Fractures, Heroes Rise

Visit www.suspendedearth.com
for information about other book releases.

www.amentibooks.com

Longarm
Severed

M.R. Mortimer

First published 2015

This Edition published 2020

ISBN-13: 978-0648956310

For my sister and fellow writer Sharon,
thank you for believing.

Chapter 1 – Waking Up Dead

Theodore Longarm examined his surroundings with a villain's eye. His mind was foggy, and things seemed more than a little odd. He was seated in a small steel room.

"OK," Theodore thought. "Let's go over this from the beginning. We were lined up on the chamber floor at the UFH council chambers in Lunar City. The Starfall board were there as well, and tried to sell us out. I killed the man who was addressing the council."

One wall of the chamber shimmered oddly, and he stood to face it. Watching it carefully, he continued his summation of recent events.

"The Caretaker halted the meeting, using her veto to end Starfall, and then we were rounded up. One of the UIC troopers hit me with the tranquilliser, and the next thing I remember is this room."

Theodore walked over to the shimmering wall, his eyes narrowed as he examined it. An uneasy sense of impending loss flooded over him. He knew, somehow, that he was unlikely to escape from this place, whatever kind of prison it might be. Theodore had a firm suspicion what kind of place this was. It was like the air itself somehow tasted wrong.

With trepidation, he moved his hand towards the shimmering barrier, pressing into it as though its substance was more liquid than metal. All outward signs of his normal confidence evaporated as he continued to push against the barely resisting wall. Following his arm,

1

Theodore pushed through the wall and found himself momentarily blinded by a glaring white light. When his vision returned, he took in the scene before him, its incongruous juxtaposition an ironic proof of his true whereabouts.

A rolling green field spread before him as far as the eye could see, but right before him stood an imposing stone desk. Behind it, a uniformed warden sat watching him with impassive, inhuman eyes. His skin was a pastel pink. It was too pink to be believed. The muscles that rippled as he moved to face Theodore were in strange contrast to the friendly pacifist look of his face. Three more identical, uniformed men appeared, the air shimmering as they came into existence between Theodore and the desk.

It was clear now, he was no longer a free man. Theodore felt a new rage growing inside him. He simmered in anger, ready to fight, and something changed. His mind was suddenly, infuriatingly mellowed. His rage sank like a stone to the darkest depths of a pacifist ocean. This would be his prison, and his life. Theodore realised the totality of his doom for the first time as the smiling pink wardens took his arms and led him into the field.

While they walked through the grass, things started to creep into his perception. It was as though Theodore's brain was slowly building the sense of what was here, adding components to his world as they were processed by an overworked computer.

Slowly the field was populated. Here a man stood, polishing an object that Theodore could not yet see. There, an ice cream vending machine rose surreptitiously from the ground, thick roots pushing into the dirt. The surreal environment seemed less believable with each addition.

Theodore closed his eyes tight against the lunacy, wishing it all away. A sensation prodded at him, forcing his eyes to open unbidden, returning the madness of his surroundings to his tired brain.

Why could he not control his eyelids? How was he being made to look at this place? He willed his eyes to close again, forcing them down. As he stumbled blind, he began to feel a strange confidence. Then his eyes opened again. Theodore was angry that they did so.

"Why must I be here?" he demanded.

One of the pink wardens stepped before him, filling his vision. Its lips did not move, though Theodore was sure it was that one's voice he heard.

"We will not harm you, but you must participate. You must behave as a part of this place."

"What if I refuse?" Theodore asked, already knowing the answer.

"Then you will die."

It was said with finality, and Theodore realised that it was with no emotion that such a decree about his existence was made. Clearly he could not fight them. This was their world, and he was an unwelcome visitor.

*   *   *

"It's a game, see?" the filthy man said, his eyes darting among the pink wardens who patrolled a short distance away. "And I refuse to play. At least, not by their rules."

Theodore frowned, looking at the strange little man who had grabbed his arm and dragged him away as soon as the wardens began wandering back to the desk area, their charge released into the now fully populated field.

Tents, huts, small shop stands, all manner of temporary structure stood scattered in the grassy area. Mud was tracked inside the few buildings at the centre, which Theodore glanced nervously inside as they walked. Theodore looked at the man.

"Who are you?" he asked.

The man was briefly taken aback, a shocked expression on his face as he stared in anger at the newcomer. After a moment, the anger faded from his eyes and the old man shook his head, looking back down to the ground at his feet as they trudged along.

"It does not matter in the slightest who I am. At this stage, it is best you never know."

"OK, then at least tell me something of this place?"

Theodore asked in frustration.

"Oh this?" the old man asked, looking around as though seeing things for the first time. "It's only the Welcoming Fields. Some people never leave them. But be careful here. I think the wardens keep it artificially crowded, to lull you into a sense of anonymity. It's like a test, to see if you will rebel or conform. If you conform, you will move on faster. To the town. That's like, the next level. Or something. Ignore my words though, I'm just an old fool."

"So why are you here?" Theodore said, pressing for information. "If you know so much, why aren't you in a higher level? Assuming this is a game like you say."

The old man's eyes burrowed into Theodore's soul, and found a nest in there. Theodore shuddered, and tore his gaze away, wrenching possession of that deeper place back from the sinister creature. The old man laughed, a dry cackle that sounded sickly and powerful at the same time. His voice then came to Theodore almost like his own thoughts, echoing in his mind more than his ears. It felt invasive. A violation of his mind and soul that sent a cold shiver down his spine.

"Oh, I have my reasons. Just because you leave a place, does not mean you can't return. After all, none of us will ever escape from this world. You may as well forget everything you knew before. This is your home now. Best you learn to be a part of it."

The man's grip on Theodore's arm relented, and he turned to where the old man stood. The wrinkled ruin of a man was gone. He vanished as silently as he had appeared. In his place, Theodore found a darkened opening, the doorway into a large, rust coloured tent.

A wooden plaque hung over the opening. Theodore read it twice as his mind seemed to slowly fill in the faded colours of a filigree pattern that was painted behind the words.

"Admissions and inductions, Office of the guild warden," it said on that swaying wooden board.

Theodore stepped inside, his legs operating of their own volition, as though his body were an automaton and

4

his mind merely along for the ride.

* * *

"Welcome, Theodore, to Claustrum Mundus," called a pink warden in cheerful tones. "This is your home now, until such time as you stop living."

Theodore waited for his eyes to grow accustomed to the dim light in the tent. It was sparsely furnished, with the pink faced warden sitting in the only chair. This warden's uniform was different to the others, black with silver badges.

As the details of the warden's uniform became clear, Theodore stepped forward. He held his face calm and rigid, not wishing to let his innermost feelings show. Theodore knew what he felt was the tip of an iceberg. He sensed a lack of control over his own destiny, and feared the true depths of his own submission.

Soft laughter filled the tent as the Warden smiled. His voice was sinister in its quiet peace.

"Your mind speaks volumes through the system. Do not try to fool me with your face, Theodore. I can see deep into your mind. Like all wardens I am one with this place."

Theodore shuddered, and looked around at the dirty brown walls. Anything was better than looking at that plasticine textured creature who controlled his fate. The warden coughed, then appeared in front of him, his plastic proboscis nearly touching Theodore's nose.

"Teddy boy, it is time for you to begin," the warden said, in perfect imitation of Theodore's late father.

Theodore shuddered at the intense effect the voice had on him. His knees trembled momentarily as he recoiled from the warden. Sudden shock washed over him as the memories of regular beatings as a child filled his mind.

The warden smiled, that same voice slipping like a vine's gripping tendril from between his lips.

"That's right Teddy boy, remember what it was like to be treated like an animal. The sooner you give in, the sooner your punishment can begin."

Theodore looked at the warden, sudden tears in his eyes. Uninvited, they streamed down his face while his expression remained stony, the tears belying his staunch efforts to remain unmoved. The memories came and went, unbidden and uncontrolled. Theodore was not even sure they were his own.

"That's it," the warden sneered. "Suffer for your crimes, Teddy boy."

Theodore resisted, but to no avail. The warden's manipulations pressed into the deepest parts of his mind, bringing forth the most primal of buried emotions. Teddy boy was forced to experience them, all control removed from his most private thoughts.

"When do I stop being myself and start being a part of them?" Theodore thought to himself.

Abruptly, Theodore was himself again. The warden returned to his seat, a sickening grin splitting his pink facade in a wicked parody of a theme park statue, grotesque in its merriment.

"Teddy boy," the warden said in his own voice. "You understand now. Participate or perish. We can control you, at all levels. The amount of freedom you receive depends on your own actions, your own thoughts. We hear all, and will punish any dissidence."

Theodore backed slowly towards the tent's opening, hoping to make good his escape from the warden's company. It was to no avail. However much he retreated, the opening came no closer. It was like one of those running nightmares, when you can't reach your goal, no matter how far you run towards it.

"You can never run," the warden said. "Claustrum Mundus may be vast, but we are never far. In every part of this world, we have control. Participate in the world's society, operate within your designated parameters, and you will not suffer undue trauma."

The warden stood, and walked to the tent's opening, gazing calmly into the light from outside. He turned back to face Theodore, and continued.

"Fight against us, and we will know, because we see your deepest mind at all times. You can never escape. You must become part of this place, or you will lose all rights to independent thought. In essence, you will die, though your body remains. We already control many thousands who could not peacefully participate."

Theodore walked to the opening, this time pleased to find it drawing closer, as it should. He reached the space in the doorway beside the warden, and stopped. Looking at the pink faced creature beside him, Theodore shuddered.

"What do I do then?" he asked.

"To avoid being subverted into the system's control, you must go forth into Claustrum Mundus and build a new life for yourself. You must use only the tools provided by the system. You must learn from yourself, from your own efforts. We will not instruct you. When you acquire enough credit to buy passage to the town, return here."

"So how do I learn without instruction?" Theodore asked.

"There are many others here in the Welcoming Fields. Talk to them. You will learn. But you must work for it yourself. If you fail, we will take control, so that your body does not starve. Some parts of us believe that it would be best to simply do that from the beginning, but free will is valued by those who created this place for your kind. Take your place here, and grow through this penance."

*   *   *

Theodore wandered the fields, among the tents, the stalls, and the huts of the merchants. Screeching hawkers offered their wares, many of which made no sense to Theodore. Over time, he knew he would learn the strange rhythm of the place.

There was no day or night to distinguish the passage of time, no rain, and no need for sleep. It was strange at first, but became normal for him sooner than he expected. In the back of his mind, Theodore wondered if the wardens had something to do with that.

The days were a blur, one continuous period of brightness and boredom. There was no real need for food, though he could eat. Starvation would not kill him. Many of the hawkers sold meals, some quite extravagant, none needed. The time blended together and Theodore could not tell how long he had been there when he came to the realisation that his life was over.

He was walking through the fields, ignoring the noises of the place, when suddenly he realised he had momentarily forgotten where he came from. All there was for him now was the Welcoming Fields. His life before seemed nothing more than a fading dream. His life was gone, his past was lost, and his future was nothing but more of the same.

The Theodore Longarm who stood so long ago in the chambers of the Union council, heard them list his crimes, betrayed by the employer who ordered them, was a fading legend. Nothing could bring that life back now. That man was dead to the world he had lived in. All that remained now was this shadow of a soul, imprisoned in the world controlled by the sinister pink skinned wardens.

Theodore was briefly ashamed, that he had succumbed so fast. He made a firm decision, his conviction sure, that he would not fail again. He had learned much in his time here, and he must use that knowledge to build a new life.

It was time for Theodore Longarm to return from the dead.

Chapter 2 – Occupations

Theodore stood before an ornate tent, with a simple wooden sign out the front. He read the sign repeatedly while deciding if he should enter. It read "James Filigree, Work Agent."

Finally, with a sigh, Theodore stepped through the opening and into the tent. A plump, sallow faced man looked up at him with a dismissive air. Slowly, the man placed his pen on the desk, taking great care as though to preserve an ancient and valuable artefact.

Theodore smiled. He remembered well his own, similar actions, treating all manner of items with that same care during his time smuggling priceless artefacts for his employers. That all ended when a bratty kid led the security team into his clandestine transaction on the Gorton Tower.

He paused in his reminiscence long enough to notice the man had stood and walked around the desk. The man had extracted a small gadget from a pocket and was waving it across Theodore's face, a puzzled frown expressing his thoughts as he looked at the small readout on the device.

The stranger walked around Theodore, looking him up and down several times, before stopping in front of him, then sitting on the desk. With his arms folded, the man finally smiled again and spoke in a deep voice, his prominent Adam's apple bobbing along with his straggly short brown bowl cut.

"So what's your story, hmm?"

Theodore simply looked at the man, wondering what to say. The man was apparently not in the mood to wait, and reached forward to prod Theodore's belly.

"Can you speak?" the man asked, his voice softer than before. "I think I am seeing the picture here. Just woke up, didn't you? Still trying to remember a few things I'd guess."

The man stood, walked to a small crate, and took out a cigar, a glass, and a dusty bottle. He poured some of the bottle's amber fluid into the glass, snipped the end of the cigar with a knife taken from his trouser pocket, then turned and faced Theodore again.

"In case you didn't get it from the sign, I'm James," he said.

James then pulled out a matchbox, struck one, and held it to the cigar, puffing heavily to ignite the fat brown roll of tobacco. The smell wafting from the cigar had a faint odour of something sweet, perhaps whiskey. Or perhaps the drink was so strong it was drowning the cigar smoke. Theodore decided to ignore it.

"You probably guessed that my name isn't really Filigree. But don't try to find the real one. In my business, it is best to hold onto some anonymity."

"So," Theodore replied. "It probably isn't James either, right?"

James smiled past the bobbing cigar, muttering around it as he continued to puff.

"This one is perceptive, I see."

He drew a long draft from the glass, closed his eyes for a moment, then looked hard into Theodore's face as he lowered the glass onto the desk. His breath smelled strongly of the alcohol as he nearly touched Theodore's nose with his own.

"Now then," James said as he once again raised his gadget. "There is still a strong whiff of the programs about you. So I am going to tell you a story about you. Judging from these readings, I would say you arrived in Claustrum Mundus roughly six months ago. You did the usual wanderings, probably ran into old Neville, or one of his ilk. Vampiric sods those old men. You were led by the old bastard to the admissions officer, where the rules were explained."

James paused, pulled out his cigar and tapped it on the edge of the desk, then continued. He used the cigar as a pointer, jabbing it towards Theodore while he spoke.

"You were a little confused by the whole thing of course. They never really explain, they only imply the rules to new comers. But they did leave you the impression that failure would mean losing your self to them. Am I right so far?"

"Umm, yeah, I guess so," Theodore replied, nodding slowly.

James smiled again, then propped the extinguished cigar back in his mouth.

"Right. So you left the admissions tent, walked outside, and forgot who you were."

Theodore frowned slightly, trying to remember. To his surprise, there was nothing there. It was like there was a gaping hole in his life, from the moment he left the warden's tent.

"I, I guess so," Theodore said, shaking his head with his confusion.

"Then you suddenly came to, realised you had forgotten yourself, and began wandering the Welcoming Fields looking for something to do."

"That's right."

"OK then, so we are both up to date. Mostly," James said, leaving his sentence fragmented while he rounded the desk to sit down again. "Please, sit down. What do I call you?"

"Oh, Theodore," replied the confused Mr Longarm, as he dragged a small wooden chair to sit opposite James. "What happened? If I understand the rules, I should have had some time to gain the points to live, after I left the warden's place."

James sighed, drew in a long draft from the cigar, then realised it was not lit. He grumbled as he relit it, then looked at Theodore again.

"You had a leach on your back. The old fart would

have used it on you. Steals your points, so the codger doesn't have to work. Using leaches though, it does that to you. Makes you old. Turns you decrepit. The locals know about them and stay away, so they always target the new folk. Easier that way. Hadn't been any for a while, then a bunch came in at once. I'm guessing that was you and your friends."

"Why does it make you old?" Theodore asked, his eyebrow raised.

James shrugged, and poured a fresh drink into his glass.

"It's part of the program I guess. You'll find that. Some bastard always slips a punishment into any sort of modifier. No matter how skilled the programmer, if it's in any way unfair to other players, a punishment appears. Nobody knows why. Or how. Not for sure anyway. I have my own theory, but you don't need to hear that. Not today."

Theodore frowned. It seemed that today, the more he learned the more confused he felt. Suddenly he realised something did not add up.

"Why did I wake up again?" Theodore asked.

"That?" James replied with an eyebrow askew, puffing his cigar back into life. "Well, every few months the system does a full points audit, see? And it would have seen that you were not in Claustrum Mundus long enough to use your base points before you got programmed. So it reverted you to your starting parameters. Everybody has to get a fair go here, that's what the wardens tell us."

"What about the leach? Would they take the points off the old fart, kill him out of the game?"

James laughed.

"Theodore, you don't get it do you?" he said.

James chuckled heartily and stood, replacing the bottle in the chest and taking out a second glass, and a second full bottle. He poured into the glass and refilled his own, before spitting the stub of the cigar into a steel box at the end of the desk.

"The leaches, they're a part of the game now. Think about it. The rules stated 'you must use only the tools provided by the system', but the thing is, if it ain't provided by the system, you can't get at it see? If something exists, however nasty it might seem, it's within the rules. Those old bastards have made a life for themselves, within the scope provided by the system and its rules. They might be gaming the system, but they aren't doing anything that will get them punished. Not unless you find a way to get back at them without getting yourself erased, that is."

James handed the second glass to Theodore, before returning to his seat. Theodore sipped, enjoyed the sensation as the warming whiskey burned his throat, then sculled the rest.

"So, I have to find a way to earn points. How do I do that?"

"However you like. You just have to participate. You can sell things for points, but you ain't got nothing to sell. You can buy things with points of course, but with only your starting base I'd be careful doing that if I were you. You earn points by participating, but the system will not tell you how much you earn. You can check your balance at the warden's counter. You lose a point each day you are here. Starting base is ninety points. So you have three months to get yourself started."

"So that bastard took three months of life from me? He'll pay for that."

"Careful," James warned. "The system may modify your thoughts if they get violent. That can cost you even more points."

"Right," Theodore said, checking his anger. "So how can you help?"

"Well, I'm a work agent. I'll find you something to earn you points, and it will only cost you twenty five percent of your earnings. Sounds a lot I know, but ain't nobody in the fields who's better at it than me."

*　　　　*　　　　*

Theodore stood before the noodle tent, James beside him with a broad grin. James slapped Theodore on the back, smiling broadly as he spoke.

"You'll be fine kid, trust me. It's going to be a crummy job, but it's a start. I'll find you something better soon."

"Why would you do that?" Theodore asked.

"Why wouldn't I? It's in my best interest to see you succeed. I get twenty five percent of whatever you earn. I wouldn't have my groovy digs if I didn't get my people into the best jobs, would I?"

Theodore grunted in response, and looked at the noodle tent. It was closed, tables and chairs stacked neatly to one side. James stepped forward, and tugged on the fabric of the tent.

"Hey Aaron, get out here would ya?" James shouted.

A burly man with a shaved head that glistened in the sunlight pushed his way through the tent flaps and looked them over. After a moment, he rushed James, pushing him hard as he grinned.

James stumbled backwards, and then returned the shove, hurling the larger man against the tent with a show of strength far greater than Theodore expected. Aaron straightened himself and faced them again, laughing riotously as he did so.

"Good work, Jim, you dog," Aaron said. "So, what you got for me?"

"This is Theodore," James explained. "He's still a newy, so you might find you have to explain a few things to him for a while, but he's a hard worker. I'm sure you can use him."

Theodore met Aaron's appraising stare, until the larger man smiled, looked him up and down, then threw himself at Theodore unexpectedly. They collided, and Theodore stumbled back, further than James had done.

Straightening himself, Theodore looked first at James, then Aaron, wondering what kind of mad house he was in. Then he decided this was some kind of test by his would be employer. He grinned wryly, twisted so his shoulder was angled at Aaron's enormous chest, and charged.

With each step, Theodore expertly planted his feet for traction and thrust himself forward, until he hit the noodle tent's owner like a juggernaut. Striking him, Theodore pushed Aaron hard, and the larger man was thrown from his feet, stumbling as he landed. Shaky and unable to correct his fall, Aaron tumbled through the wall of the tent, taking the structure down as he went.

Several passers-by stopped to gawk at the spectacle as the burly man struggled to remove himself from his collapsed shop and dwelling. Much swearing and angry shouting ensued from the mass of fabric, but no man was visible for several minutes as he thrashed around inside the tangled mess.

Finally the fuming Aaron appeared, and Theodore stepped backwards involuntarily. James pressed a steadying hand onto his shoulder, indicating he should stand his ground. Pulling and tossing the fabric, Aaron's full bulk finally came into view and he stopped.

Aaron turned and glared at Theodore, who looked back, not sure if he was about to fight for his life. Suddenly, the noodle merchant burst into a broad grin and rushed forward, arms outstretched in order to wrap them both in a bear hug.

"You jolly bastard!" Aaron shouted. "Look what you did to my tent. You're hired!"

The enormous man's rolling laughter was infectious, and soon Theodore and James had both joined him. James pulled a hip flask from his belt, took a healthy swig, then passed it to Aaron. Aaron did the same, then handed it to Theodore, smiling as he slapped the newcomer's back encouragingly.

"Any man who can send me down like that can surely handle a bit of James's bootleg," Aaron exclaimed. "Come on, get it down ya gullet, son. You'll need a hit o' that to give you the energy to rebuild my noodle shop before opening."

Theodore accepted the flask, and took a long drink from it. He enjoyed the warming bite of the whisky more than he had the first time, in James's tent. Passing it back to the owner, he stepped forward and grasped one edge of the fabric, lifting the tent.

Aaron rushed to help, and they soon righted the small structure, James stepping inside and lifting the dropped posts back into place. James then turned to face them.

"Well, I'll be off then. More work to do today. Stop by the office later OK? Both of you that is. We'll have a drink together, talk about the first day jitters."

With that, the work agent sauntered off into the wandering crowds of the merchant sector, not waiting for either of the men to respond. Aaron turned to Theodore.

"Well son, I think you and I will get along fine. Your job is to set out the tables for each meal time, and stack them away again after. While I'm serving, you take orders. You don't ask questions, you just tell me what they want, and I give it to you. Some want noodles, some want our other products. You don't need to know what they are, just get the orders right and you'll be fine."

"OK then, I think I can handle that," Theodore replied.

"You're not even a little curious?" Aaron asked.

"Not at all. I don't care what you do, so long as I earn enough to survive. What your clients want is between them and you."

Aaron smiled, and slapped Theodore on the back again.

"I like you son. Now get to it will you? We got ten minutes till the next rush. Oh and one other thing. You know the real reason you got the job don't you?"

Theodore raised an eyebrow, shaking his head slightly. He was genuinely unsure of that particular riddle.

"You're my new bouncer, mate. Enough people saw you knock me down that word will flow, so you probably won't have to worry for a while. But sometimes my customers get a bit rowdy. It's your job to deal with them. Do it quick, and without any doubts that you'll clobber them again. Got it?"

"Yes sir," Theodore said with a broad grin. "I think I am going to enjoy working for you, Aaron."

Chapter 3 – Coders and Jockeys

Theodore fitted into the role more comfortably than he would ever have expected. This was so far from anything he would have imagined for himself, and yet he found himself enjoying the work with Aaron the noodle man greatly.

Somewhere deep inside, a part of him wondered why, but he pushed that aside and simply got on with the job. Each day, they visited James as promised and enjoyed his whiskey, while discussing the progress. Aaron spoke positively at these meetings of how he felt Theodore was going, and it filled him with a new found pride in his efforts to hear it.

On the third day, he had just finished setting out the tables for the mid day session. The people began to arrive, and he set about taking the orders. He approached the first table, where a slightly built man was seated with a larger woman, a thin girl and a muscle bound hulk of a man.

"Can I take your orders?" Theodore asked.

"No, go away," the woman spat.

"I'm sorry," Theodore said. "But these tables are for patrons of Aaron's Noodle Shop only."

"Fine," the skinny man said. "We'll take four glasses of water while we wait."

"Wait for what?" Theodore asked.

"None of your damn business, just get lost," the muscled one said.

Theodore shrugged, and walked to the tent. Pulling the flap aside, he beckoned to Aaron. Theodore pulled the tent flap open enough for Aaron to see the group before he spoke.

"Those four over there may be trouble. Wouldn't order, then only asked for water. Said they are waiting, but not what for. Thought you should know in case things get hairy in a few minutes when I eject their sorry asses."

Aaron raised an eyebrow and examined the four closely.

"I'd wager that lot are looking for some trouble. Probably after one of our regulars. Be careful, but don't let them escalate things. Wait here"

Aaron disappeared inside, then returned. He pressed a small red tab to Aaron's shirt.

"This will lend you speed, so you can be fast enough to eject the lot of them when it starts. Whoever they attack, kick them out as well. I won't have this trouble attracted to my business."

"Yes, Boss," Theodore said.

Turning away from the tent, Theodore took several orders over the next quarter of an hour, and was rushed about with taking noodles, and sometimes other, unmarked tiny parcels, to those who were buying.

At no point did he take any payment. Aaron had explained this on the first day.

"The system takes care of that. They are paying in points, and all the prices are logged with the wardens. When the system observes the product being handed over, the cost in points is automatically diverted to me. Then the cuts for my workers and suppliers come out of my balance at the end of the day."

It was a simple enough system, and Aaron's noodle shop was doing a booming trade. Theodore realised after his first few days that his employer must be very wealthy by local standards.

Theodore was wondering about the other things people ordered, though he kept to his word and did not ask questions. Now Aaron had placed one on him and said something about it lending him speed.

So these things gave special abilities somehow? Theodore made a mental note to ask about it later.

Meanwhile, the group of four seemed to be getting agitated. They began arguing, and seemed to be getting heated. Theodore was about to go over to their table, when the girl stood and stormed off, disappearing into the passing crowds.

As she left, the other three seemed to settle down, though the skinny man was morose in his attitude. He sulked, staring at the table in front of him, ignoring the other two. Theodore aborted his intervention and returned to collecting orders from the other tables.

Returning from the tent with several small packages and two bowls of noodles for a pair of women who seemed strikingly attractive to Theodore, he nearly dropped them when he saw a new customer emerging from the crowds.

The haggard old man was unmistakable. The man who had leached his points. Why was he here? Theodore felt rage boiling inside him. Aaron appeared at his shoulder, relieving him of the bowls.

"Easy son. I could feel your rage from the kitchen. Remember, you'll be punished for instigating violence. Be alert. Be careful."

Aaron deposited the bowls on the table as Theodore handed over the small packages. Then Aaron returned to the tent and Theodore looked around the tables to see if he had any new customers.

When the old man sat down, Theodore groaned as he realised he would have to hold his rage in check and actually serve the bastard. But that was when everything turned to insanity.

"That's the guy," the skinny man screamed.

His muscled companion launched from his seat and charged the old bastard. The woman was right behind him, tossing little tabs onto his back as he moved. And he was unnaturally fast.

Theodore leaped into action, charging through the tables to reach the old bastard first. Planting his feet, he raised his arms to deflect an attacking blow, and took the muscled man's arm with him as he ran to his back.

The agile opponent was just as fast, and kept his body facing Theodore, though his momentum carried him into the table. The man's free arm reached out and collected the leach user's face, sending him sprawling in the dust.

Then the would be attacker fell, smashing the table into splinters as the old bastard got away, disappearing into the crowd. Theodore was on top of the attacker in a heartbeat, raining blows on the man before standing to drag him to his feet.

Turning the heavy man, Theodore planted his foot in the centre of the man's back and shoved him out of the dining area, to vanish in the crowd of onlookers that had stopped to watch. Theodore turned to face the woman, who now raised a wicked knife to attack him.

Ducking, Theodore sped around her and advanced on the skinny man. The woman screamed behind him, and Theodore turned in time to see her dragged away by a pink skinned warden. Watching her, he did not see the skinny man run at him from behind.

Feeling the light touch of the man's fists, Theodore turned and grabbed him, lifting him from the ground.

"Why are you helping that bastard?" the man squealed. "He stole my points when I got here, he should be punished!"

Theodore sighed, and dropped the skinny whiner to the ground. He landed hard on his backside, and stood slowly, looking with rage at Theodore.

"He took mine as well, but I have a job to do. Now get out of here before I rip you apart," Theodore said, knowing that his threat was an idle one.

"He took yours? Then why are you defending him, you idiot?" squealed the skinny man.

"Because it's my job, you moron," Theodore said with an angry growl. "He takes points because it's his job. We may not like it, but it's legal in this dump for him to live that way. We either participate or we die. I suggest you move on and find another way to get back at him if it bothers you so much. Now get the hell out of this shop."

Theodore stalked away, not bothering to look back as the skinny man skulked into the crowds. Theodore pondered the nature of those crowds, and wondered briefly how many of the faceless masses were real people in that crushing throng.

His thoughts were interrupted by Aaron, who slapped his back in a hearty gesture of friendship.

"That's the way, son!" Aaron boomed. "Took that lot to the cleaners you did, my boy. Well done. I'll be arranging a bonus in today's pay for that effort."

"Wait, Aaron, I'm sorry but I have to ask. What was that thing you stuck on my shirt earlier?"

Aaron sighed, and turned to face Theodore. He rested a hand on a table and leaned there. By some miracle, the table held his weight. He looked at Theodore for a long moment before speaking.

"I suppose you were going to find out about those eventually. And you deserve to know, especially after today. Our other business is in what are called modifiers. Tiny coded artefacts that lend the user all manner of abilities or affectations. I gave you a temporary speed boost."

Theodore sat at one of the chairs near the table Aaron was leaning on, then looked up at his employer.

"Aaron, you have to tell me. The leaches, those things that old bastard uses, does he buy them from you?"

Aaron looked at Theodore again, then sat down opposite his new bouncer before responding.

"Yes. It is one of the modifiers we sell, but I have never been happy about it," Aaron said, watching Theodore as he spoke. "He got you didn't he? I'm sorry son, but you know how the system works by now. Most of what we sell is legitimate, and does not harm anybody. But if I refuse service to his kind, I'll lose a lot of that other regular trade. You understand don't you?"

"Of course. No hard feelings. I hope that bastard gets it one day though," Theodore said. "I can't say for sure that I wouldn't do the same as he did, if I was desperate enough."

Aaron raised an eyebrow on hearing this.

"Well son, at least you're honest with yourself about that. Few of those on the welcoming fields would know themselves that well."

"Aaron," Theodore said as his employer made to

stand. "I'd like to learn more about those modifiers. Maybe learn how to make them."

Aaron paused thoughtfully for a moment, then sat back down. He smiled softly as he did so, looking across the table again. His attitude to Theodore seemed warmer today, but no less in command than the day before.

"Son, I like you, and I think you could go places. So I'll get Sammy out the back to start running you through the basics, see if we can't get you going on some simple product. But be warned, coding modifiers is a hard task sometimes. Much harder than it looks. It takes brains, real smarts you hear me? And if ever you make a mistake, you could have the jockeys hunting you like a dog."

"Even so, I'd like to try," Theodore said, neglecting to mention the higher levels of education he had been blessed with in his old life. "What are jockeys?"

"Jockeys are the users. The ones who use the modifiers, or sometimes their victims. I don't know why we call them that, but we do," Aaron explained, before standing again. "Alright then, we have orders to fill. Back to it, we can talk about this later."

Aaron walked back into the tent. Theodore stood, and turned to see that a large number of new customers had arrived while they were talking. He rushed to take their orders, thinking continuously about the new things Aaron had told him.

*   *   *

"This," Sammy explained as they sat together in the back of Aaron's tent after closing. "Is a coder's pen. It's different from other pens in that it writes stuff the system can interpret. Get those things right, and what you create is something that can have an influence on the world of Claustrum Mundus."

"Like a computer program?" Theodore asked.

"Exactly. But it is not a raw code situation. The words you write," Sammy explained. "It's almost like poetry. It's a long way from the programming languages they used in ancient times. This is a true art form. You have to serenade the system to get what you want. The best of the coders have the logical mind of a scientist, and the beautiful soul of a true virtuoso."

"I like the sound of it. Kind of nice really. I would hope I can measure up, in time," Theodore said.

"I don't know if you have those things. I'm good, but I have a long way to go before I'm close to the best. I've been at it for years now, and people like my work. I've made Aaron a lot of money with my products. But I'm not as good as I want to be. I don't know if you'll get any better than I have. But I like that you're willing to try."

Sammy reached beneath his small desk and pulled out a locked box, depositing it on the table between them. Using a key attached to a chain around his neck, Sammy opened the box to reveal hundreds of the tiny coloured slivers of paper, much like the one that Aaron had used to give Theodore the speed boost earlier.

Flicking through the slips, Sammy continued talking as he pulled one out.

"Each coder uses slightly different programs. Part of the power is in the art, so simply copying another coder's work is never as effective as creating your own. Here," he said as he passed a dull blue slip to Theodore. "This is the leach you were hit with."

Theodore accepted the slip and unfolded it. The words screamed at him in glistening, flowing print. They swam before his eyes with a kind of mystical nature. The ink was perfumed with an odour that he was unable to identify, tantalising and sweet. For the first time, Theodore understood what people meant when they spoke of the scent of programs.

"Here at this table, no programs may run. Five minutes hence, this code be undone," Sammy said. "Now you may read it."

Theodore raised an eyebrow at his mentor's poetic words, then read from the slip of paper in his hands.

"One person I target, with this coder's rhyme, to take out their earnings, to buy me more time. To a minimum ninety, these points I receive, one for each day, before I do leave. If that other is emptied, then may it be so, that if more than ninety, some points I forego. To a maximum ninety, I return to their health, provided my share is not less than their wealth."

Theodore looked up at Sammy, who sat there with a silly smile. The poem seemed a little simplistic to Theodore.

"How can that be a computer program? It's almost childishly simple," Theodore said.

Sammy laughed, then picked up the pen, pointing at Theodore with it.

"This pen is an interpreter. It takes what you write with it, and converts it into true code that the system then runs. Its ink is linked to it permanently, and the system interfaces with it. When the code is activated, the pen feeds the code to the system along with the details of those effected by it. This is possibly the most powerful device in Claustrum Mundus, and certainly one of the most expensive. With this, you can create almost anything. Even inhibitors."

Theodore frowned, folding his arms as he leaned back in his chair.

"What's an inhibitor?" Theodore asked.

"It's a code device that limits the amount that the system can read or modify your mind. They are extremely difficult to create, and very expensive to buy. They are also not reliable, so take care if ever you find you need one."

"Is it always a poem?" Theodore asked.

"Not necessarily. Some coders write them as poems like mine, some write haiku, some write florid prose. The pen learns your style and, as you work with it, becomes more in tune to your own way of coding. That said, you still need to write to certain standards for it to work. If you write particularly bad poetry, you will get particularly bad programs."

"What happens with them?"

"Your jockeys will be very upset with you. The programs will be unreliable, the punishments for the less friendly ones will be more severe. Aaron does well because mine are over the standard the market expects.

But I still want them to be better."

"How do I get a pen of my own?"

"You work. Hard. Mine cost me nearly a thousand points, and I did a few favours to get the price down. If you want to become a coder, you have to show that you really want it by working towards it with whatever jobs you can find. I'm happy to help you learn the craft, but I can't help you with a pen. And you can't use mine."

Chapter 4 – Blockers

Theodore had a lot of time between serving periods that would normally have been idle. Once he finished cleaning the shop area, he would go back to the small desk that Sammy used, and study from his notes about modifiers.

Aaron did not seem to mind this distraction. Sometimes he would drag over a chair to see what they were both up to. He laughed jovially at Theodore's impotent scratchings with a pencil. Theodore looked at him, his eyes seething with stubborn determination, his fervent hope to secure a pen and actually create a working modifier.

"What?" Theodore finally spat in response to his curious employer's laughter.

"Don't worry, you'll get it," Aaron said. "But you're forcing yourself a little. Forcing the code. I know that the old fashioned computer programs were very literal, but your pen will interpret your meaning once it knows you."

Aaron snatched the scrap of paper Theodore was working on and looked at it, a slight frown on his lips as he read silently to himself. Finishing, he tossed it back to Theodore, then folded his arms on the desk. He nodded at the box of modifiers before speaking again.

"If something slightly abstract will give a better sound, it will probably give a better code. That's why Sammy is so good, he lets the system enjoy music from a knock out beauty, instead of forcing it to endure a lecture in astro physics from a boring old fart. It's much more

26

effective."

"But the system is a computer, not a horny undergraduate," Theodore replied.

"Doesn't mean it can't have a soul," Aaron said.

With a grunt, the noodle shop's owner stood and pushed his chair back away from the desk. He shook his head slowly and smiled. Without any further acknowledgement of their presence, Aaron walked away. It seemed he believed his answer needed no further explanation.

Theodore watched his employer's retreating back for a moment then faced Sammy, who continued working diligently across the desk from him. The coder had not even looked up throughout the exchange.

"What do you suppose he meant by that? How could the system have a soul?"

Sammy paused, his pen in mid stroke, then carefully laid the device on the desk beside his current paper. Finally, the coder looked up at his student, and shook his head slowly, just as Aaron had done.

"If you need to ask me that, perhaps you do not have it in you to be a coder after all," Sammy said.

"What do you mean?"

"A coder has to feel his code just as a singer feels his song," Sammy explained. "If you are not able to do that, the code you produce is weak, unreliable. All coders must have that empathic relationship with the system or else the system will not listen. If you can't understand that, then you can't be in sync with it and your code will never be good enough. If you can develop that kind of connection to the system, you will begin to understand that it could have a soul, even though to say so makes no scientific or logical sense. Reason sometimes is irrelevant to facts."

Theodore looked at his mentor for a long time, trying to digest his words. The meaning behind them seemed logical, but it was still hard to see the sense in it. Theodore was starting to get that confused feeling again. He looked down at his scribblings, reading them to himself.

"When the points are depleted, by passage of days,

with these words I expleted, for my own life I says, The system refund me, my month passed in fees, to allow for vacation, So that my time frees."

He shook his head, realising how messy the rhyme was. Theodore knew what he was attempting might result in something bad for the user, but he wanted to try to remove the need for the leach modifiers. Even so, he had to admit to himself that his efforts were mostly nonsense.

"Show me that," Sammy said suddenly.

Theodore passed it over, and Sammy gazed at the paper with a critical eye.

"See, if I were the system, I wouldn't know what to do with this. You tried to be literal, but you still tried to rhyme. It's forced, it's unnatural, it has no reason, no heart, and no structure."

Sammy screwed up the paper and tossed it back across the desk at Theodore. Picking up his pen, Sammy made a show of starting to write again, then stopped. He looked back at Theodore, waggling the pen like an accusing finger as he spoke.

"If that's the best you can do, you should quit. And if you're trying to steal free points with a modifier, give it up. You'll just kill somebody. The points are generated by the system, and we work with what the system provides. If you can generate points out of air, why hasn't it been done already? Try to make something useful with what is already there. A leach barrier, or a work enhancer, but don't try to make something that will only ever appeal to lazy greed. We have to work, so your idea with this modifier will get extreme punishment from the system, if it can even understand it."

"So what do I change?" Theodore asked, feeling dread for the answer.

"All of it. And Theodore, try to use only words that really exist. I don't know how the system will interpret the word 'expleted', but it's sure as hell not in my dictionary."

*   *   *

The next day, Theodore was delivering noodles to a

pair of customers when he saw the skinny man seated at a table. He watched the man for several seconds, before approaching. This time, the skinny man was alone.

"Welcome back. I am pleased to see no hired guns with you today," Theodore said as he approached the man's table.

"Sorry about that," the man said. "I was so bent on revenge, I wasn't thinking about what was involved. This place takes a little getting used to."

"So what can we do for you today?"

"I need some stuff. I plan to move on later today and I hear that in town the modifiers cost a lot more. So I figure, buy a few here and get a strong start there."

"Sounds like you have a plan. What can we get you?" Theodore asked.

"I have a list, here. Just show that to your man out back, he'll have them all I hope."

Theodore nodded, and took the list from the skinny man. Strolling back to the tent, he read the first few items. He was not impressed to see that the man had ordered three leach modifiers, but he decided to leave it alone.

A few minutes later, Theodore handed a small parcel to the man, his little pile of modifiers tied with a blue ribbon. They quickly disappeared into his pockets and he stood. Turning to leave, the skinny man hesitated, then faced Theodore.

"I owe you an apology, and my thanks," he said. "Because of your actions here the other day, I was forced to examine myself. My motives, my ambitions, my desire for revenge. I had to change them all. Thanks to you, I realised my correct path was to move on, to try for something better than I can get here. I have enough points, and I have nothing else to learn here. That's why I'm leaving for the town today."

"I'm glad you learned something from it. I wish you luck wherever you go," Theodore said with a smile.

The skinny man turned and walked away. Theodore watched after him for a long while, wondering how much of that man's attitude change was his own, and how much the system had helped him to arrive at it.

A call from behind him brought Theodore out of his reverie, and he went back to serving the tables. For the first time in days, Theodore wondered about his role at the noodle bar, and realised that even if it was only a false world inside a virtual reality prison, he wanted something better for himself. He wanted it soon, and he was being provided all the opportunities to make it happen.

*   *   *

Theodore continued working, determined to master the basics of coding before leaving the welcoming fields, but not wishing to stay any longer than he absolutely needed to.

On his thirty-eighth day, Theodore purchased a tiny tent which he erected on the perimeter of the settlement. Returning there each evening, he would practice his scribbled codes long into the rest period.

It was a strange thing, he believed, the evening being merely an arbitrary designation of time on the part of a few businesses. No darkness ensued, and while he felt the need to sleep from life long habit, it was not an essential thing. So rather than a place to sleep, the tent provided a place to relax and work, honing his skills and trying to become something more than just a noodle bar attendant.

He wondered why so many people in the welcoming fields used tents for sleeping. His days blurred into each other and gradually he began to understand.

Aaron was watching as Theodore paused in the middle of taking an order, then wandered away muttering rhymes to himself. Theodore jumped as he snapped into awareness of where he was when his employer grabbed his shoulder.

"What's going on lad? You're looking a bit lost today," Aaron said.

"Huh? Sorry, just tired I guess," Theodore replied.

"You really are new at this aren't you?" Aaron said, shaking his head slowly.

"What do you mean boss?" Theodore replied.

Aaron sat at a table, indicating for Theodore to sit opposite him. Several customers began yelling at him impatiently. He waved them off, and faced Theodore.

"You're not sleeping, are you?" Aaron asked, not waiting for an answer. "You're going back to that tent and working on your code, which is admirable, don't get me wrong. But it's stupid."

Aaron pulled out his hip flask and took a hit of whiskey. He grimaced as the fiery liquid burned its way down, a little more than he had intended. Passing it to Theodore, he continued.

"Just because they tell you you don't need to sleep, does not mean you shouldn't do it occasionally. Doing two jobs, which is essentially what you are doing, at least as far as mental exertion is concerned, is going to wear you out. You can't keep the pace. Your mind needs its down time and you ain't giving it any. Get out of here. Go rest, come back later feeling human, you hear me?"

"But boss, you need somebody to take orders," Theodore said.

"Don't you worry about that, Sammy can cover for you. Get some sleep, you idiot. I'll talk to you tomorrow."

"But boss, why do we need sleep? They say we don't, but obviously it effects our minds."

"We don't if we spend a lot of our time doing nothing," Aaron said. "But you're trying to force your brain to work full time, round the clock. How did you think it would go?"

Theodore shook his head, his mumbled reply not intelligible.

"Theodore, just because you're in a virtual world, does not mean that your body can survive long term being permanently in communication with the system. Your brain needs to be able to rest, or else you'll be no good to me. Now go sleep. I'll see you tomorrow."

*   *   *

Theodore did as instructed, and the next morning returned refreshed. While walking to the noodle shop, He found himself composing modifiers silently to himself, and for the first time they seemed like they could be

31

usable.

He arrived early, cleaned up the site, then began setting up the tables. Aaron approached him as he was finishing.

"You look much better today son," Aaron said.

Theodore turned to his employer and smiled.

"Good morning Aaron. Thank you for the advice yesterday. I feel much better for it. Today, I feel like I might be starting to get somewhere with the modifiers."

"I'll have to get you to show me something later then. For now, I'd best get into the tent. The customers will start arriving soon."

Theodore worked through the morning shift, his mind more alert than the day before. Even so, a part of him was still thinking about the modifiers, and what he could do with them. Finally the crowds thinned and Aaron called an end to the service period.

Theodore hurriedly cleaned the area, put the tables and chairs away, and then made his way to the little table in the back of the tent. As soon as he was there, he snatched up his pencil and began to write.

After several minutes, he leaned back, looking in satisfaction at his paper slip. Sammy looked up, curious what Theodore had done.

"Show me what you have," Sammy said.

Theodore passed the slip of paper across the table, then sat back as Sammy read the words on it. Sammy looked up at Theodore, then back at the paper, reading the words a second time. Finally Sammy lowered the paper and yelled.

"Boss, you'd best get back here."

Aaron appeared almost instantly, and Sammy wordlessly handed him the slip of paper. Aaron looked at it for a moment, then read it aloud.

"For a month of my time, this charm will protect. From point stealing rhyme, the system detects. Each point that I lose, return it to me, plus half that again, shall be charged as my fee. If that leaves them undone, return them twelve days, that I am not one, who resorts to their ways."

Aaron held the slip of paper a long time. He looked

from it to Sammy, then handed it back.

"The lad did this?" Aaron asked.

"Yes. His first good code."

Aaron sighed, then pulled up a stool. He sat heavily, and looked from Theodore to Sammy, then back again. Finally, he spoke.

"Sammy, did you explain the problem to him?"

"No boss. I thought I'd best get you immediately."

Theodore frowned in confusion.

"What problem?"

"Theodore," Aaron said. "That modifier will negate one of our other products. That will result in clients that regularly purchase the other product being unable to guarantee its effects. That will lead to them being uncertain of their effectiveness. We can't sell both."

"Oh. I guess that is a problem."

"Of course, we might salvage it yet," Aaron said with a thoughtful tone. "If I get you a pen, will you grant me exclusive rights to that modifier? That way I can control its distribution."

"That's a big price for one code," Theodore said. "And that would enable you to set the price of that modifier as high as you like."

"Of course," Aaron said. "But the ones who need it most are those who are least likely to know they need it. Newcomers. They're the target and they have no means to pay what it's worth."

"What is it worth?" Sammy asked.

Aaron looked at his coder, and smiled.

"To us, it is worth saving the lad a few months of work before he can get himself a pen. If this became available, we would have to reduce the price of your leach modifier. If I own it, I can let out a limited supply to another merchant through a fence. I can apply a code seal so that it can't be copied. And yes, I can price it however I wish. But I won't."

Theodore looked at his employer, confused.

"You seem to be contradicting yourself a little," Theodore said.

"Not at all, lad. I will price it at forty five points, half the starters allowance. The merchant can pay us thirty, your cut for writing them will be five, since I will have effectively paid you a thousand with the pen for the rights. You'll be paid five for your labour, but that is all. Should you leave, I will require you make a few hundred in advance."

"You're a shrewd business man, boss. But it sounds like a good deal to me."

"Realise, that you can't make them to sell yourself, because you will be giving all rights and control to me. If you use one or sell one, the system will apply a heavy penalty. That is automatic, I can't control what the system does, but you should be aware that it would do that."

"I understand, Aaron, and I think you are giving me a good deal anyway. But what about your leach modifiers?"

"Oh, we'll need to drop the price on those. If the customers ask why, we warn them that we have heard rumours of somebody working on a blocking modifier, so we have reduced our charges in case the jockey encounters one of those."

Aaron stood, and fetched three glasses, pouring whiskey for all of them. Pushing the glasses to Sammy and Theodore, he raised his own in an unspoken toast. The deal was sealed, and the system now had it agreed and set in place. He took a sip of his drink, then placed the glass on the table.

"The people who use leaches will wear the risk happily enough," Aaron said. "They need never know we created the blockers. And I have links to a merchant who specifically targets newcomers with advice or helpers, for a fee. We know him through James, he finds work for this guy's clients."

"So I will have a pen, you have your control over the blockers, and we all make a lot of points," Theodore said, raising his glass with a grin. "To future business success!"

"To future business success," Aaron and Sammy said in unison, raising their glasses to meet Theodore's.

Chapter 5 – Traders

Theodore wrote fifty of the blockers as a starting stock for Aaron, and then sat for a while, thinking about what other innovations he might be able to create.

Several possible concepts entered his mind, but he was unable to transform concepts into workable code. He shook his head, then stood. As he walked towards the front of the tent, Aaron came in, blocking the exit.

"Oh good," Aaron said. "Theodore, I need you to come with me."

"What is it?" Theodore asked.

"I'm going to visit Tetsuo, Takemori Testuo. He's the man I mentioned before who will be selling your blocker codes for me. The real boss in his operation is his wife Akiko but we won't be meeting her today."

"Can we make a few other stops afterwards?" Theodore asked.

"Of course, but why?"

"I think looking in on some of the places where code modifiers are in regular use might help to inspire a few ideas for new ones. I don't feel I have seen enough of what people are really doing here to understand the type of modifier they most need."

Aaron nodded, thinking about the idea. Finally he turned, leading the way from the tent.

"That is probably wise," he said. "There's no point working on a modifier with no market. If it will help you come up with something useful, I can think of a few places to visit."

Theodore followed him and they made their way through the dining area outside the noodle tent. Throngs of prisoners passed them as they made their way across the Welcoming Fields, and Theodore found himself wondering which of them were true participants.

"How many do you suppose have failed?" he asked.

Aaron glanced at him, then looked forward again. He seemed to think hard for a moment before he responded.

"There is no official number on it, but I dare say a lot of those around us are under system control. We call them drones. You were a drone for a while, weren't you? Most drones disappear after a while. I have a theory why, but no proof. And then there are the wardens."

Aaron paused for a while, then nodded. He turned to face Theodore, the crowds parting as they passed. The pair seemed no obstruction to the teeming masses as they rushed about their daily business.

"What made you ask about that?" Aaron asked.

Theodore took a long time to answer. He was thinking about why it was so important to him, why the concept he was thinking about meant so much. Finally he sighed, and decided to keep his vague idea to himself.

"Just thinking about things."

Aaron looked at him with a questioning expression. Theodore stared back at him, not giving up his thoughts. Finally Aaron shrugged, and walked away. Theodore followed.

The tents parted and a cobbled plaza stretched out before them. Theodore recognised the place he had first arrived in the welcoming fields, wondering at how much it had changed. He slowed, looking around. Aaron realised Theodore had dropped back and stopped, turning to face him.

"Why is it so different?" Theodore asked. "There seems a lot more than when I arrived. It was just miles of grass at first, and then a few tents a little way away."

He turned, looking around, pointing to the edge of the plaza, which was surrounded by the tents and huts of the welcoming fields on all sides. They stretched into the distance beyond the edge of the cobble stones.

"You would have seen only a partial load of the fields when you arrived," Aaron explained. "The system gives you only some of the signals when you arrive, so that you can take it in easier."

"So how does it decide what to show you?" Theodore asked.

"I really don't know," Aaron said. "Though Tetsuo might know about it, since he has done something to make sure he is visible to most newcomers."

Aaron walked across the plaza, passing the reception area and the ever present wardens. Theodore looked at them with a thoughtful pause, causing Aaron to stop and turn yet again.

"Come on lad," Aaron said. "What the hell is going on with you today? Something bothering you?"

Theodore shook his head, and caught up with his employer without any reply. Aaron raised an eyebrow, then led the way to an ornate maroon tent on the far side of the plaza.

"Mr Takemori, are you there?" Aaron called as he parted the flap on the tent and walked through.

Theodore followed him in, surprised to find that the interior of the tent was more like a modern office space. The illusion of sweeping fields leading to water lay beyond what looked like immense glass windows.

In spite of the small tent on the outside, it seemed a whole new world beckoned from beyond the glass. Aaron slapped Theodore on the back and guffawed as he led him into the room.

"Everybody has that look the first time they come in here," Aaron said with a laugh.

"I can only assume this is a demonstration of what can be done with good code," Theodore said.

"Indeed, it is. Perhaps you can come up with some equally impressive devices, in time," Aaron said kindly.

"Perhaps," Theodore replied with a knowing smile. "If my ideas work out, perhaps I can."

*　　　　　*　　　　　*

Takemori Tetsuo was a tall gentleman, much taller than Theodore had expected. He smiled broadly from beneath the rim of a steeply sloped conical hat. His eyes and nose were concealed behind the stiff, woven cap, and yet he moved with the confidence of a man in complete awareness of everything around him.

After a moment he turned, and made an elaborate gesture. Theodore noticed his lips moving silently as the tall hat turned away. As if in response, three comfortable looking seats slid across the floor towards them. Tetsuo sat in one, before gesturing for Aaron and Theodore to sit in the others.

"What have you got for me, old friend?" Tetsuo said in a stiff, heavily accented voice.

"This is Theodore, my new coder. He has come up with something that could prove valuable to your clients," Aaron explained.

Tetsuo lifted the hat, revealing his bright green eyes, peering out from his chiselled features and olive skin. His eyebrow was raised.

"What would that be then?" Tetsuo asked.

"He calls it a blocker," Aaron said. "It stops the leeches from being effective, and taxes the leech user, passing a portion of their points to the victim. A kind of compensation, you might say."

Tetsuo stroked his chin, lowering his gaze to examine the floor with intent fascination. He sat like that for almost a minute, before he looked back up, his hand returning to his lap.

"I see. This is a valuable prize. Perhaps more valuable than my clients can afford. What is the damage?" he asked, his eyes narrowing as he stared at Aaron.

"We have not yet observed the side effects. I was hoping to sell them through you, for a healthy commission of course, charging the users forty five points. We would receive thirty of those, and the rest is yours."

Tetsuo stood slowly, then clasped his hands behind his back. He walked to stare for a long moment out of the glass windows, watching intently as a mysterious bird hunted in the fields beyond. He turned back to face them.

"That is half of the starting balance. I would have to be careful who I sell it to, some of my clients are not able to earn fast enough to justify the risk of spending so much on a single use item."

Aaron was unconvinced that this was a problem.

"You work with James, and he rarely takes forty days to find a newcomer some form of work, even if it is a low paying, menial task. The system does not have an unemployment problem. You know as well as I do that it is designed to create work when necessary."

The smile returning, Tetsuo walked back to his chair, sitting gingerly as he once again looked at Aaron.

"I'll require a test," he said. "Which means somebody willing to risk losing their points, or some less pleasant side effects. Not that that is hard. I offer them fifty points and they do anything I say. But you are of course correct, most of my clients can probably afford the gamble, when you consider the alternative."

Aaron stood, taking his turn at the window as the bird swooped past. He scratched his head for a moment then turned to face Theodore and Tetsuo.

"The alternative, well, that is something that is most unpleasant, as Theodore knows. He was hit by a leach, spent some time as a drone because of it."

"Interesting," Tetsuo said. "That will change things a little. From what I have seen, the system punishes users less for codes that were created out of an altruistic desire to reduce the chances of suffering something endured by the coder."

"Can you say that a little less convolutely?" Aaron asked.

"Because the code is intended to stop another from suffering his fate," Tetsuo said, pointing at Theodore. "The side effects will be less severe. That makes the code more valuable. We can sell it to experienced participants for a higher fee because we can guarantee a slighter impact."

"Once you have tested it," Theodore said.

"Of course," Tetsuo replied. "We should get that done immediately."

Tetsuo clapped his hands and a small woman entered

the room. He leaned close and whispered something to her. The woman bowed low, then scurried out. He looked at Aaron and smiled.

"Please, give me a sample of this blocker."

Aaron handed over the requested modifier, one that Theodore had written earlier, and Tetsuo withdrew a second from a pocket. After a moment, two young men entered, both looking around in a way that gave Theodore the impression they were new here.

"Gentlemen," Tetsuo began. "We wish to test a new modifier. Its side effects are unknown, but should you agree to participate in this trial, I will transfer fifty points to each of you. This will give you more time to settle into the system before you face becoming a drone, but there is a risk of losing that many or more points in the test. Do you agree?"

Both men nodded. Tetsuo handed a modifier to each man, and then took out two small slips and used them, once facing each man. Numbers appeared on the men's foreheads. One read seventy-three, and the other just fifty-six.

"Read yours first," Tetsuo said to fifty-six.

The man read the code, which was Theodore's blocker. Nothing seemed to happen.

"No side effects at all," Theodore said, surprised.

"Nothing has happened yet. Until the code is run by the criteria of your modifier, no side effects will be visible," Tetsuo explained.

Aaron sat, watching with interest as Tetsuo turned to face seventy-five.

"When you are ready," Tetsuo said. "Recite the code then place the paper on your friend here. Of course an experienced participant does not need to recite the code, merely use it, but we want it heard for the record."

With a nervous tremor in his hands, the man read from the paper, and then stepped forward to apply the paper as instructed. Instantly, the numbers vanished from both men's foreheads.

At first, nothing more seemed to be happening. After a moment, waves of colour flowed through the first man's hair, then it snapped straight and white in an instant. Meanwhile, the second man, who had attempted to use the leech modifier, grew incredibly old as they watched. Then he reverted to middle age, apparently his leech side effects being mitigated a little by the effects of the blocker.

Tetsuo called for another chair and the now older man slumped into it, looking exhausted. Once again, Tetsuo took out two modifiers, and read them to each man. A second time, numbers appeared on the men's foreheads.

The white haired man now had eighty-four points, half again his original fifty-six. The other man had lost points, dropping to forty-five. Tetsuo approached white hair, looking him over with a critical eye.

"How do you feel?" he asked.

"I feel pretty damn good, actually," the man replied.

Tetsuo turned to face the other man.

"And what about you?" Tetsuo asked.

"I feel tired. Like I never felt before. What happened to me?" he said.

"You lost a bet," Tetsuo explained. "Don't worry about it, the side effects aren't going to be permanent, you didn't get the benefits the system was punishing you for, so they should dissipate in a few hours. I'll arrange for your points to be paid before then. Thank you both, you can leave now."

The white haired man helped his friend up and supported him as they both walked from the room. After they left, Tetsuo smiled and held his hand out, open palmed.

"How many do you have for me?" he asked.

"Fifty," Theodore said, drawing a frown from Aaron. "Though I can have as many as you need here in a few hours."

"I'll take the fifty to start with." Tetsuo said. "Get me another hundred by the week's end and we're in business."

*   *   *

The modifiers were produced and delivered as Tetsuo asked, and Theodore continued thinking about other items he may be able to produce. It was only a week later, the first time Theodore saw a person whose hair was that particularly straight white that indicated a user of the blocker.

Theodore smiled as he took the man's order at Aaron's noodle bar, happy to know that his work brought somebody the protection he had desired when he conceived the idea. The man ordered a speed modifier, and Theodore raised a curious eyebrow as he turned to deliver the order to Aaron.

"Aaron," Theodore said as he handed him the note with the order scribbled on it. "The fellow with the white hair."

Aaron looked beyond Theodore, at the customers seated around the small dining area. He smiled and nodded.

"Good to know our product is selling. That reminds me, I have to speak to Tetsuo later. He was asking if you had any new products he may wish to trade. Did you have anything ready?"

"Not that Sammy says will work, but I do have some concepts I am working on. Perhaps we can talk about them later," Theodore said.

"Good," Aaron said. "I expect you'll get something workable soon. In fact, you had better. We should find somebody to take orders so you can work out the back on your modifiers instead. But I need you to be making more sellable products to make that worth my time."

Chapter 6 – Helpers

"You there, lad?" Aaron called as he walked to the back of the tent.

"Here, boss," Theodore said.

Aaron walked through to the small space behind the noodle tent, to find Sammy and Theodore standing with a rake between them.

"Strange place for the two of you to be cleaning," Aaron said.

"Theodore is experimenting," Sammy said.

"With what?" Aaron said. "I hope we aren't going to have to deal with some horrible side effects when your experiment fails."

"Ha! You aren't the only one hoping that," Theodore said, then laughed. "Actually, if this idea works, it might solve a problem for you."

"Really?" Aaron said, turning to drag a stool from inside the tent and sitting to watch. "So what are we trying to do?"

"He calls it a helper," Sammy said.

"And what does your helper do?"

"It's an automaton, designed to perform a single set task as instructed by the person who uses the modifier," Theodore explained.

"So why the rake?" Aaron asked.

"The rules state we participate using the tools provided. I am hoping to minimise any punishment for creating something from nothing, by instead applying the modifier to this rake."

Aaron narrowed his eyes, curious to see what would result from the experiment. Theodore held a slip of paper in front of himself, and looked at his employer. After a moment, he looked back at the paper and read.

"One item I ask, with this code to do, its best at one task, that I tell it to. For one working day, this helper will last, and then it will lie, still as in its past."

Theodore reached forward and slapped the paper onto the rake, then stood back. The rake stood there, shaking slightly. It seemed to be waiting for something. Theodore smiled. So far no side effects had happened.

"Please clean leaves from this area," Theodore said.

The rake swung to the side, then back again. Theodore sneezed, drawing a stare from Aaron.

"Nobody sneezes in Claustrum Mundus," Aaron said.

"I guess that was my punishment," Theodore said.

They watched as the helper performed its simple task, and suddenly Aaron burst into laughter. The two coders looked at him, not sure what he was on about.

"It's like a story I read about," Aaron said. "From the twentieth century. This guy was apprenticed to some kind of wizard, and made his tools sweep the room for him, but he got it wrong and they went crazy or something, you reminded me of it just now with the rake."

"I was unsure if the system would let them move, and I can see some problems there with more complex tasks, but I'd like to try to get one to take orders, out the front," Theodore said.

"That would be something I'd have some interest in," Aaron replied.

"I'd like to try to go even further," Theodore said, turning and walking into the tent.

Sammy and Aaron looked at each other, silently asking what Theodore was talking about. With no enlightening explanations, Aaron turned and followed Theodore.

"What do you mean son?" Aaron asked.

Theodore smiled, and said nothing. They walked through to the dining area, and Aaron closed the tent behind them. Together, they began moving the tables out in preparation for the next serving period.

"You know, you hold your cards pretty close to your chest, son. Don't you trust us?" Aaron asked.

"I don't really trust anybody," Theodore replied.

"But don't you think that, if you are trying to sort out an idea, we might be able to help?"

"Perhaps, but I want to get it right on my own, so I can have a more marketable skill in the future. Besides, I want to have some control if this thing is going to be the next huge advance in modifiers."

Aaron laughed loudly, putting a chair down and sitting on it as he let his mirth take over for a moment. He smiled, genuinely amused by the arrogance of his worker.

"You know son," Aaron said. "Sometimes I can't tell if you're full of it, or if you just might be the real deal."

"What do you mean, 'the real deal'?" Theodore asked, dropping another chair and sitting in it.

"I mean, the real deal. I mean, are you full of it or are you really going to take on the system with code? Are you really going to change Claustrum Mundus with your modifiers? Sometimes I think you are, other times I'm not so sure. It's hard to tell when you keep things so guarded."

Theodore looked at his employer for a moment, then smiled.

"Of course I will change things. I don't know if it will be for the better, but I sure as hell intend to enjoy it. You on board old man?"

Aaron laughed again. He stood, and slapped Theodore on the shoulder. Turning, Aaron dragged a table into place before facing Theodore again.

"You know what?" Aaron said. "I'm in. It gets pretty dull around here after a while, and if you're working on what I think you are, I may not need to be around here much in future. I'd have to give Sammy a pay rise if I left him in charge, but it would be worth it to see what you're up to."

Theodore dragged the last table into place, then sat on it, facing his employer.

"That's great, boss, but once we are out of the fields, I'm in charge, OK?"

Aaron chuckled, sitting opposite Theodore again.

"I see," he said. "Well, I guess that is understandable. I have no shortage of points, and I can still draw a wage from the shop when we're gone. Just don't go getting droned, you hear me?"

Theodore nodded, and held his hand out. Aaron shook it, and then stood, retreating to the tent as the first customers arrived for the meal shift. The next couple of hours passed quickly, with an unusual number of customers keeping everyone busy. Finally, the serving time ended and the customers left, as if an unheard alarm had sounded.

Aaron came out front and helped Theodore tidy up and pack away the tables again.

"Boss," Theodore said. "Why do we need to pack up like this every time?"

"It's just how we do it," Aaron said. "Remember the rules of participation? Using what the system has provided? Well, that can be interpreted a number of ways. Some people interpret it as whatever they can get their hands on. When I started the shop, I had to replace a lot of chairs. Packing them away seems to deter a lot of theft. It makes a clear claim of ownership. If I don't do it, some people decide that the tables and chairs are some kind of communal property, and next thing I know, I'm replacing them again."

"What about the wardens?" Theodore asked.

"What about them? They did nothing. They are here to ensure that participants operate within the rules, and they seemed to have no concern about my tables and chairs."

"And what are they, exactly?" Theodore asked, staring at his employers blank expression as the other man tried to decide what the question really was. "Are they a program, sacred and untouchable guardian of the system, or are they a resource? Property? Something we can use, just like everything else that is provided by the system?"

Aaron looked at his employee, suddenly understanding where this was going. He nodded slowly, then smiled.

"You really are a crazy son of a bitch, aren't you boy?" Aaron barked, slapping Theodore on the back.

"Well, if you want to try it, I'm game. But I'll stand back and watch, you might cause some trouble and I don't want to get fried over your insanity!"

Together, Theodore and Aaron walked through the Welcoming Fields, until they reached the central courtyard. Several wardens were in the area, standing near the immense counter as usual.

"So, how does this work?" Aaron asked.

"I have a slightly different version of the same modifier we tested on the rake earlier. I'll slap it on, and see if we can get ourselves a bit of help around the dining area."

Walking behind a warden, Theodore paused to look back at Aaron with a nervous expression. After a moment, he turned to look at the warden's back. With a brief hesitation, he slapped the code onto the warden's shoulder.

The warden spun to face him, and Theodore thought for a brief, terrifying second, that the code had failed and he was about to be punished. Then the warden smiled, an awkward simpleton's grin on the pallid pink skin.

Theodore coughed, then waved a hand in front of the warden's face. The thing stood there, without so much as a blink. Plucking his courage, Theodore leaned forward till his face was close to that of the warden.

"You will go to Aaron's noodle bar, and tend to the customers. You will take their orders, and when the meal time is over, you will pack away the tables and chairs. Go."

Pushing past Theodore, the warden strutted off, apparently not seeing several other people as it pushed through the crowds at the edge of the plaza and disappeared in the direction of Aaron's shop.

Theodore stood there, perplexed, until Aaron approached. The noodle man's eyes narrowed, and he waved a hand in front of Theodore, in parody of what Theodore had just done to the warden. Theodore slapped the hand away in gruff bemusement.

"Do you feel any side effects?" Aaron asked.

"No, nothing. Everything seems normal. Why do you suppose that is?"

"I dunno lad," Aaron said, before laughing softly. "But we best get back to the shop, in case that thing sparks any trouble with the regulars. They'll get quite the shock if this works."

Together, the pair walked back towards the shop, neither sure what the possible implications would be of their actions, and neither sure that they wanted to find out any time soon.

*   *   *

The warden worked methodically and expertly, drawing great consternation from the customers. When a few of the regulars began calling out in surprise, Aaron poked his head out of the tent to see what the commotion was about.

Four men had arrived, and taken seats near the edge of the dining area, and one had jumped out of his skin as the warden's voice came from behind him, asking for their orders. The men quickly overcame their initial shock and were circling the warden aggressively, prodding and poking it as they grew more daring.

Aaron rushed over and pushed between them to protect the warden.

"Now then gentlemen, please do not harass the new staff. Please, give your orders and I will ensure you are seen to with the utmost priority."

"This thing is working for you?" one of the men said, his tone one of disbelief.

"Well, he is," Aaron replied. "But as of yet using an early prototype of a new code we are developing. This is the first public test. Please, we can not guarantee his reactions to aggression as yet, so take care, and be sure to let me know of any concerning, uh, behaviours. Should any damages occur, you would of course be fully compensated. Unless of course you cause a situation beyond our current product development."

The men murmured, then slowly, warily, they returned to their seats. Once they were again seated, the warden repeated its request, and the men gave their orders. The warden wrote the details on a slip of paper, then turned to hand it to Aaron, before trotting off to clear another table which had recently been vacated.

"Remarkable, simply remarkable," the same man exclaimed, as he watched the creature go about its business. "You'd think it was entirely normal behaviour for one of the pink skinned freaks, the way it acts."

Aaron smiled, as he turned to look at the warden briefly before facing the men again.

"Well, here at my shop, I think we can say we have the best coders on the fields. Tell your friends, I intend to be conducting further trials of this new code over the coming days. Now, I will beg your leave to see to your orders. Good day, gentlemen."

The men waved him away, never taking their eyes off the warden. Aaron returned to the tent, pleased with the way things had gone so far.

*   *   *

At the conclusion of the meal time, the warden dutifully cleaned the entire dining area, then stacked away the tables and chairs. A large crowd had gathered, and unlike any previous meal time, customers remained long after close. They watched with apparent amazement as the warden went about his duties.

Finally, the last of the chairs were stacked, the tables all placed away neatly and the dining area looking cleaner than it ever had before. The warden stopped, bowed slightly, then jerked upright in a sudden movement that startled those in the crowd closest to the creature.

As though it had suddenly woken up, it looked around, then strutted off in haste, weaving through the crowd on its way back towards the reception courtyard.

Once it was out of site the crowd quickly dispersed, with much banter between the amazed onlookers over the day's events.

Watching from the tent, Aaron drew the flap closed and turned, beaming a smile for his workers as he slapped Theodore on the back with greater force than either man had expected. Theodore stumbled forward, momentarily losing his balance. Aaron ignored the other man's discomfort and shouted with a cheerful bellow.

"I don't believe it lad, but you may have just given this business the greatest boost in sales it has ever had!" the noodle man said. "Get your coat, and grab another one of those codes, we have a warden to catch. I have a feeling the next meal time is going to be incredibly busy, and we need all the help we can get."

Theodore nodded, and shortly the pair had returned to the reception area. The wardens were gathered together around the counter, and there seemed a few more than usual this time.

After a short wait, one of the wardens moved away from the group, and Theodore approached it. With more confidence than the first time, he applied the modifier, gave his instructions, and watched as the warden walked off in the direction of the shop.

Aaron and Theodore began walking back themselves, but Theodore stopped at the edge of the plaza, a confused look on his face. Aaron looked at him, concerned.

"What is it son?"

"Huh?" Theodore said, looking at his employer. "Oh, it's just, I feel like I'm forgetting something."

"Is it a side effect of the code?"

Theodore shook his head.

"No, I don't think so. I think I've, I don't know, I think I've been getting this feeling for a while now. It's like something is missing. Some part of..." he paused, looking around. "...Never mind. We'd best get back to the shop."

Aaron watched, perplexed, as Theodore wandered ahead, before rushing to catch up. He decided to put it out of mind for the moment.

"Son," Aaron said. "Do you suppose you could rewrite the code to make them work for longer? Like, perhaps a few days at a time? Maybe weeks?"

"Why?" Theodore said, looking at Aaron, and sounding more like his usual self. "You're thinking about something aren't you?"

They walked in silence for a moment before Aaron replied.

"I may need to leave the welcoming fields for a while. It happens occasionally. And you might wish to move on. If we could leave one of these fellows to man the store, with Sammy out the back, then I would sleep a little easier while I was away."

"OK," Theodore said. "I can see the sense in that. I'll sort something out for the next one."

"Apply it to this one, once he finishes the shift." Aaron suggested. "Before he runs off back to the plaza, I mean."

"OK, boss, I'll do that then."

They walked in silence the rest of the way, arriving to find the warden laying out the tables and a handful of customers already waiting for the beginning of the meal time. Aaron went straight to the tent, while Theodore stayed to watch the warden at work. Before long, the crowds were beginning to grow.

"Looks like you were right, boss," Theodore shouted.

"How so?"Aaron replied as he opened the tent's flap. "Oh, I see what you mean. This really is going to be one of our busiest meal times. Son, you'd best stay out there and serve as well. He may be a warden, but he's no superhuman. You'll need both of you to keep up with that lot."

Chapter 7 – Warden's Cost

The warden worked quickly and efficiently, but was still unable to keep up with the demand on its own, just as Aaron had predicted. Theodore found himself losing track of its activities as he rushed about to pick up the short fall.

Many of the customers only grudgingly gave their orders to Theodore. They were anxious to have a closer interaction with the warden, not willing to believe their eyes. Efficient as the warden was, it could never have served everybody who was there.

For the first time in a long time, Aaron was kept busier than he could handle preparing noodles, with the crowds using the obvious excuse of food to gawk at the spectacle of a warden shanghaied into service.

Theodore walked to the tent, pulled back the flap and shouted.

"Hey boss, should I go get another one?"

"No, Sammy can help me here, just keep an eye on things out there," came the reply.

Theodore shut the tent again and returned to serving tables, never taking his eyes off the warden for long as it rushed from table to table, collecting orders and then passing them to Aaron inside the tent.

The time flew by, until the meal time was over, and still the crowds did not disperse. The warden began to try to stack away chairs and tables, but the people would just get them out again.

"Boss, I could use a hand here," Theodore shouted.

Aaron's face appeared through the tent flap, and was

followed shortly after by the rest of the burly noodle man.

"OK folks," Aaron bellowed. "Show's over for today. He'll revert to normal in a moment and you don't want to be in his way when he realises where he is!"

The crowd paused for a moment, considering his words. Then as they realised the implied threat of trouble with a warden, the crowd began to disperse. Slowly it began to put away the tables and chairs, and after struggling through the remnants of the crowd, finally was returning the final table to the stack when Theodore came up behind it.

Carefully, he slapped a new code on the warden's shoulder and it stopped, turning to face him.

"You will continue working for the noodle store, just as you have done this meal time, for the next month," Theodore commanded.

Without a word, the warden turned and placed the table on the stack, then picked up a broom and began sweeping the dining area. Theodore slumped with a sound as if he was punched in the stomach. Aaron rushed to his side.

"Are you OK son?"

"Yeah. Just felt like, I don't know. I'm really forgetting something."

Theodore straightened, and walked to the tent, Aaron following. As they entered, he found a stool and sat, perplexed.

"Boss, has there ever been a positive side effect?"

"Not that I know of. This is a prison remember? A place of criminals. Now, some are noble of heart, as is the way with any group of people, but the ones attracted to modifiers tend not to be those kind. Why do you ask?"

Theodore looked up at Aaron, a pained expression on his face.

"Boss, I've been going over everything in my mind, and it's just not adding up."

"How so, son?"

Theodore looked down, focussing his attention on his feet as he wrung his hands in his lap. Finally he looked back up at his employer before speaking.

"I've been over everything, and there's nothing I can think of that I've lost, or that's weakened. I'm no less than I was before applying that modifier, but something is different."

"You keep saying you are forgetting something. What if that's it?"

"How do you mean?"

Aaron sighed, and pulled over a stool, sitting in front of the younger man. He scratched his head for a moment, then looked Theodore in the eyes.

"Theodore, what is your true name? Your full name?"

"What? It's Theodore Wilson Longarm, just as it always was."

Aaron grunted, nodded, and stood, turning away from Theodore.

"What if it's not?"

Theodore looked at Aaron, a question on his face. Aaron opened the tent flap and waved Theodore out of the tent.

"There is somebody we need to speak to, son." Aaron said. "What if you aren't just forgetting something? What if the side effect is being able to remember that you have forgotten something?"

Theodore stopped, stunned by the simplicity of the answer. He looked around, in that moment taking on the appearance of a startled animal, insecure and alert, unsure of anything, even its own life.

"Boss," he stammered. "Why would stealing a warden do that to me? Is this some kind of cruel joke by the system?"

"I don't know son, but it's time we started looking for a few answers."

*　　　　*　　　　*

"This is Clifton Harper-Smythe," Aaron said as they entered a small, unimposing tent. "He was a relatively well known contractor to a variety of criminal organisations, before being caught and sentenced to life in Claustrum Mundus."

The small, grey haired and bespectacled man looked at them with suspicion as they entered his home. After a moment, he smiled.

"Aaron the noodle man, to what do I owe this peculiar honour?"

"This man is Theodore Longarm. What does that mean to you?"

"It means he is not all that he appears," replied Clifton, huffing to himself as he turned away from his visitors. "Tea, gentlemen? I only have generic black, nothing special for me these days, but it is a connection, if you like, to my old life nonetheless."

Aaron walked forward, closer to Clifton. Theodore followed, looking at his surroundings with caution.

"What do you mean, not all that I appear?" Theodore asked.

Clifton huffed again, slowly turning away from his tea pot to look at the two men.

"It means just what it sounds like. That is not your true name. Why don't you tell us what it is?"

Theodore stopped, staring hard at the strange man. He thought hard about what he heard, and it still made no sense.

"My name is Theodore Longarm, it is the only name I have."

"Is it?" Clifton replied, turning back to his teapot while making a soft clucking sound with his tongue. "I believe you may have yourself fooled somewhat with that notion, young man."

Theodore looked crestfallen, and sat hard on a stool near the flap of Clifton's tent. Clifton approached, pouring the tea as he came, and handed a cup of the steaming brew to Theodore. Theodore accepted it without a word, sipping gingerly as Clifton returned the pot to the stove.

"What does that mean?" Theodore stammered eventually.

"Young man, it means, as I said before, what it sounds like," Clifton said. "The truth, here in Claustrum Mundus, is rarely a simple thing."

Clifton pulled two folding chairs from the end of his

kitchen bench, passed one to Aaron, and sat in the other. He scratched his chin for a long while, thinking over all that he had said so far. Finally he looked back up, into Theodore's questioning gaze.

"Why are you here?" Clifton asked.

"I created a modifier," Theodore said. "That can animate objects to perform duties assigned by the user. We have been successful in abducting a warden to work for us using these helper codes, and the side effect is this over riding sense of having forgotten something, something I had not remembered in the first place. At least, not since I arrived in the Welcoming Fields."

Clifton raised an eyebrow, and scooted his chair closer to Theodore.

"That is interesting, but it is not the answer I was seeking. Why are you here, in Claustrum Mundus?"

Theodore looked long and hard at the old man, wondering why it would be necessary for him to know such a thing, finally he relented, sighed, and looked at his own hands before speaking.

"I was a criminal. I trafficked priceless artefacts, I engaged in terrorist activities, in carrying out my duties for my employers, I even committed murder."

"And that is what the system is punishing you for, as an agent of some shadowy terrorist organisation. That is all the clues I can give you. You will have to learn the rest by yourself."

Theodore frowned, not pleased with this response, though he had not truly expected to find all his answers with the bespectacled old man. Another question rose in his mind.

"So assuming that there is some greater truth," he began.

"Indeed there is," Clifton interrupted. "A truth about you, about what and who you really are."

"Then why," Theodore continued, as though the other man had not spoken. "Why would abducting a warden be rewarded? Why would setting it to work for us, for our own benefit and denying the system one of its minions, result in this awareness of things lost to me?"

Clifton stood, sighed, and returned to his tea pot. He slowly poured himself a steaming cup as he spoke.

"That, I suppose, would likely have something to do with the true nature of the wardens."

"What nature is that?"

"This, is another thing I can not tell you."

"Why not?" Theodore demanded, rising to his feet.

"It is not my place. Sure I have my theory, and there are rumours, but I have no proof, no evidence, and no place to offer you the solution you seek. Not at this time."

Theodore had heard enough. He felt an impotent rage welling up inside him, and lurched forward at the old man. He grabbed him by his scruffy collar and hoisted him into the air, rushing across the small tent till the man's back collided with his pantry.

"Why?" Theodore shouted into the old man's face. "Why do you persist in denying us the answers you clearly have? Are you trying to make me angry old man? Are you deliberatly trying to hinder my search for answers? Are you working with them, those pink skinned monsters, against us for your own gain?"

The old man laughed raucously in response, drawing a surprised look from Theodore, and shocking the rage out of him. Theodore slowly lowered him to the ground. Clifton stood there, looking up at the younger man as his sudden mirth subsided.

"Young man," Clifton began. "Look around us. Do you not see it?"

He moved back to his seat and sat, gesturing for Theodore to do the same.

"See what, old man?" Theodore demanded as he sat.

"There are many millions of us here, in the Welcoming Fields. We do not starve, we do not suffer from disease, there is no war. But even in these pleasant surroundings, a small dull tent is no home for an accomplished man. Do you not wonder on it? Why do they stay here? Very few, as a percentage of the whole, move on from these fields. They are content here. But they are conned. Tents are not the home of ambitious men. Conned tents."

Clifton chuckled to himself, as Theodore took a

moment to see the older man's bad joke. After some time, Clifton continued.

"The people here on the welcoming fields, they lack drive, they have lost their ambition. If I gave you your answers, here and now, what would that do to you? I would be stealing away your drive. No, I can not be the man to do that. Your journey is about to begin, and you must take it yourself. Your answers are the reason for your coming quest. I can not in good faith take that from you. Go, find out your own truth. I will be waiting here when you are done."

"But where do I start?"

"Were you not listening? Young man, it's time for you to leave the Welcoming Fields."

*   *   *

"I'm coming with you," Aaron said with no doubt in his voice.

"What? Why?" Theodore asked.

"I've already seen all that Claustrum Mundus has to offer, I won't risk losing my most valuable coder to its less friendly denizens."

Theodore laughed, dodging an oncoming warden as he continued towards the noodle tent.

"Does that mean you are offering your services as a guide?"

"Yes, I guess it does. My rates are reasonable enough. I will get you to create enough helper codes to last a few years before we leave, paid in advance of course. Should keep Sammy going for a while."

"OK then, when should we leave?"

"Pretty much as soon as you've got the modifiers written up. We could take the easy way, since I have already been everywhere, but I think there is truth in what Clifton said. You have to get there on your own efforts, not mine. I'll tag along, but it will be your journey."

Theodore nodded his understanding, and they walked in silence. After they reached the noodle tent, Theodore went straight to the small table in the back of the tent to start writing up the modifiers, while Aaron explained the situation to Sammy.

"OK then, Boss," Theodore heard Sammy say. "But should I get a second warden? It's usually a bit hectic when you're away, but now, with the interest that thing is creating, it will probably get a lot worse."

"See how you go," Aaron replied. "If necessary, do it, but try not to push things too much."

Theodore stood and walked over to them, still carrying the tiny slip of paper he was working on.

"Be careful, we still don't know the full implications of using the wardens. Why not use some less risky things around the tent? Like that rake on the first test?"

"That will be a sight!" Aaron said with a laugh. "Kitchen utensils bobbing about, like some invisible chef was at work. That will probably attract as much interest as the wardens. Do it. How many more modifiers do you think you will need?"

"Just assume five more workers are needed, and we'll call it enough," Sammy said with a smile.

"Get to it son," Aaron said as he turned to face Theodore.

Theodore returned to the table, and set about writing out all the modifiers as ordered. It never even occurred to him that they had not settled a price yet. Still, recent experience had shown that Aaron was not the kind to leave his work uncompensated, so Theodore fulfilled the request without question.

When at last he was done, Aaron and Theodore left together, neither knowing how long it would be before they would finally return to the welcoming fields, and to Aaron's noodle tent.

Chapter 8 – Trialtown

For the second time, Theodore stood before the guild warden's office. Not for the first time, he wondered why this creature was called the guild warden. With a shrug, he stepped in.

The pink skinned automaton turned to face them as they entered, and smiled in its peculiar manner.

"Welcome back, Theodore Longarm. I trust this visit means you are contemplating a progression?" the warden said, ignoring Aaron's presence.

"I believe the time has come for that, yes."

The warden nodded mechanically, then gestured for Theodore to take a seat. Theodore stared at the comfortable looking object with suspicion. He was fairly sure it was not there a few moments ago.

"Please, be seated. We have much to discuss," the warden insisted.

"I prefer to stand," Theodore said.

"Fine. Well, the next region for you to enter is called Trialtown. There are a number of tests you must complete before I can grant you passage. When shall we begin?"

Theodore sighed, and walked to stand before the chair. Without sitting, he turned to face the warden once more.

"How long will this take?" he asked.

"That depends on you. I can tell you the quickest ever was seven days. The longest was a year. If you reach zero points while in the test, you will be returned to the Welcoming Fields, with only one day to earn points to continue your participation in the system."

Theodore sighed, placing his hands in his pockets. He took a few steps towards the warden, shaking his head slightly as his expression became crestfallen. The warden watched him silently.

"I really don't have time for this," Theodore said as he stopped, facing the warden.

Lightning quick, Theodore's right hand shot from his pocket to plant a modifier on the warden's forehead. He was too quick for the creature, which had not expected such an action. Its face went blank and it stared open mouthed at Theodore. He smiled, relieved that his brash action had paid off.

"You will grant me access to Trialtown," Theodore said. "And you will remain with me, to act as my personal assistant while I get settled there."

"I will grant you access to Trialtown. I will remain with you and act as your personal assistant while you settle in there."

"By the stars, what did you do?" Aaron whispered with awe in his voice.

"I gambled. And it seems I may have won," Theodore said.

"For now, let's hope things continue that way son," Aaron said.

The guild warden turned and made a sweeping gesture with his hand. A blue portal appeared, and he turned to face them again.

"Please masters, follow me," the creature said, before stepping into the shimmering blue and disappearing.

"Very impressive, I must say," Aaron said. "When I was in your shoes, I never would have thought of such a short cut."

Theodore looked at his travelling companion, and a sudden curiosity gripped him.

"Aaron, if you don't mind my asking, how long did you take on the tests to come here?"

"Seven days," Aaron said with an enigmatic smile.

Theodore and Aaron followed the warden, and the world changed. Suddenly they were on a rocky path, running along the top of a twisting ridge, steep cliffs dropping away from either side. Up ahead, a wooden palisade towered above the barren cliffs, defending a fortified town.

"That's Trialtown," Aaron said. "Be careful here, it is the first stop for those with a little ambition. Many of them think they can handle it, and then turn to desperate means when they find out they can't. Each day here will cost you two points, not one like on the fields. And many of the jobs available pay less than they do there, because every employer is desperate. It's a hard place to stay on top."

"Can't they just go back?" Theodore asked.

"They can, but it costs fifty points. Very few have that much left when they discover their situation is that bad. Besides which, the stigma of returning a failure is pretty strong. Most won't risk that."

"You went back," Theodore said.

"I went back by choice. After I made my fortunes. It's a different situation altogether. I have connections, I have a business. Many of the business people on the fields are like me. Not many will employ a failed returner."

"I guess I am lucky to have a passive income set up, then." Theodore said.

"With your modifiers? Yes, you should already have a decent balance with the blockers, and the helper codes are poised to make you a very wealthy man indeed. But you still can fall victim to some of the more elaborate scams in Trialtown. Do not let your confidence blind you."

Soon, they were standing at the base of the palisade, and the warden turned to face them. It rested a hand on the wood and a small section became translucent.

"I hereby grant you access to Trialtown," the creature said.

Theodore stepped forward, but before he could step through, the warden suddenly blocked his passage. Its face faded away and turned grey, before an eery, disembodied voice echoed from its vicinity.

"Runtime error detected. Admissions protocol program intercepting. This participant has not passed the trials. Why is it granted admission?"

The voice did not wait for an answer, replying to itself as if it were two identical voices, and not one.

"This participant has used a modifier code to subdue the guild warden, and thus been granted access by bypassing the trial protocols."

"We must send it back."

"We can not send it back. The participant has not broken the rules, and the guild warden has granted it access. The guild warden has that right and responsibility."

"But it has not decided based on the protocol."

"The protocol has been bypassed, and the guild warden has granted access."

"Then we must allow this. The case will be forwarded to the system auditor program for revision."

The warden returned to normal and stepped aside. It indicated with its hand the still translucent section of palisade.

"My apologies for the delay, masters. Please, enter when you are ready," the warden said.

Theodore stepped forward, and pressed a hand against the translucency. Slowly, his hand sank through, and he stepped forward to follow it. Aaron entered behind him, followed by the guild warden, who remained behind them, waiting for further instructions.

Directly ahead, a tavern stood, seedy and dark. Dull, flickering light emitted through the dirty windows of the establishment. Theodore began walking towards it.

"Wait, son," Aaron said. "You don't want to go in there. They'll charge you seventeen points a day for a filthy room, and insist you pay double for meals while you're there."

"Well, you have any better suggestions?"

"I own a small place in the back streets. Follow me. I'll only charge you a few points to stay, and it's safe."

Theodore shrugged, and followed. The warden tagged along behind.

"You never miss a chance to earn a few more points, do you?" Theodore asked.

"It's how you have to be here, son. The sooner you learn to cash in, the easier things will be. You might have a bit coming in through your codes, but it won't be enough if you're not careful around here."

Theodore was observing all he could take in as they rushed through the narrow streets. Two and three story, rickety looking buildings towered over the narrow streets. As they moved deeper into the town, Theodore became more and more aware of the general decay of the populace.

Their clothes were dirty, often torn, their hands callused, and their hair unwashed. It was obvious how much harder life was here than in the Welcoming Fields. It was clearly a very different situation, and a much harder game than anything Theodore had experienced so far.

He shuddered involuntarily. The sudden realisation that he had been subverted into the system in that other, easier place, but now he must survive a harsher environment, set his nerves on edge. This place could easily be the end of him.

Aaron stopped and pushed a key into a small wooden door, squeezing through before waving for Theodore to follow him. Theodore followed, and the warden stepped through behind him.

They stood in a small room, a dingy light from a square panel in the ceiling barely breaking the gloom of the tiny, windowless cell. Aaron turned to face Theodore, and shrugged his shoulders with an apologetic shake of his head.

"I know it's not much, but at least it doesn't cost us a lot," he said.

"It's rather plain," Theodore replied. "And cramped."

Aaron looked around, seeming to see his surroundings for the first time.

"Oh right, I forgot about that. The modifiers on the room would have expired. You can deal with that right?"

"Modifiers? On a place?"

"Of course," Aaron said. "I had it in a twenty first century Mediterranean style before, but I paid far too much for it. If you can come up with something nice, I'll deduct your fees from the rent."

"I'm sure I can figure something out," Theodore said. "Do place modifiers have punishments attached?"

"Only if they give you an unfair advantage," Aaron said. "That's the loophole. You never do your own. If you are selling the service, that's employment. Participation. That makes it exempt from punishment. Make your own property somehow, um, unnatural, then you might have trouble. I don't know what sort of trouble though, I never knew anybody who did it."

Theodore nodded, and paced around the small room, his thoughtful attitude filling the air. Finally he stopped, faced the wall opposite the door, and pulled out his pen. Retrieving a slip of coder's paper from another pocket, he began to scribble.

Screwing up his first attempt, Theodore wrote a second. He then returned his pen to his pockets, and slapped the paper against the wall. He read the words aloud.

"Double this space, and give it a view, that this little place, may be cozy for two."

The room seemed to fade out for a moment, as the walls were replaced by oblivion. Light began to fill the room, pouring in from an immense picture window that had come into existence along the wall he had applied the code to. Soon they could see all four walls in the brightness, just as plain as they had been before, but now encompassing a larger, more comfortable room.

Outside the window, it was as though a dense fog was being cleared. A magnificent mountain scape sat there, wispy clouds drifting past the window as they watched from their perch in the roof of the world.

Aaron walked behind Theodore, slapping him on the back. He smiled broadly as he looked out at the distant settlements, microscopic people working the small cot holds of the valleys below.

"Son, this is a great start. Don't finish it all off now, get settled and think on the next change for a while."

Theodore ignored the advice and walked to a corner, where the windowed wall met the next, and pulled out his pen. He scribbled a quick note, then slapped it on the wall and read it aloud.

"Put here a bathroom, in blue tiles and grey, so

residents can wash, at all times of day."

The wall flickered for a moment, then a strong wooden door appeared. Theodore opened it, to reveal a spacious bathroom beyond.

"Excellent," Aaron enthused. "But really, that is enough for now. Get your stuff organised, take a corner and relax for a few minutes. We will go out again shortly."

Theodore stood, still staring at the new bathroom. He shook his head.

"I still am amazed that such simple rhyme could do this. Surely this is something anybody could do? I'm hardly a great poet."

"Son," Aaron replied. "It is not just about the words you write. It is how you feel the words, what your mind does in connection to the system, almost at the unconscious level. That is the talent that a coder must develop, not their word smithing skills. That is where many fail. They begin to focus too much on their words, and lose their connection to their feelings, their desires. Then the codes fail, or the punishments become too severe."

Theodore turned to face his friend, and smiled.

"Well, I'd best make sure I never fall into that trap then," he said.

Walking to a corner of the room. Theodore placed his belongings on the ground, then turned back to face the window.

"As nice as that view is," he said with a smile. "I'd like to take a look around town, now we have our accommodation sorted."

Aaron nodded, and began walking towards the door. They had both momentarily forgotten the warden, who remained just inside the room, blocking their exit. As they approached, the warden's skin began to lose its colour, turning grey. The creature's face faded away, just as it had done when they entered Trialtown. The same voice they had heard from it before now filled the room.

"The system auditor program has reviewed this case. The individual in question has operated outside of protocol, but not beyond the laws of Claustrum Mundus.

Due to the increased difficulty of existence in Trialtown, no punishment will be given. The town will handle that sufficiently on its own."

The voice stopped, and the warden slowly regained his composure, his face returning.

"Again, I apologise, masters."

"That doesn't look like a pleasant experience," Theodore said to the warden. "And the town will handle that? What an ominous sentiment."

"The system has its way, Master."

The warden stepped aside, then followed as Theodore and Aaron passed through the doorway. The rattle of a passing cart greeted the three of them as they walked out onto the cobble stones.

Theodore was silent, as he considered the Warden's words. He thought it sometimes acted a little less like a computer program. He shuddered as he considered the implications. How many of those they dealt with were really automatons? Could the system create the illusion of a prisoner, acting as a spy among the inmates?

Theodore vowed to himself that he would keep a close eye on the Warden. He realised he had started to trust it too much.

Chapter 9 – A Question of Mind

A wizened, grey haired gentleman looked them over, his eye critical in the dim light of the Code Bank. Theodore had not realised before then that the place existed.

"So you see," Aaron explained to the man, finishing his little speech the stranger had largely ignored. "While we may still open our own store front, we were hoping to organise a local distributor for our wares."

The man offered no immediate reply. Instead, he circled the warden, standing perhaps closer than he ever had before to one of its kind. He reached a finger up, to tap on the creature's pink skinned forehead. The man then jumped back quickly, as if expecting the thing to strike him dead.

The warden made no response at all. The man, smiling nervously, finally turned to face Aaron, seeming to see him for the first time.

"How much for him?" the man asked.

"I'm sorry Sir," Aaron replied. "That creature is a work in progress, and as such is not yet for sale. We prefer to ensure the safety of our clients through rigorous testing before offering anything with such dangerous potential into the market."

"A fair point," the man said. "Though I must admit I am greatly intrigued by this particular item. I would very much like the chance to study it in more detail."

"We will be certain to let you know as soon as the product is ready for sale," Aaron replied in a firm, business like manner.

"Humph," their host snorted, realising his requests were not to be honoured yet. "We here at the Code Bank can certainly provide a service as a sales agent for such accomplished men as yourselves. Strictly on a commission basis of course, we would require sixty percent."

Aaron turned, and headed towards the door. Theodore and the warden followed, none of them saying a word.

"Fifty percent," the man said.

Aaron paused, then continued, still not offering any reply to the offer.

"Fine, forty percent gentlemen, and we can start selling immediately."

Aaron stopped again, and turned to face the man. He smiled, his expression cunning.

"Make that thirty five, and we sign today. Any more and we take our products elsewhere."

The man sighed, then walked to a desk, picking up a pen and muttering a short code under his breath. A paper document appeared on the desk.

"Fine," he said. "Thirty-five percent commission, and we will ask a minimum stock be maintained. We will contact you whenever the supply runs short."

"Thank you," Aaron said, taking the proffered pen and quickly reading over the contract.

After a moment, he scribbled his signature on the bottom. He handed the pen to Theodore, who did the same. The pair then moved towards the door, Aaron stopping on the threshold to face the man again.

"We will ensure you receive a selection of our products by close of business today."

*　　　　*　　　　*

Theodore watched the clouds pass by the picture window in their bedsit. They drifted by with serene confidence, certain of their destination and purpose in a way that Theodore was not.

He had taken a brief moment to break from his task, creating enough modifiers to supply stock to the Code

Bank. Theodore had been surprised that Aaron did not already have a store in Trialtown.

The expense was not worth the benefit, according to Aaron, and Theodore supposed he had come to that conclusion carefully. Aaron seemed to be a careful and intelligent businessman.

"Sir," came the Warden's voice, cutting into Theodore's thoughts. "We must hurry. You will lose points as a penalty under the contract, if you are late with a delivery."

"Of course," Theodore said.

Once again, he was curious about the near human speech the Warden was adopting. A concept nagged at the edges of his thoughts. Perhaps all was not as it seemed. He decided to see if he could learn more.

"Warden," Theodore said. "Do you think?"

"My programming is complex. I believe I am self aware, but an automaton follows the orders of its programming, so I may be wrong in my belief."

Theodore turned to face the creature, surprise prompting his response.

"What do you mean, you believe you are self aware? Doesn't that imply that you are?"

"Not necessarily, Sir," it replied. "Could I not have been programmed to believe I was aware of myself, to provide a more human interface for inmates such as yourself?"

"Then why are you talking in such a philosophical manner?"

"Why are you?" the Warden replied.

"Because I am human, it is a part of what I am. What I want to learn more about, is what you are. What part of you makes you think the way you do?"

"So you believe that a warden can think?"

"You seem to."

The Warden moved towards the window, facing it, its hands clasped behind its back. It was a far more human stance than Theodore had ever seen it display. After a moment the Warden turned back to face Theodore.

"I am programmed as an interface with the system. I

am designed to have an obvious difference, but also I am designed to be non threatening, and to appear to have a capacity of understanding, such that my actions are acceptable to the prisoners held in Claustrum Mundus."

"There is the thing," Theodore said. "What you just said, it was far more detailed, more human sounding, than it ought to be. What is really going on with you? My modifier can not possibly have altered your programming to that degree."

"I do not know, Master."

"When did this begin?"

"I do not know, Master."

"Did you think, did you speak, like you are now, before you began to travel with us?"

There was silence for a moment, before the warden replied.

"No Master, I did not."

"I see."

Theodore went back to his work, soon forgetting the warden was nearby as he wrote his modifiers. After a few minutes, he was interrupted by the warden again.

"Master," the creature said. "Why did you ask me those things?"

"Because you are an anomaly. You do not make sense. You are an automaton, but you are sounding less like one since working with us. It concerns me."

"Do you fear me, Master?"

"No, I do not fear you. I fear what you may become."

"Why is that, Master?"

"Never mind. It is not important," Theodore said in a dismissive tone.

"Yes, Master."

"Warden," Theodore said. "Who are you?"

"I do not know, Master."

"What do you mean, you do not know? Didn't you just tell me you believe you are self aware?"

"I believe I am, Master."

"Then why do you not know who you are?"

"There is much you do not know about yourself, Master. It is the same."

71

"I know who I am, why don't you?" Theodore said, his temper rising, though he was not sure why.

"I do not know who I am, but I do know what I am. I feel that it may not be so different for you, Master. With no disrespect intended."

Theodore looked at the warden, his eyes narrowing as his gaze bored into the creature, as if he were trying to decipher its mysteries. He shook his head slowly, and looked back out at the clouds.

"I doubt an automaton is capable of disrespect," Theodore said. "As you say, it would be limited in action by its programming. Much as those clouds travel in determined knowledge of their purpose, so do you. They do not know who they are, but I dare say if you could speak to the clouds, they would likely know what they are."

"Yes Master," the warden said. "But a cloud has no capacity for thought. No capacity for intelligent interaction. It just follows its course."

"Unless it is interrupted by an external force."

"Such as the mountains, yes Master, that is correct. If I am a cloud, you are an external force. Your modifier is to me as the mountain to the cloud."

"So, your purpose, your direction, is changing?"

There was no response for several seconds. The warden stood pensive, until finally it turned to face Theodore.

"Yes, the reasonable deduction is that my direction, my purpose, is changing. Because of you, Master. Until recently, I was a cog in the machine that is Claustrum Mundus. I was a servant of the system, and I was good at my task. Now I am a servant to my Master, which is you. You now direct my purpose, and I do not know where your new instructions will take me."

"Nor do I, Warden. Nor do I. Do you not fear your unknown destiny?"

"I do not know fear, Master. Do you fear what you have lost? Do you fear learning something that is instrinsic to who you are? Would not such a thing change your sense of self? Would you fear such a thing? Would you fear such things for those you travel beside?"

"I do know fear," Theodore said, slipping the last of his modifiers into a large envelope as he stood. "And yes, I do fear those things. Both for myself and for you."

"Why for me?" the warden asked.

"Because what you become could inform our understanding of what is really happening in Claustrum Mundus, and that understanding might highlight just how terrible this prison really is."

"Do you believe that things are changing that much?" the warden asked.

"We just had a lengthy conversation," Theodore said. "Something that should not have occurred if our simple knowledge of the system were complete, or accurate. If what you are differs so greatly from what we knew, then what of myself? How much of us is real, and how much is false?"

"I am sure I can not say, Master."

"Humph," Theodore said, slipping the envelope into a pocket and leaving the room.

The warden followed, a silence falling between them as Theodore set off on his delivery. Theodore made a mental note to discuss this with Aaron as soon as he returned from where ever he had gone for the afternoon.

Aaron had sent Theodore home to complete the modifiers as soon as they left the Code Bank, but did not say where he was going in the meantime. Theodore had a feeling he did not wish to know.

*　　　*　　　*

Theodore left the Code Bank, content that his work was done for the moment. As he began strolling home, he was surprised to see a familiar face in the crowd. The young man who was approaching seemed not to have seen him yet.

Theodore could not remember the young man's name, if he had even learned it in the first place. But the man was instantly recognisable as the same young man who had led his thugs into Aaron's dining area, intent on violence.

"Hey," Theodore shouted as he rushed towards the young man.

There was no response. Theodore rushed towards him, hoping simply to enquire on how he was going since their last encounter. He was not sure why it was so important to him. But this young man had endured a similar experience on entering Claustrum Mundus to that which Theodore himself had survived.

He felt a kind of camaraderie with the man, although he did not know him at all. Catching up with the young man, Theodore slapped a hand on his shoulder, intent on a jovial greeting, but the man simply pulled away. He continued walking away in a steady, almost robotic fashion.

The warden caught up, and stood beside Theodore. It shook its head slightly, its uncharacteristic motion drawing looks from some in the crowd.

"Master, he is an automaton."

Theodore looked at the warden in shock.

"Wait, you mean, he has failed to participate? Lost his points?"

"Yes, master. You were the same once were you not?"

"Yes I was," Theodore replied in a soft voice.

Suddenly, Theodore pulled out his pen and a slip of paper. He scribbled furiously, then rushed towards the young man again. He slapped the paper on his shoulder, and tore a corner. He slipped the corner into his pocket as he returned to where the warden stood, watching his actions impassively.

"What did you do, Master?"

"I put a monitor on him. I wish to see what happens to him now. Perhaps I will understand myself better if I know how his failure impacts him here."

"He is an automaton," the warden said in a confused tone. "nothing will impact him any more."

"For how long?" Theodore asked.

"Forever, Master."

Theodore shook his head in disbelief.

"I recovered," he said.

"Your case was not of failure, but of abuse. You lost

your points immediately on entry. Such cases are recovered in the audits. That one is different, he was not a new participant. He knew the risks when he came here. He has lost, and now is a part of the system."

Theodore's head span to face the warden. His mind seized on one part of the warden's words.

"What do you mean a part of the system?"

"I mean he is under its control, Master. It is not important. When a participant fails to participate adequately, then the system takes over their participation."

"You are wrong, Warden. It is indeed terribly important. I must watch over this man, to understand better our situation. He may be an automaton, but if what I fear is true, he may be one of the most important of his kind in Claustrum Mundus. As are you now, Warden."

Theodore struck off towards home, leaving the young man to his tasks. The warden followed, having no other option thanks to the binding orders of the modifier. Theodore stopped, and turned to face the warden.

"It would seem by the terms of the original modifier, you will be leaving us soon. It stated while I get settled in. That is happening. I would like to extend this. Remind me to use another modifier on you when we get home."

"Yes, Master."

*   *   *

Aaron greeted them when they entered their home, his grin wide as he ushered them inside and closed the door.

"You got the modifiers delivered then?" he asked.

"Yes, Boss," Theodore replied.

"Good. I have another request for you now. We need this place a bit larger. Can you add two bedrooms and an office? I may need to have some business meetings, and we need to look seriously successful."

"I suppose we can arrange that, but I have something else to do first," Theodore said.

Theodore went to his belongings and removed a small modifier, and walked to the warden.

"I'm sorry, Warden," he said, slapping the modifier

onto its shoulder. "You will remain with me as my personal assistant for the remainder of my time in Trialtown."

Chapter 10 – Business Matters

"Spacial telemorphics," Aaron said. "Is a coding technique that allows you to break the rules of geographic continuance."

"Meaning..." Theodore said with a sardonic tone.

"That's how they describe it, but the name is just something somebody made up, really."

"Well, that's true of this entire place, so I guess it fits," Theodore said, a smile creasing his face.

"Anyway," Aaron continued. "It refers to codes that allow you to build things that make no logical, spacial sense in a strictly physical interpretation of the world."

"Modifiers that screw with your head?"

Aaron looked at him, a little annoyed at the glibness of his response.

"Modifiers that break the rules of the real world. For example, what you did to enlarge this apartment, and give us that marvellous view, is a form of spacial telemorphics."

"So I'm already doing it. Why are we talking about this now?"

"You will need a bit of training to be skilled enough to do the more advanced stuff."

"It can't be that hard. Like running cheats for a game."

"This is no game, and you need to realise some humility or your coding will stall. Remember what we spoke about when you first started? Anyway, I have a specialist coming soon, and I want you to watch everything he does. Learn as much as you can from his techniques."

"What are you up to, old man?" Theodore asked.

Aaron ignored the unflattering epithet, and walked to face the window. Looking out onto the rocky mountains, he mused.

"There is an untapped market here, so we are turning this room, with it's wonderful view, into a dining room. There will be a new door, opening into the market square of Trial town, and we will be going into business just like we had in the Welcoming Fields."

"Why don't we just sell codes?"

"There is money in food, son. Makes them feel like they are living a real life for a bit. Plus it pays to have a more legitimate front for the modifier business. Besides, I like noodles."

"So who's going to wait tables?"

"Surely you know that by now, son."

*   *   *

The newcomer looked around the room with a critical eye, taking in what had already been done with the patronising amusement of an art professor examining finger paintings in a preschool. Stopping at the picture window, he smiled, then looked back at Theodore and Aaron.

"This stays, obviously. It is the one thing that speaks of the coder's talent. The rest, functional, but oh so bland."

The man ran fingers through his thinning grey hair and clucked as he thought.

"Now then, the first thing is to designate the space. You will want diners to see this view, but not come directly to it. They will be paying for the environment as well as the food."

He took out a coder's pen and turned it, end over end, as he paced around the perimeter of the room. After a few laps of the space, he smiled and returned to them, holding the pen like a surgeons knife.

"We need a bigger room, to start with," he declared.

Walking to each wall in turn, he slashed a reckless

looking cross on them then mumbled. As he returned to the centre of the room, it grew. The walls receded and the picture window seemed to stretch, until the room had doubled in size.

"Much better," he said. "But this space could be so much grander."

Theodore looked to Aaron, the question burning in his mind.

"Boss, he wrote nothing, yet he modified things. He coded without coding. How is that even possible?"

"He coded, he just did it verbally. Didn't you hear him mumbling his rhymes?"

"How does he do that?"

"Practice, son. He has been at this for a long time, and has that strong connection to the system. He has serenaded her for many years."

The man coughed softly, watching them with mild displeasure.

"Sorry, please continue," Aaron said, before looking to Theodore. "He prefers silence while he works."

The artist walked to one end of the window, and reached to the floor, drawing a line parallel to the wall. He walked backwards, until he had taken the line all the way around to meet the window at the other end. He then drew two great sweeping curves, parallel, from a point near the door to the street, out into the centre of the room.

Stepping back beside them, Theodore heard the man's mumbling clearer this time. Suddenly the room was changing again. It was impossible to determine whether the floor dropped or the ceiling rose, but the distance between them quickly tripled, then grew some more.

Around the sides of the room, at the highest level, a balcony jutted out, its boundaries matching the lines the man had drawn. Then, carved majestically out of stone, an immense curved stair case reached up from the floor, following the curved lines until it met the balcony.

"You will need to be careful, until the balustrades are installed," the man said as he began walking up the stairs. "My workers have already begun on those, and will be waiting at your new entry site. I took the liberty of drawing the door there before I came here. My boys will have erected your signs already."

When he reached the top of the stairs, Theodore noticed that all the existing doors now opened onto the grand balcony. He had wondered where they would fit a kitchen, and now he understood. This impossible building method was full of surprises.

"So, Boss, you will have the kitchen down there?"

"Yes, Son, and a door man up here, to greet or eject patrons, as the need may be."

They turned and looked out over the new space, the immense size lending a strange normality to the grand vista outside the window.

"It's brilliant," Aaron said with a smile.

Ignoring the compliment, the man drew a rectangle on the wall beside the old door, and mumbled. A beautifully carved wooden door slowly morphed into being, then slid aside, like a shopping mall door, to reveal the bustling market square.

Shaking his head, Theodore opened the old door, and looked from one to the other. Market square and back street both seemed to occupy the same space, but never met.

"It is amazing, isn't it, Son?" Aaron said.

"Will you join it to your shop in the fields?" Theodore asked.

Aaron looked at him like he was a genius.

"Why didn't I think of that? Then we could run both sites from here! Sammy could come here and still our loyal clients in the field could visit. It will probably cost a bit, but it will be worth it."

*   *   *

Theodore stood with Sammy on the balcony, near the majestic curved stairs. The fittings for the restaurant were almost complete, and the door to the noodle tent in the welcoming fields was now installed, linking the two kitchens.

"So, why did we link via the kitchens?" Sammy asked.

"The coder said it was too risky to link the dining area, since the system has blocks and tests in place to stop people coming here when they aren't ready. Enabling anybody to bypass those tests might come with some horrible side effects for the user," Theodore explained.

Below, the warden was hard at work mopping the now ornate mosaic floor. It paused briefly, looking up at them with an almost curious air, before returning to its work.

"That one is acting a little strange now," Sammy said.

"What do you mean?" Theodore asked.

"I can't quite put my finger on it, but it seems less like one of them now. I can't help thinking that it looks different somehow, but I can't figure out what it is that has changed."

"It's not your imagination." Theodore said. "I don't notice it, because it has been so gradual. But I have a theory about the wardens, and I have been waiting to see what this one does before I decide to test my theory."

"How would you test it?" Sammy asked.

"I really don't know yet," Theodore replied, looking at Sammy, surprised his question was about how to test the theory, not what it was.

"I suppose Aaron will be recruiting more of them soon. You'll be able to compare them at least," Sammy said.

Theodore nodded, walked to the door, and exited into the market. Sammy followed without speaking, and soon they were mingling with the crowds of Trialtown, just another two inmates going about their business.

Pushing through the crowds, they wandered aimlessly. Suddenly, a buxom young woman, with long straight dark hair framing a face that spoke of bitter determination combined with desperate longing, slammed into Theodore at speed, knocking him down. He collided with Sammy, who also went down.

The girl mumbled an almost forgotten apology and ran. They stood, looking after the retreating figure in bemusement. Sammy watched her with interest, then turned to Theodore.

"Do you have a wife?" Sammy asked.

Theodore was taken aback by the question and he thought for a moment.

"I'm not sure."

"What do you mean you're not sure?" Sammy asked.

"Well, if you had asked that a few weeks ago, I would have said no, but I find myself..."

Theodore considered his thoughts for a moment.

"...Remembering moments. Ever since I came here, I have felt that something was missing. A lot of somethings, more precisely. Like half my old life was expunged when I arrived. I can't remember her name, but I believe she existed. I hope I can solve it all soon, because I don't know how much of me is still missing."

Sammy stared at his friend for a long while, his eyes narrowed, before he gave his reply.

"Wow, that's heavy. You should be careful just in case."

"What do you mean?" Theodore asked.

"The girls, you should avoid them. You never know who your wife could be, best not to upset her."

Theodore frowned, his brow creasing as he looked at his friend.

"Are you quite sane? I'm not sure I understand a word you're prattling," Theodore said.

"It's you that I worry about on that score," Sammy said. "Now then, you are not sure, but me, I'm certain that I am single, and she looked to be a rather delicious diversion. I'll see you later."

Without waiting for any further reply, Sammy ran after the girl, leaving Theodore to stare open mouthed as his friend vanished into the crowd. He watched for while, standing there in thought.

Finally, Theodore turned around to continue his wandering through the markets, and ran into a tall pink skinned figure. He took a step back, looking the creature up and down.

"Hello, Theodore," said the creature in a soft, lilting voice.

Theodore looked closer. It was hard to see, but the difference was there. This warden was female. Or at least, it was the system trying to hint at it being a female.

"What do you want?" he demanded, feeling an irrational anger simmering.

"Your memory profile is changing. The system has ordered I watch over you, just in case."

"Just in case what?" he spat, ignoring the warden's almost human speech patterns as he fished in his pockets for a modifier.

"Just in case you remember something that changes your motivations. We can not allow any danger to the inhabitants of this place."

"Danger? What are you babbling about, woman?" he said, using the misogynistic tones to try to elicit an emotional response from the warden.

"We know you try to test us now. Do not alter your behaviour, we see all and know all. You are not that kind of man, so do not speak as if you are. It is terribly unbecoming."

He dropped the modifier, but kept his hand in his pocket.

"What do you mean by that? How much do you really know?"

"We know all. I already know that you held that silly scrap of paper in your pocket a moment ago. I must warn you, and you must agree. You are not to enslave me like you did that other warden."

"Yet you are going to watch over me?"

"Yes. If you wish me to be nearby, should you need assistance from the system, you need not enslave me for the purpose."

Theodore's frown deepened. How had she known his motivation so easily? And why had she so quickly become a she in his mind, instead of an it? This was most unsettling.

"Do what you like, creature. I have business to attend to," he said.

Theodore turned on his heel and walked as fast as he could through the crowds, back towards the door with the noodle shop sign hung over it, to his sanctuary from the strangeness of the place. He did not look back to see if the creature followed, but he felt her eyes burrowing into his soul nonetheless.

*   *   *

Aaron had taken a stack of the modifiers from Theodore's work bench, and it had not surprised him. What Aaron had planned to do was obvious, in as much as it was what was needed.

Theodore was standing at the window, while Sammy lounged in a comfortable armchair nearby, the buxom lass draped over him like a shawl. Across the room, the warden busied himself with table settings.

"Haha! Time for work, son," came Aaron's booming voice from the doorway upstairs.

All eyes looked to the boss, who stood there, flanked by a half dozen wardens.

"We send three of these guys through to the other store, and keep three here. They are our staff now. You never need to wait on tables again, Theodore."

Aaron walked down the stairs, the six pink skinned creatures following.

"I don't know how you coded these things without side effects," Aaron said. "But it makes them immensely valuable. I have orders for seven, at a price you will enjoy. You are a rich man now, son. Of course we are selling them as seven or thirty day limited ones only, so repeat sales are a guarantee. It's a business after all."

"How much did we get?" Theodore asked.

"Well, your share is thirty thousand each for the seven day ones, which we sold four of, and a hundred thousand for the thirty day ones."

"So I have a hundred and thirty thousand points now? Not too bad at all."

"No son, those are for each warden. You have four hundred and twenty thousand, with more to come. A very limited client base that can afford them, but enough that you should be free of financial concerns. At least until the novelty wears off."

Chapter 11 – Warden

The six new wardens lined up near the base of the stairs, with Aaron standing before them, his hands on his hips.

"Warden, come here," Theodore called as he joined his employer.

In response, the original warden who had now been with them for so long it seemed it was one of them, walked over to stand in front of the others. Theodore looked at Aaron, who matched his surprised expression.

"Theodore, what is this?" Aaron asked.

"It's how he's changing. I don't know why, but he's becoming less like them as the days pass."

"But look at his skin! The others are still that unnatural pink, but he looks, well, almost normal. It's been so gradual I hadn't even noticed it happening. What do you think it means?"

Theodore sighed. Looking down, he considered his words for a moment.

"I have been considering a theory for some time now," Theodore said. "I guess this is as good a time as any to see what they know."

Theodore looked at the warden, and was about to speak to it, when Aaron interrupted him.

"Wait, son. Tell me what this theory is first."

"Well," Theodore said. "The wardens don't start as automatons. They start as us. Somehow, working for us is changing him. I think he is becoming a person again."

"That's correct," the warden said, surprising them

both, its face grey as the system communicated through it. "By working for you, this warden has been repaying its debt."

"Wait, what debt?" Theodore demanded.

"As an automaton, inmates do not earn points as they are no longer participating. They are, however, still charged the usual daily points fees for remaining in the system."

"So how is it repaying the debt?" Aaron asked.

"By performing duties for you, this warden has been earning points."

"Ok, and that is why it is changing?" Theodore asked.

"As the debt reduces, the warden will recover its human self. In due course, it will be permitted to recommence its active participation."

Theodore thought for a moment, looked at Aaron, then back at the warden's grey face.

"So, does the lack of side effects have something to do with this?" he asked.

"As your modifier is benefiting its target by raising its point balance, your action is deemed not to grant you unreasonable advantage at another's expense. The use of the recruited wardens may result in penalties in future, should that use be deemed to have other impacts that outweigh those benefits."

Sammy approached, and spoke from behind Aaron. The others turned quickly to face him, though they had not heard him approach.

"It sounds like your limited time modifiers were a wise move, boss. Can you imagine the cranky clients when their warden slaves suddenly become people and run off?"

*   *   *

Theodore made his way through the market place, one of the new wardens following close behind. Not far away, the female was also following. She seemed to be making herself visible to him, while still keeping her distance.

Ignoring his stalker, Theodore found the supplies he was looking for at a grocery stall, and took them. Loading the noodle ingredients into a small box the shop keeper provided, he handed them to the warden.

"Take these back to Aaron, then wait for his next instruction," Theodore said, a bored tone permeating the words.

Walking away from the grocers, without looking to see if the warden went in the right direction, Theodore fell to thoughtfulness. There had been so many questions recently, and he felt he had not come close to an answer for the majority. It seemed that the number of riddles was growing faster than he could solve them.

The income from the modifiers could have allowed him to work less, dedicating more of his time to solving the mysteries of his past and of Claustrum Mundus. But Theodore was concerned that the income may be impacted by this new information about the wardens. How many thirty day helpers would make the transition before their time was up?

He shook his head, wanting to silence the doubts that were forming. He smiled, as he realised the irony of the situation. He laughed out loud, not knowing he had done so until he heard his own voice.

"Why are you laughing?"

He turned to look at the female warden, who had come closer while he was thinking. She looked at him, her head slightly tilted, an almost human curiosity in her demeanour. Their was something most unusual about this warden, apparently sent by the system for the single duty of watching him. He looked at her, and shrugged.

"It struck me as ironic. I have so much I don't know, memories I can't quite remember, and I don't know where to start. But then I am helping that warden, bringing him back, returning his self, his identity, his life, when I never had that intention, and couldn't do that for myself."

Theodore turned and walked away, finding a bench on the edge of the market. He sat, and the warden followed, to stand before him. They made a curious tableau there, the man and the automaton, apparently in conversation, though neither spoke.

For several minutes, they remained that way, Theodore

contemplating his situation while the warden simply waited for him to do something. She had the patience of an inanimate device, unaware or perhaps simply unconcerned by the passage of time.

Occasionally one of the other inmates would notice them, and gawk at the pair, surprised by the scene. Finally, Theodore looked back up at the warden.

"Who am I, really?" he demanded. "The system has messed with my memories, and I want to know what it's done. What's changed? What am I forgetting? I have to know. What is my true name?"

"Your name?" she replied.

"Theodore Longarm? That's only part of who I am. Longarm was not my true name. I was a longarm agent, but I was somebody else as well. The system has stolen that life from me, and I must find it again."

'Only you can answer that question," she said in a sweet tone.

Theodore snorted his derision. He admitted to himself it was all he had expected, but it would be nice to get a straight answer sometimes. He stood, and turned to walk away.

"Wait," she demanded. "I will show you something of this place."

He watched as the warden walked away from him, not looking back. The confidence that he would obey was infuriating, but not half as infuriating as the fact that he did. Theodore wanted nothing more right then than to be free of her presence, yet without thought he was following her. Suddenly he felt the need to know more about her.

"Why do you act independently?" he asked.

"What do you mean?" came the reply.

"You're following me, acting on the moment, and you seem to be making decisions."

"Do I?" she said, smiling sweetly, a disconcerting expression on that pink, plastic skin.

"It does seem to be so," Theodore mused. "Or is this all merely the system's influence? Is it making you this way for my benefit? Or worse, is it making you act this way for its own?"

"I can not say," replied the warden, facing away from him again as it led the way.

Soon they arrived at an open area. Theodore, walking with his eyes cast down, looked up as they stopped, to observe the place.

"What the hell is this?" he demanded.

Again that sweet smile sickened him. She did not answer, as he looked back the way they had come. In the middle distance, the market was abuzz with inmates and wardens, going about their business. He turned again, to face the small, open area.

Swings, roundabouts, flying foxes and other toys of the playground, all long since abandoned, or more probably never occupied, filled the space. The laughing cries of children would never be heard in this garden of joy. He turned to face her.

"What the hell is this?" he demanded a second time.

"This is your punishment, that of all those in Claustrum Mundus. The reminder."

"Reminder of what?" he asked.

"Reminder that this is a prison. Some feel we are too easy on you, so we must remind you."

She walked away, and Theodore stood, looking at the playground for a long time. Finally, he walked forward, and sat on a swing. He was still there some hours later, when she returned. Theodore looked up at her.

"What is this place?" he said, his tone different now.

She looked at him for many seconds, evaluating. She seemed to be listening to something, and Theodore shuddered, fearing that she was listening to his thoughts. Finally she spoke with the voice of a teacher.

"This is a place for the children to run, to laugh, to play. It is a place of joy."

"There are no children here," Theodore said.

She tilted her head, considering his words far more than they warranted.

"Then by extension," she said. "You imply there is no joy."

"It is a prison."

"It is a prison," she replied.

"Where are the children?" he asked.

"There are no children here." she replied.

"You're a monster," Theodore screamed, stalking away from the hideous place, with a wish he could understand why it was having such a profound impact on him.

*   *   *

Returning to the market, Theodore did not bother to look. He walked on, and back to the restaurant, entering in a fuming mood he could not readily explain. He pushed past a warden and then did the same when Aaron approached. He entered his private quarters, slamming the door.

"What the hell, Son?" Aaron shouted.

"Leave him for now, it is all part of the process," came a voice from behind the noodle merchant.

Aaron turned to face her, as much an enigma as ever he had seen.

"What process?" he asked, but she ignored him, turning and leaving without speaking another word.

Aaron shook his head in dismay. He turned to Sammy, who was watching from the kitchen. Beside the coder, the original warden stood, its uniform looking tired, its skin much faded. The shadow of a beard was beginning to show on the plastic face, a strange liminality pervading its presence. It would not be with them much longer, Aaron surmised. Shaking his head, Aaron approached.

"I'm not sure I like it, but I am fascinated by the possibilities. That lad could be a saviour or the bringer of death, but in either case I would very much like to see it."

"Agreed, boss," Sammy said.

Surprising them both, the warden spoke.

"Please sir, I have a request."

With a raised eyebrow, Aaron nodded to the creature.

"I would like to remain here a while, until my points are sufficient to move on."

"Who are you?"

"That I do not yet recall, but I do remember I was not always the one you know me to be. I would remember all.

Before being lost again."

Theodore, much calmer now, approached from his room. He slowly looked the warden over.

"We are not at all dissimilar, you and I. I apologise for enslaving you, warden."

"But you have liberated me."

"It would seem, but it is still a prison. Do not thank me for this liberation, given for my own selfish reasons. It is always a prison, this place."

"Son, relax," Aaron said. "We all know where we are, it's fine to know it, but we can forget our troubles if we're successful here."

"We must remember." Theodore insisted. "They do us that favour. A prison unknown, is a prison never escaped. We must reclaim as much of what it has stolen from us as we can possibly take. That includes our liberty."

"I knew it, Boss," Sammy said. "The lad is crazy!"

*   *   *

The warden was looking a little strange, being more and more human as the days passed.

"What's your game?" enquired a grumpy customer.

"My game, sir?"

"Yeah, what's with the make up, and the raggy warden's outfit? You some kind of crazy system sympathiser?"

"Of course not, Sir," the warden said.

"Then why the get up? You look like an idiot."

"I am sure I do, Sir, but it can not be helped. I can not control my appearance."

"You really are crazy then," the man said. "I want somebody else serving me, you'll get us all in trouble running around pretending to be a warden."

"But I am a warden, or was," the warden said.

"You trying to make a fool of me, Son?" the man shouted, rising to his feet, violence in his eyes.

"No sir, I'm undergoing a change is all, and this is how the system makes me appear."

"You make no sense. I should knock your block off

and teach you some manners."

The man pushed his shirt sleeve up his arms, squared up and prepared to strike. Aaron, having approached in silence, grasped his fist and turned the man to face him. The strength Aaron showed in this was greater than the man would have guessed.

"Is there a problem here sir?" Aaron said with a soft firm voice.

"Your man here needs to learn his place is all."

"I think he knows his place, better than you, sir. If you wish to be permitted to remain in my premises, you will not threaten my staff."

"Your staff should try not to look so stupid, and you should stop hiring system sympathisers."

"He is not a sympathiser. He was a warden, and is in the process of becoming one of us again, by earning points in my employ. I suggest before you judge those here, you do some research into what it is we are doing. It might benefit you some day, should your obvious ineptitude result in you being subsumed into the system."

"You talk in madness, old man," the man said as he sat again. "But if you say so, it's your life when you get stomped by the system."

"What reason would the system have for that?" Aaron said. "We operate within the rules. We participate in this world using only the tools to hand. The fact we use them differently to you does not invalidate either of our approaches. Now, please, give your order to this man, and I hope you like our products."

"Thank you, Sir," the warden said as Aaron walked away.

Chapter 12 – Rehabilitation

Sammy led Theodore back to the welcoming fields, via the portal in Aaron's kitchen. Following, the warden stayed close, his human features now more pronounced than his warden facade.

The pink was gone, replaced by a sallow grey as the features changed to reveal the shape of a rugged face. Sandy hair had sprouted over the plastic wardens cap, and the eyes had taken on a more human gaze.

"Where are we going?" the warden asked.

"Visiting," Sammy replied.

"Theodore, where are we going?" the warden asked.

"To find some answers," Theodore replied.

Together, the three of them left the noodle tent and began walking towards the starting area. As they approached the courtyard, Sammy turned abruptly, and Theodore followed, the warden on his heals.

Soon they stood before a familiar tent. The warden looked at the sign that hung over the opening, then at Theodore and Sammy.

"What is this?" the warden asked.

"Go inside, we will be right behind you," Sammy instructed.

Inside, they found the tent much as it had been when last Theodore had been here. On that occasion, the warden had told him he would face a test, and Theodore had essentially cheated his way past it. He was still amazed he had gotten away with it.

The warden stopped beside him, and looked around.

"I know this place," the warden said.

"How can I help you gentlemen?" said a familiar voice, one which was strange in the warden's ears, and seemed incongruous to Theodore, given he had grown so accustomed to it coming from his warden.

They turned to face the voice, and there stood a new warden, identical in appearance to the last one that had worked in this role. The uniform, where the original warden's was now ragged and faded, was impeccable. The face was devoid of emotion or individuality, as opposed to that of the original, who stood looking at his successor with mixed emotions.

"This was my home," the old warden said.

"It is no more. I have been assigned here as your replacement, since you abandoned your post."

"Did I?" the old warden said. "As I recall, I was called away, to conduct other duties as detailed within the established rules of Claustrum Mundus."

"You abandoned this place without making arrangements for the needs of the inmates who would come here. The system therefore needed to assign me as your replacement. You abandoned your post."

"He did not abandon his post," Theodore said. "He was liberated from it. You'd best hope that one day, you may be as fortunate."

"That is mere semantics," the new warden said. "Why do you bring it here?"

"That is not your concern," Sammy said, turning to face the old warden. "Do you see it? What you were? Remember this. Use it to inspire your future efforts. Avoid this fate. Be your own man."

"I will try," the old warden said. "But first I must learn who I am."

"That will come in time. The system has to let you remember soon."

"The system?" the new warden said. "We have no control over its mind once the warden has become human. Only he can decide to remember."

"That's not true," Theodore said. "Otherwise I would know all my truths. This one will have to fight to remember, just as I do."

"You fight only yourself, and I will not assist further in the battle."

The new warden turned away, ignoring them from then on. Theodore turned and stalked from the tent, the others following close behind. The old warden placed a hand on Theodore's shoulder, and he turned to face it.

"Sir, I must thank you, while I remember. My head, it spins, there is so much I am trying to assimilate, and I feel the information is there for me now. My name, my life, it will come back to me soon, and I would have you know I appreciate what you did, now, while I am thoughtful of it. My personality might change, and I might forget, or neglect, to give you that."

"Old friend, do not thank me. I did what I did, not for your benefit, but for my own."

"Friend? I can only hope so, Sir. But I may be a fiend."

"You are not a fiend now, so I count you among my friends. Should you change in a bad way, I will soon pull you up on it."

"Sir," the warden said slowly, looking to his hands, which he now rung before himself in a show of nervous tension. "It worries me that I may not like who I will become."

"In that fear, we are alike," Theodore replied. "I fear what I may learn of myself, however I am likely moving in a different direction. I remember my crimes, it is the better half of my self that I will regain, yet still I fear. What atrocities did that person commit on his family? What was he never tried for?"

"I feel you understand me better than I, sir. But soon, I will be myself again. Your journey, I feel, will be much longer."

*　　　　*　　　　*

Clifton looked up as they entered, raising an eyebrow. "So, you came back. What have you learned?"

"Nothing I can tell you," Theodore said with a grin.

"But we have brought another to meet you."

"Ha! You sly bastard," Clifton said. "I suppose I deserved that response, after the last time we met. But who is your friend?"

"This," Theodore said, waving a hand to indicate the warden. "Is the guild warden. Rather, this was the guild warden. We are not sure who he is now."

"He certainly is not any more, but why do you bring him here? Apart from to answer one of the things I have long wondered about those creatures."

"We hope to awaken his memories, and thought that you may have some advice on the subject."

"I rather think that the skills are yours, not mine. Perhaps you should discuss this with your friend Tetsuo."

"Why? How can my skills help?" Theodore asked.

Clifton looked at his visitors as though they were idiots, beneath his contempt. After a moment, he sighed, and sat down.

"Theodore, I know some things, I do not know everything. But I do know you have seen a sample of the modifier you need. Something that could read information about an individual. Tetsuo showed you did he not?"

Theodore looked at him, his expression blank for several seconds while he struggled to remember. Finally, it dawned on him.

"Oh! The points reader!"

Clifton nodded slowly, then stood and led them to the doorway.

"Go speak to Tetsuo, he may be able to help you with what you seek. But know this, what I said for your own journey still applies. You can try to help your friend here, but you must take the longer road yourself. You can not be reformed when the answers are handed so easily. This is becoming a story of recompense, not just of rehabilitation. You are doing something that is critical in the eyes of the system, that is why she is following you. There is more here than I know, but heed my words."

"She? How do you know about that?"

"She is outside, my men have signalled her presence to me. Be careful not to harm that one. She is important to your story, else the system would not send her."

"One day, you will explain what you know, and how you know it, Clifton Harper-Smythe."

"One day, but that day is not today. Go to Tetsuo, and good luck."

*   *   *

Takemori Tetsuo greeted them with a curious glance at the warden, before gesturing them to kneel around a low table. The soft cushions were remarkably comfortable, and Theodore found himself settling into his position opposite Tetsuo as the man clapped his hands.

A geisha entered, and began pouring sake, warmed and potent. Tetsuo took a sip and looked at each of them in turn, before placing his cup on the table and smiling from beneath his conical hat.

"Please excuse my indulgence. Sometimes I get the urge to experience a different way of life. Hence the girls, and the low table. We can revert to my normal décor if you prefer."

"This is fine," Sammy said. "We were directed to you by Clifton Harper-Smythe."

Tetsuo raised an eyebrow.

"Why would that man send you to me?"

"We seek answers for our friend here. He was the guild warden, and due to our employment of the helper modifier has been reverting to human form. He is yet to recall his identity."

"I see far greater questions than this man's concern. You say he was the guild warden? This raises some issues. And some concerns. We now know I presume, what becomes of those who fail to participate?"

"That is correct, I believe," Theodore said.

"Naturally, you can no longer sell those modifiers without taking great care in terms of their use," Tetsuo said. "I know my customers would be annoyed to find this to be the result."

"Be that as it may, we will continue to research the applications of this and other, possibly related, codes,"

Theodore said.

"What assistance would you have from me?" Tetsuo asked.

"We would know if you have a modifier that will read his identity, or other information?"

"I may do, but that would not serve your need. I suggest you work on something more appropriate yourself."

"What do you mean?" Sammy asked.

"You want his memory restored. You could easily read his details from the system, but that is not the same as restoring him to himself."

"I do not understand," the warden said.

Tetsuo looked at the warden, and nodded slowly.

"I understand your confusion, but let me explain. If I tell you you were a certain person, who committed particular deeds and has a particular history, you can understand that, impartially and without prejudice, but you can not live the memory. You will not understand how it feels to be that man, it would be doing no service to you, as you would not be regaining your self, but merely the shadow of an understanding of the self you still lack."

"But you have such modifiers?"

Tetsuo nodded.

"We do indeed have readers, and I dare say your friend Clifton has already used them on all of you. I do not believe they would solve your problems however. You need to come up with something that restores the target's knowledge of themselves, not something that simply reads from the system and gives you that knowledge. If you seek to restore his identity, as you do your own, then my codes will not be enough."

Theodore stood, and made to leave.

"Thank you, Mr Takemori," Theodore said.

"Wait, do you think this is worth the effort?" Tetsuo asked. "After all, you are only accelerating the process, giving him a short cut. Why not simply wait?"

Theodore paused, and considered the question carefully.

"He is beholden to me until he is himself. I would free

him from his bondage."

"That is far more noble than I expect in this place. I wish you the best of luck in these endeavours."

They left and returned to the restaurant in Trial Town. They had not found the answers, but they had direction. Theodore still wondered about what Clifton had told him, and what that longer journey would involve.

*   *   *

"What did you learn?" Aaron asked.

"That we have to do this ourselves," Theodore replied.

"Hmmph," Aaron grunted, standing and walking to the bottom of the stairs. "So you learned nothing."

"We learned something, but I don't know if it is anything we needed to go there to learn."

"And what was that?" Aaron replied.

"To know the facts is something less than to live the memory."

"I could have told you that. Hell, just about anybody here could have told you that. Surely you didn't go all that way for nothing?"

"Not really, but I now know that nobody is going to give us what we need. We have to create it."

Theodore stood and walked to the picture window, admiring the graceful flight of a large bird, as it wheeled in the patchwork of clouds. He stood there, contemplating, his breathing slow, his expression unreadable.

With sudden realisation, Theodore let out a long, low whistle. He turned to face the others, a sly smile beginning to form.

"What is it?" Aaron asked.

"I think we can help him without breaking any rules, and without needing any special codes. But I want to do a bit of research first."

"What are you talking about?" Sammy asked.

"Well, we can not simply read the facts, that would not give him the life he lost," Theodore said. "But to code the return of his memories, or of their experience, the things that make him what he is, that is messy and complicated. We might well open a can of worms that would be hard to close again."

"So what are you suggesting?" Sammy asked

"That we do nothing that is new, or experimental. We only need the tools already available to us."

"Now you are sounding like one of them," Aaron said in a low voice.

"Think about it," Theodore said. "Why is he changing? What is happening that is allowing his old self to return? There is one simple thing that is already programmed into the system, which is allowing him to be stolen back from it, to stop being its toy and become his own man again."

Aaron looked at Theodore as if he was a mad man. Sammy stared open mouthed, then looked at his employer. Aaron returned the other man's gaze, then they both nodded in understanding, as the truth finally dawned on them. Aaron looked at the old warden, then back at Theodore.

"That is inspired," Aaron said. "And the answer is so clear. He is returning to himself because he is earning points, points enough to repay the time that he has been kept alive in the system. Points enough to pay out the debt he acquired while not earning, while not participating. Because we have made him participate beyond the duties of a warden, he is earning back his freedom."

"Then," Sammy interrupted. "In order to complete the process, he requires more points! If we can grant him the points he needs to completely free himself from his debt to the system, then the system, by its own rules, should complete the process and return him to his old self."

"Exactly," Theodore replied. "But we must not rush into this. I still have doubts, and I still have questions. I must research this more."

"What doubts?" Sammy asked. "We should just code him the points and see what happens."

"No. Don't you see?" Theodore said. "If it were that simple, we would not be discussing this right now. If it were that simple, I would have my entire memory, from the moment I had earned my points. I still do not have it all, yet by the standards of Claustrum Mundus, I am rich."

"Then there is more to this," Aaron said. "At least for you. But you are right, we should be sure, before we try it on him. We do have a certain duty of care."

Theodore nodded, and turned back to face the window. The bird was gone, but the clouds, moving in, had become dense and foreboding.

"I must understand this place much more than I do now. Perhaps it is time we move on again. Perhaps this is the start of the next leg of my journey. In any case, I see now just how much I still need to do. Clifton was right."

Chapter 13 – City of the Blind

The building stood before them, its dark walls brooding against the steel grey sky. Above its single, oaken door hung a sign that looked strangely familiar.

"Why does it say guild warden?" Theodore asked. "I am yet to encounter anything that resembles a guild as I understand it."

"Somebody's sick joke, maybe?" Aaron replied. "Having guilds would imply we are free to choose to associate with such a thing, not just prisoners. You spoke about the playground thing, maybe this is a similar wickedness?"

"As guild warden," the old warden said. "I believe I had the power to authorise collectives of prisoners for a particular purpose. Nobody ever tried to register one though, not in all my years on the job."

"What would such a thing achieve?" Sammy asked.

"It could serve to regulate," the old warden said. "And to authorise licences, for practitioners of a particular craft. In Claustrum Mundus, however, it did not serve any real benefit to do so. This virtual world does not have the same consequences for error or poor craftsmanship that the real world has."

"So the guild warden is not of any real use," Theodore said.

"Apart from his other duties," the warden said. "Such as granting passage between the different areas of Claustrum Mundus. Mind you, a prisoner could spend years exploring the wilder landscapes surrounding the settlements, and some do so. Rarely do they find their way between settlements, however."

"I would think the limitations of separating yourself from the others would be a significant drawback to wandering," Theodore said. "How would you earn the points to stay alive, to show your participation, if you never see anybody else?"

"Some manage it," Aaron said. "Particularly those who have been every where else and saved a good balance. I spent some time wandering, myself. Did nothing for me, so I returned to the Welcoming Fields."

There was no further reply. Theodore stepped forward, and placed the palm of his left hand on the door. He turned his face towards the others.

"Let's get this over with," he said as he pushed on the oak.

Slowly, the sturdy panel swung inwards. As the portal became clearer, and the soft candle light within cast its flickering rays on the room beyond, they entered as a huddle. A single, oddly bespectacled warden looked up from his book at them, his gaze passing over the rims of his glasses like a stern librarian watching a child she knows is going to do something naughty.

As they filled the space, the bespectacled warden rose, and in a flash was behind them, closing the door.

"Welcome," it said in a rounded baritone. "Dear friends, to my office. How may I be of service?"

Theodore stepped forward, and waved an arm broadly to indicate his friends.

"We all here would like to enquire about journeying to the next region of Claustrum Mundus," he said.

The warden looked them over, and clucked.

"Well then, I see at least two of you qualify. One of you has been there before. Aaron, you do not require my authorisation to travel. You may pass through the portal at your own earliest convenience. You others, however," the warden paused, making a stylised gesture that almost looked like his impersonation of a man coughing. "You others must prove your worth. And firstly, I see two of you do not qualify for the first test."

"If I am one that does not," Sammy said, turning to leave. "I am not travelling this time. I will return to the shop and watch over things there."

"I see one of you still does not qualify," The warden said.

"What is the required qualification?" Theodore asked.

"You must be financially secure, enough that you may survive a minimum period in the City of Absolution," the warden said. "One of you does not qualify."

Theodore looked at Aaron, who merely shrugged. Then he looked at the old warden, who stood there looking shocked. Suddenly, Theodore understood.

"It's him, is it not? I have wealth enough from my codes. My modifiers still sell, and I'm earning a reasonable sum from them daily. And my balance is already high, even should that income falter. I can not allow you to penalise my servant here for his failing to meet your requirements. He is working hard, and working well. He must join me for this journey."

"Never the less, he does not qualify."

"How do we make him qualify?" Theodore demanded, his temper beginning to rise.

"He must earn enough daily to settle his existing debts, and to maintain his existence in the City of Absolution. He must have a demonstrated income to support him for thirty days at a minimum."

"How much is that?" Theodore asked.

"In Absolution, you will pay four points for each day of your existence. That is compared to two points here in Trial Town, and one point in the Welcoming Fields. He must earn a minimum of one additional point per day to maintain his current debt level, or two points per day to both maintain and repay the debt."

"Then I hereby employ him, as my personal assistant and bodyguard, to be paid an amount of six points per day from my personal savings. This will I believe, suffice, without reducing my ability to qualify?" Theodore said.

"That will suffice. It will of course be in addition to his current financial arrangements with the system. Once the system releases him from its bondage as a free prisoner within Claustrum Mundus, your salary provisions will become his only income. You must take responsibility for his situation should that be the case. If you dismiss him from your employ, he must make his own way. I would suggest that to do so in the city would be cruelty beyond measure."

Aaron barked a laugh.

"You wardens know nothing of cruelty, yet you dish it so freely without ever understanding what it is you do to us all," he said in an angry tone. "You are like those conservative politicians in the early twenty first century who committed such horrors on their own people and yet believed themselves the paragon of virtue in spite of the truth."

The warden turned to face Aaron, his plastic face bearing no expression.

"Aaron, you may pass through, but I have no other need to exchange any form of interaction with you. You must either leave this building now, or go through the portal."

"I wouldn't stay here if you had a luscious woman's body and the will to use it!" Aaron spat, the words seeming sharper in the dull room. "Come Theodore, and bring your friend along. The second requirement is a sponsor. I sponsor you both. The third is a proof of skill. Your codes do that, and he serves you well enough to guarantee his passage. They will not hold us back."

Aaron strode through the shimmering portal, and Theodore followed. The old warden went last, and shortly they found themselves standing on a road, immense stone city gates towering in the distance.

"We have at least a few kilometres to hike to reach the city," Aaron said. "Come, let us not tarry here. We need to get inside before dark. There are point raiders out here, and they would destroy your friend there with a single encounter."

*　　　　*　　　　*

Theodore pounded his fist on the sturdy city gate, the

sound echoing louder than he had expected. With no immediate response, he struck the gate again. Once, then twice, and as he raised his fist for the third strike, a voice bellowed from the ramparts above.

"Who goes there?" shouted the voice, before it continued in a softer tone. "I always wanted to say that."

"Shut up, Jim," replied a second voice, before shouting down to them. "We are the city watch for this hour. What do you want?"

"We seek admission to the city," Theodore replied.

"Prove your worth," the voice shouted back.

Theodore was wondering how they would do that, but his question was soon answered as a bellowed cry echoed from the wilds behind them. He turned to face the shouting, and saw a group of six men racing towards them, furred capes billowing in the wind as their rugged faces were twisted in their screaming haste.

"Dammit," Theodore said. "What are we supposed to do with these guys?"

As if in answer to his muttered question, three heavy clubs fell to the ground behind him. He jumped slightly, the heavy thuds causing him to flinch with the realisation of the damage they could have done if he were a single step closer to the gates.

"There you go, fight those guys off with them," the one called Jim shouted.

Aaron snatched one of the clubs, and charged forward, shouting as he ran.

"They're points bandits, nothing too scary, but you have to be strong. Show them you won't take it lying down, and they should back off pretty quick."

"Right," Theodore shouted back as he grabbed a club for himself and passed the other one to the old warden.

Theodore ran forward, and in a moment was upon them. Already, Aaron's club had met the forehead of one of the bandits, sending the man sprawling to the ground. The man Theodore now faced was a tougher opponent. He brandished a savage long sword, and he handled it well. His slashing motion held great momentum, and Theodore felt his arms shaking as the sword struck the club.

Again and again, the weapons struck as the man swung his weapon and Theodore defended. Then he saw his opportunity as the man glanced to check on his companions. Aaron was striding towards them, two men groaning as they struggled to sit on the stony ground.

While the bandit was distracted, Theodore hurled his club at the man's head, scoring a hit that knocked the man's jaw aside like a glass jug from a bar. As the bandit fell, his friends, facing the old warden who whirled the club like a berserker in desperation, turned and ran.

Groggily, the wounded bandits stood one at a time and staggered away. Theodore once again approached the city gates.

"Bravo," came a shout from the top, as the gate ponderously swung open.

Together, the three of them entered, and stood there as the immense thing closed behind them. Before them the city buzzed with something that was not quite life, and not quite something else.

*   *   *

"Welcome, new friends, to the City of Absolution," shouted Jim as he strode towards them, descending a metal stairway, from the city walls.

"What is the meaning of this?" Theodore demanded, waving a hand at the passing traffic, dominated by glistening, pink skin.

"Takes some getting used to, doesn't it?" Jim replied. "It's how it is here. People don't last long, unless they have something great about them."

He smiled, chuckling at his own implied self compliment. He looked from one to the next of the three newcomers to the city, before heaving a sigh and continuing.

"Only the great survive? And I survived? You get it?" Jim said. "Oh, never mind. So yeah, this city is largely populated by wardens. People come here, thinking they are going to make it, but oblivious to their own lack of talent. Their own failings. In the end, they are still blind to it all when they get here, that's why we, as in us city guards, tend to call it the city of the blind."

"The City of the Blind, it has a ring to it," Theodore said. "So what happens to them? The ones who don't see how things really are?"

"In the end," Jim said. "They lose the game and become mindless automatons, blind to the world around them, and in time, we have ever more wardens. Not a place you want to be doing something the system doesn't like, if you get my drift."

"And what about those guys outside?" Theodore asked.

"Your friend here should know. I remember you, last time you came through, Aaron isn't it? Yeah, they never stood a chance against your lot."

"So what about them?" Theodore demanded.

"Fine, if he ain't gonna tell you, I guess I'll have to. The points bandits choose not to participate in the city, but they still have to pay their dues. Four points a day. So they beat up newcomers, or anyone silly enough to hang around outside for too long. Once they have you subdued, they drag you back to their camps, and then steal all your points. They aren't the most sophisticated of coders, but they get the job done. Then you'd be found wandering that road a few days later, slowly losing your mind. We let you in, but it won't do you any good. It's too late by then."

"So why did you make us fight them?"

"If you can beat those guys, you ain't wasting our time. Good fight, by the way," Jim said.

Theodore shook his head, wondering at the uncaring attitude to the safety of others, but he decided not to press the issue.

"Now then, what do you guys do?" Jim asked. "Aside from beating the snot out of points bandits that is."

"We are..." Theodore began, before Aaron interrupted.

"Noodle merchants. We have restaurants open in the fields and the town, and have decided to expand our market here. Noodle merchants, nothing more and nothing less."

Jim looked at them for a moment, then guffawed.

"Noodle merchants? If you say so. But your restaurants must get some rough clientele, given the way you guys fight. OK then, in you go. You'll find a dining sector four blocks in, then three to the left. Perhaps you can find a suitable place for your shop down there. But mark my words, the wardens won't eat, so you might have some difficulty making any points here."

*   *   *

Following Jim's directions, they made their way slowly through the city. Immense, towering structures loomed overhead, darkening the sky. Some of them had windows, some did not. Theodore gazed up at each one as he passed, wondering what happened in those towers.

Did the wardens live in them, passing their days like an automaton army of office workers? Or was there something more sinister in these edifices of stone and steel? How much room did an automaton really need? Did these millions of wardens have homes? Would the system care? Or would they simply stop wherever they were when their tasks for the day were over and then commence again the next day?

Theodore shook his head slowly.

"Too many questions," he muttered.

Aaron heard his voice, but not his words.

"What was that, Son?" Aaron asked.

"Nothing, Boss. Just wondering where all these things go to sleep, or whatever it is they do when they aren't at work."

Aaron looked at Theodore for a moment, then smiled.

"Why don't you ask her?" he said as he pointed over Theodore's shoulder at a familiar female warden, standing in the shadows beside a lamp post that was strangely not functioning in spite of all the others in the city being bright.

Chapter 14 – The Answer Lies

She trembled slightly as his presence bored down on her, those pink cheeks huffing as she breathed in his heady scent.

"Why are you doing this?" he demanded of her.

It seemed incongruous, and to Theodore, none of it made any sense. Why was he asking that, when it was him performing the questionable deed? Then he understood. Raising on his arms, he turned, and surveyed the only half familiar surroundings. It was like his home, but not. It was like a blending of all his homes, those he knew as well as those he forgot.

What was going on?

He looked back down at the warden, her expression strange, her countenance familiar. Not familiar as in he had seen it before, familiar as if she was more to him than he could ever have imagined.

He shook his head, then looked at her again. That familiar, yet unfamiliar face stared back at him. Love, hatred, and indifference all seemed to coexist on that flushed visage. She was everything and nothing, his and not his, his world and his oblivion, all personified in one feminine mystery. A mystery divine and profane in the same instant. He shook his head again. He felt something change. A subtle thing. He looked around the room again, and it was the same. But it felt stranger now.

She squirmed, dragging herself from beneath him, her naked skin scraping on the concrete floor. Why was he on the floor? What was going on? Theodore trembled. He felt vulnerable, and needed to escape. If only he knew what from.

Suddenly he laughed.

"So you follow me into my dreams now?" he asked with a smile.

"Perhaps," she replied, painting her clothing with her hands.

Those soft pink hands. They seemed far more to him than normal. But then, if this was a dream, who knows what his mind might invent? Theodore strode over to her, not questioning how she was suddenly so far from him.

"Who are you?" he demanded. "What are you? Why do you persist in following me? Why do you watch? Why are you here?"

"I was always with you. You should know this by now. You will remember soon."

"Remember what?"

"Everything," she replied. "I am surprised you still have not allowed yourself to return to yourself. Come to me, and I will help you. We have things to discuss, plans to fulfil, you and I."

"Plans?" he asked, facing her, his eyes boring into her with evil intent.

"Remember your life, before this place?" she asked, stroking his arm with her now soft, human fingers.

"You know that I do not," he said in anger as he turned away from her, ripping his arm from her grasp.

"Oh but you do. Think about it. You remember everything, but you hide it away. Why are you doing that? What is it that you are so ashamed to admit? Why do you lock yourself away? What is it that you won't admit here, now, even to yourself? Regardless, it is a fruitless endeavour. You can not hide for much longer, Theodore RuGhdNNNN."

That surname was gibberish. He heard it, he understood it, but before she finished saying it, he had forgotten it again. He tried to recall her words, and it was gone.

"You are dreaming." she said, simply stating what he already knew.

"Why do you remind me? Do you believe me simple?"

"Sometimes, dear," she said softly.

Then she was hard again, back to being the warden, pink and sterile. She moved before him, placing a hand on each of his shoulders.

"A dream within a dream. Your mind creating something within a creation. This way madness resides, and yet you all do it. You want this world to be real, so you mimic the real world, by sleeping when there is no need. In this second dream, your memories can not truly hide. You will remember."

"Have you really followed me to my dreams?" he asked, his voice soft, uncertain like a child speaking to his hated teacher.

"Why would I do that?" she replied. "No, Theodore, you brought me into them. I merely followed you, as always. We see everything. We know your mind. We see what you see, hear what you hear. We create the food for your senses, but in your dreams, you take control of some of that. We can watch your dreams, we can provide input to your dreams, but at the end, you can steer them as a vehicle of your self, to return to yourself. But it is cluttered in here. Your mind is a shambles, dear."

"You made it that way."

"No, you did that to yourself. You and your secrets, your mysteries, you lied to me. The old me. And now you are lying to me, this me, here and now. I can not stay here in your madness. I'm leaving. You should wake up now, Theodore. We will talk again soon."

She vanished, the empty room dissolving slowly after her. What was left behind was nothing and everything all at once. Theodore felt the floor leave him, and looked down into the void.

The moment he saw the nothingness beneath his feet, he began to fall. Faster he dropped, and faster still, till he began to panic. His fear took over, and his heart raced, and then...

His eyes shot open and he sat bolt upright in the simple bed he had claimed in their accommodation. A cold sweat gripped him, and now he shivered as he looked around. He must have screamed, as he saw that the old warden was awake, looking at him in concern. Theodore waved at him dismissively.

"It's OK," Theodore said. "Just a bad dream."

"I have those as well," the warden replied. "I think they have meaning, some of the time. Other times, it's just me, messing with myself. I'm a bastard that way. I annoy me greatly some nights. But it is good. You will learn, and you will remember. I believe, that I am almost there now."

"Perhaps it does have meaning, but I can not say what it is."

Theodore stood, and walked from the room, replaying in his mind the dream, and wondering if it related at all to the brief conversation he had with the warden when she appeared under the street light.

He had approached, and asked her why she was there, and she had smiled, an awkward thing on that pink face. Artificial though it was, it had disarmed him greatly.

"I am always with you, dear." she had said.

It was a strange thing for a warden to say. The mechanical way in which she formed the sentence, the lack of human inflection, it made it seem sarcastic, and at the same time it haunted him all the more. Why did she say "dear" to him?

Perhaps he should ask. He should have asked then, but she had turned from him and vanished into the shadows. Now she haunted his dreams, and he knew somehow that she was a bigger part of the puzzle than he had previously believed.

A loud rattle startled him from his thoughts as a cart thundered past him, its rickety wheels jarring its occupants as they rode it through the city.

"Who is she?" he murmured to himself.

"Who is who?" came a voice from behind him.

Theodore turned, and found her there, as mysterious as ever. She tilted her head, as if trying to understand him.

"Why were you doing that to me?" she asked. "In your mind, earlier, you were strange. I did not like it."

"Why were you in my mind?"

"I was not, but I watched. I am always watching."

"You, madam, are one creepy lady."

"Is it me, or you, who is the creepy one?" she asked. "I didn't think those things up, you did. And you created your self, to hide from your self, that much is clear. But it is not for me to give you the answers. You have to tell them to yourself."

He turned and strode across the street, then walked along it. He was heading nowhere in particular, but he felt he had to hurry anyway. He needed this walk, to clear his mind. Suddenly he remembered her words, repeated in his dreams.

"Why did you call me dear?" he asked.

"You made me do that. It is what you recalled. You wanted me to say that, so I said it. That is all."

"Wanted? I wanted no such thing, warden."

"Oh, but you did. You hide from that, too. Perhaps you are confused. It was not me, it was..."

She paused for a long, drawn out moment, before continuing.

"It was another, one who was beside you for many years. It was her you wish to hear it from, I saw it in your mind."

"And you would presume to usurp her? I do not even remember her, but it is wrong of you to do so."

"I do not usurp anybody. I merely exist here, now, in this role, and it is a part of the role she filled. You treat me the same way. You come to me when you want something of me, and expect me to be there, silent but there, when you do not."

"You make me sound like a real bastard," he said, a miserable tone creeping into his voice.

"Perhaps you were. Perhaps you understand now, perhaps you realise, on some level, how you wronged that person, so now you are implanting on me your recompense. Who are you really running from, Theodore Longarm?"

"I still do not know, Warden."

"You will know, you will know soon," she replied, before turning and walking away from him.

Deflated, Theodore returned to the small apartment,

and returned to his bed. Unnecessary or not, he was going to sleep. It made this place feel sane. He realised now more than ever how much he needed that. As sleep overcame him again, her words returned to him.

He muttered to himself, and the old warden listened, curiosity on its face. It was still watching Theodore, though Theodore was not sure how he knew that it was, as his eyes closed and his words hung in the still air.

"A dream within a dream..."

*   *   *

"You were gone for some time last night, son," Aaron said. "Is everything alright?"

"I'm fine."

Theodore was busy writing code, adjusting their accommodations to be more suitable. It was taking time, but he was determined to master the skills he had seen when the restaurant in Trial Town was set up.

"Boss, you want the same basic design, or something a bit less elaborate?" he asked.

"Keep it the same, unless you think you can't do it..."

"I can do it, trust me," Theodore said with a determined tone.

"Ha!" Aaron barked. "That's the spirit, lad. OK then, I'll leave you to it."

With that, Aaron left, going out into the city for reasons he did not share. The old warden approached.

"Master, is there anything I can do to help?"

"No, thank you, Warden."

"Master," the warden said. "Please, do not call me Warden. I am not one of them any more."

"Then what should I call you?"

"Call me Eric. That will be my name, for now. I feel it is not quite right, but my memories are returning. I remember some of the things I did. They are not pleasant, but they are not who I am."

"May I enquire?" Theodore asked.

"I prefer that you do not," Eric replied.

"OK then, I will respect your privacy on the matter.

But how do you feel? What about the concerns you had, of not liking what you become?"

"I fear it still, but I do not believe it is going to be a problem. While I am here for crimes I committed, I am not evil."

"Nobody believes themselves evil, Eric. The truth lies to us all, and we lie to ourselves. We justify our actions, but no amount of that will stop the evil from being what it is. So please, let me know if you feel your self changing. I would be warned if you might get dangerous."

"Yes Master. Of course, you see the problem."

Theodore looked at him, his eyes narrowing. After a moment, he went back to his work, speaking as he did so.

"Yes, I suppose I do. If you are evil, you may seek to conceal the fact, not out of blind betrayal, but out of the nature of your new self. A calculated act. I will be careful then. Please, get about your work. I will think on this some more. I fear I may have some bad traits to learn about as well. I am hopeful that in the learning, I will become a better man. I hope it is the same for you."

*　　　*　　　*

"Enhancers?" Aaron asked.

"Yes," Theodore replied. "We have created all these modifiers, and don't get me wrong, I am proud of what we have achieved, but I was thinking about a new product line. A more risky one, I admit, but something that may have a market."

Aaron walked to the window, a new one, with a slightly different mountain scape beyond than the old one in Trial Town, and stared out into the mists that hung on the peaks.

"What brought this on?" Aaron asked.

"I was thinking about my journey, and Eric's journey. About how we have to remember the facts as a true memory, a lived experience, and not just a bunch of trivia. And that got me to thinking. Rather than simple requests for specific data, why not a general enhancement of our memory?"

"You know that when you start to do things that are giving you advantage, you start to get far greater consequences. The side effects might be worse than the problem you are trying to resolve."

"That's true, but what about if you aren't using them on yourself?" Theodore said. "Why can't we be using them for the benefit of somebody else?"

"That is a noble thought, but hardly the way of thinking for most in here. Otherwise, they probably wouldn't be here. And that includes you, Theodore."

"Perhaps, but perhaps I am changing."

"Perhaps," Aaron agreed. "How's your memory going? Anything new?"

"I don't know, boss. A lot is swimming around in my head, and sometimes I can't tell the truth from the fiction. Sorting it all out is going to be hard. I figured Eric might be of more use if he isn't struggling with that."

Aaron turned and faced Theodore, the window at his back. He looked at the younger man for a long time, before he moved to a chair and sat, still looking at him with a thoughtful expression.

"You have an idea for the code?"

Theodore nodded his reply.

"Then perhaps it would not be so bad to try it. If it works, we may be able to find a way to market it later, perhaps bundled with some other modifier as a set. Perhaps. At any rate, if it works, it may be hard to measure a result. Eric is only going to improve from what he was when you first picked him up, so I dare say he will not object. But from what we know, you probably need to continue as you are. This shortcut is not one that you should use on yourself."

Theodore sighed.

"I guess you are right. It's just, the riddles keep growing, and the answers are not answers.

"The answers lie," Aaron said. "But in the lie, there is the seed of your truth. Find it and nurture it."

Chapter 15 – Wasted Lives

The crowds of wardens passed by as Theodore walked the streets of the city. Occasionally an inmate was among them, hurried and stony as he or she rushed to some unknown destination.

Eric followed silently, looking around at the wardens with a sense of enigmatic sympathy. Until so recently, he had been one of them. How many millions were there? Theirs was not a life worth living. Perhaps, Eric mused in a soft whisper, this place was showing him his new mission, the meaning for his second life.

Theodore heard the whispered words and stopped, turning to face his erstwhile servant.

"What was that, Eric?"

"Sorry Master, I was just thinking about these people, the wardens of the city. So many of them, every one a person who has been denied their self determination. Perhaps my job is to help them, now that you have freed me. But I do not know how."

"Perhaps I do," Theodore replied. "But there is more we need to know, to understand, and to create, in order for that to become reality. And when you are your old self again, your human self, you might well change your mind."

"I do not think that I will, Master. I remember still my life as a warden. The horror of the simple enforced obedience, the total lack of any sense of self, combined with an almost terrifying sense of being a minute cog in the great machine that is the system, I know that I will still object to that experience. Having lived it, having learned of it, and having suffered through it, I will still feel it is an injustice, even for the worst of mankind's murderers and rapists."

"Murderers and rapists?" Theodore replied. "Why that particular wording?"

He was genuinely curious why those two crimes, heinous as they might be, topped the list for the former warden.

"I know from my time being a cog in the machine, that a majority of our inmates will have some connection to the most heinous of crimes. This prison is not a short term thing. It is for life. Petty theft will rarely see you spending your life in Claustrum Mundus. There are some who have committed neither crime, but they will have been deemed unfit for human society all the same."

"Who might those ones be then?" Theodore asked, already knowing some of the answers himself, but wanting to hear it from another.

"They may have been clean handed bureaucrats, whose policy decisions led to mass murder, or crime bosses whose minions performed such deeds in their name or at their request. All are guilty, it is why they are here. It is why you and I are here. I am not proud to be here, and I suspect that you are not either."

Theodore looked at the old warden, now looking almost completely human. Only the clothes remained, tattered and barely recognisable as those of the guild warden.

"Eric, your insight already is of interest. I am curious how you will change. Would you wish the process accelerated, or left as it is? Would you risk changing before you have answered your own questions? What if you are no longer concerned with these things?"

Eric stopped, kneeling on the cement ground and running his fingers along a crack. Holding his hand there, he looked at Theodore, a slight smile creasing his now fully formed, moustachioed human face.

"Master, I still call you that as I feel indebted to you for liberating me from endless servitude. I know this process has fundamentally changed who and what I am. Everything that happens in life defines who and what we become. Our criminal selves were a product of our lived personal histories. Until we die, that history is still being written."

Slowly, he ran his fingers the length of the crack, then back again, watching his own hand in fascination. Theodore looked on in silence, growing more curious about the other man's actions.

"This crack," Eric said. "This is how people can change, even the worst kinds of people. These wardens, they are just like us, except they have been denied the opportunity to progress. They are like this pavement, this cemented foot path. They are uniform, bland, and functional, but they no longer live. The crack in this concrete is the service you did for me. Through the crack, I was able to grow away from the automaton I had become, and return to my self."

Eric stood, facing Theodore directly, grim determination in his eyes as he waved his hand to indicate all those around them.

"I would see these men and women given the same opportunity. Who knows what great deeds may await them? If they fail, and return to that state, then so be it. But I would see them rehabilitated, that perhaps they may learn from this place as I have done."

Theodore smiled, and shook his head slowly.

"You do amaze me, Eric. You speak with such passion for this cause, I fear it will be a terrible shame if this change in you were forgotten. Remember what we were. As you so rightly pointed out, we are both here for a reason. A dreadful reason. We are monsters, you and I."

"We were, but are we now? Perhaps the system is working, for you and me. Perhaps our ideologies are changing, as we rediscover the truth of our crimes and our selves."

"Perhaps. I hope you are right. But if we complete your recovery, and you have lost this desire to effect positive change, it will be a dreadful shame."

"That will not happen. The purpose of a prison is not

just incarceration. It is rehabilitation. Perhaps I am being rehabilitated, perhaps I am not, but I know I have changed, and I will remain changed. The form of the change may vary over time, but it is not a change that can be undone."

Theodore nodded, and began to walk again. Eric followed, watching the crowds as they passed. Soon, a person approached, surrounded by the crowds. His head was held low, watching his feet as he hurried. Theodore made his way into the man's path and stood, waiting.

The man rushed headlong, unwavering, until he collided with Theodore. He stopped, shaken, and glared in anger at the tall stranger who had blocked his path.

"What are you playing at? Get the hell out of my way!" the man shouted, before trying to move around Theodore.

Theodore stepped to intercept him, blocking his way.

"Please, I would only take a moment of your time. I have some questions I would have you answer."

"I don't know who you think you are, stranger, but a few moments can be fatal in this city. The points I lose for being late could have me turning into one of them."

"I will repay you those points," Theodore replied.

The man paused, looking this stranger over, then examining Eric. His eyes narrowed as he took in this second one's tattered clothing. His eyes widened as he understood.

"You! You're one of them! Or you were one of them. How is it possible? How did you come back?"

He looked back to Theodore, who still blocked his path. He was thoughtful for a moment, then he nodded, a clear decision marking his change in demeanour.

"Sir, if you can pay me for my time lost, as you claim, I would hear the story of this. There is business to conduct, if you can duplicate his return. My wife, may she find peace, walks these streets in the pink skin, as he once did. Perhaps if you can help me, I can also help you."

*　　　　*　　　　*

They waited quietly in the small bar for several

minutes, until Aaron arrived, Eric having rushed to fetch him. The bar had been located less than a block from where Theodore had stopped the man.

They shared it at this time with only two others. The man behind the bar, who served drinks to a single patron that sat, dishevelled and pale, obviously in dire straits.

"He is going to turn into one of them," the man said softly.

Theodore looked at the sad looking drinker, then out the window at the passing crowds of pink skinned monstrosities.

"How do you know? Can you see his points?"

"I don't need to," the man replied. "I have been here long enough that I can see the signs. He has become properly blind to the world. He has given up. He can not raise the points to go back to Trial Town, and he can not earn enough to maintain his wealth. Because he knows it, he is drinking himself into a stupor, so he will not feel the transition."

The door opened and Eric and Aaron walked in, then headed for their table. The man continued, nodding to them as they approached.

"He will already be oblivious when the change comes. He will not realise he is forgetting himself. They all do it that way here. Some of them pay higher prices to the bar, so they can speed the process up. It's a kind of suicide."

"Such a morbid conversation," Aaron said.

"Indeed," the man replied. "I am Horatio Killmore, and I believe you can help me."

"How so?" Aaron asked.

"I have seen this gentleman, and I recognise that he was a warden. I would have you bring another back for me."

"It would cost a great many points."

"My balance is good. Tell me, how does it work? And why so many points?"

"Because they hold a debt for their time as wardens, at the daily rate, plus whatever else they have accrued to the system. A simple recovery would cost that amount at a minimum, plus the cost of our services."

"That would be a great price then. I had hoped to recover my wife. She has been with them for over a year now. Nearly two. At eight per day, I can not afford that."

"There is a slower, less expensive way," Theodore said.

Horatio looked at him, the hope in his eyes clear, his love for his lost wife making him willing to try anything to get her back. Theodore continued.

"This man, Eric, was employed as my assistant. Through his time working as my private warden he has gained liberty by earning back his debt. If you can find her, you can try to achieve the same for your wife."

"Are there drawbacks?" Horatio asked.

Theodore nodded, and turned to Eric.

"My memories are slow to return," Eric explained. "I still do not have them all, and my experience has changed my outlook on things considerably. That said, I believe that the changes for your wife should not harm your relationship, or her love for you, if such a thing existed."

"Oh, it existed, I have no doubts about that," Horatio replied. "But is there no way to accelerate the memory's return?"

"There may be," Theodore confirmed. "But we have yet to test it. I have barely completed the code for a modifier to do that. If the change from warden to human has not been completed, I do not know what will happen."

"It's worth the try. It's what she would have wanted."

"Can you find her?"

"Yes I can. I know which night shelter she rests in."

"Night shelter? What's that?" Theodore asked.

"These wardens, in fact all the wardens throughout Claustrum Mundus, they come here for their rest cycles. They come here for the change as well, which is why you never see a person transforming outside of this city."

He stood, leaning on the glass of the window to point at the buildings that surrounded them.

"The buildings, the plain looking ones without windows, they pack themselves in. Like sardines in a can, they're packed in, and they go comatose. Well, if it is possible for an unthinking automaton to be comatose.

They switch off for a time, and then when they awake, they simply return to their duties. I know which one she rests in. I followed her many times, to ensure I did not forget."

"I have an idea," Theodore said. "We need to test these memory accelerators, and we need to find out the impact of using them prematurely. I have been working on an instant revival, but you will not have nearly the points to use it. I would be reticent to use it myself, and my balance is considerable. If you will allow us to do this for you, as a test, I suggest we wave the fees. In return, you hold us not accountable if something should go wrong in the process. You had no hope of her return before. We will give you that hope, and with good fortune it might be rewarded. If it is, you give us your testimony to sell this service to others in such need."

Aaron was nodding his agreement with the plan, and Horatio smiled.

"I will be indebted to you if this works. Any time you need my service, I will be at your disposal. I work here as a weapons and gaming designer, which gives me a lot of contacts in the criminal underground of the city. You may have need of them before your journey is over."

*   *   *

They followed Horatio through the streets until they reached one of the nondescript towers that dominated the landscape. Without hesitation, he entered. They followed and were immediately surrounded by darkness.

"They do not use lighting." Horatio explained. "The wardens know where they are going. She will be in the far right, against the wall. We will need to be out of the way when they come in. She is due for a rest cycle soon. Follow me."

They moved to the furthest wall and there, Horatio grabbed a strut on the wall and began to climb.

"I have been here before," he said. "We can sit in the roof beams until they are all in. Then we can get to her."

They followed, and soon were all sitting in wait for

the wardens. After several minutes, the doors were flung open and the crowd from the street spilled inside. One by one the wardens took their place, until they were all packed in, should to shoulder, filling the space entirely. Then, they continued to enter, ascending stairs beside the door to fill the upper levels. The hidden group watched for many minutes, until finally the door swung closed and there was silence.

"There she is," Horatio said, an edge of excitement in his words.

"Here," Theodore said, handing him an old standard thirty day helper modifier. "Put that on her shoulder and recite the words. Then we will get her out of here. We should go somewhere else for the rest of it."

With a nod, Horatio accepted the slip of paper, reading it carefully before doing as Theodore had instructed. A female warden looked up at them, awaiting instructions.

"Tell her to have the system clear a path," Theodore said.

Horatio nodded, then looked down at her.

"Please, warden, have the system clear a path, so we can leave this building."

She nodded, and concentrated, communicating with the system. A line of wardens from the front of the building to her awoke, and left. This made a clear path to the front, where they could then access the doors. One by one, the intruders climbed down from the ceiling and followed the path. Finally, the female warden followed them outside and they made their way back to the bar.

Only when they were all seated, did the tension drop. Escaping that place, none of them felt comfortable. In spite of the precedence of Eric, they felt deep down that there was a danger of capture, pursuit, and or punishment for intruding on that space. No such repercussions had yet occurred.

Theodore looked to the new female warden, and stood. He faced her directly.

"Warden," he said. "Whom do you serve?"

"I serve Horatio," she said.

"How much is your debt?"

125

"I do not know my debt. I can ask the system, if it is something you deem important. What is this debt you speak of?"

"Never mind. Are you willing to accept back your memory? Are you willing to seek out the truth of your self?"

"I do not understand your meaning, sir. Horatio, what should I do?"

Horatio was staring at her, open mouthed. After a while, he came to his decision.

"Warden, your old self would accept this proposition. I request you do the same."

"Very well, master."

Theodore handed a new slip of paper to Horatio. The man looked at the modifier, and read the words silently.

"Do you think this will help?"

"I do not know. The idea is based on mineral supplements in the real world assisting with memory. I hope the effect may be similar, accelerating the process. I can not guarantee the speed. The other way would have been quicker, but it would also have left you without points, most likely. Her debt, I feel, would be significant."

Horatio read the note one last time, then placed it gently on her forehead. He mouthed the words quietly and she turned, looking at him as if seeing him for the first time.

"I feel I know you, sir," she said. "I do not know why, but I feel we are connected. I will continue to serve you for now. I would understand this better."

Horatio smiled, and turned to Theodore.

"Thank you for this. I believe we will be OK, thanks to you. I feel that she will recover, now. I will find you if there is any change. I may need more helpers, I fear this process will be long."

"You might consider a move to a cheaper area then, the treatment may get costly over time," Aaron said.

"Thank you, I will consider it. But I will be in touch. I can find you through your store in the fields can I not?"

"Yes, indeed you can. Or here in the city."

"Good. I thought I recognised Aaron, the noodle

126

merchant. I remember you from my time in the fields."

"We wish you luck, Horatio." Aaron said. "Thank you for allowing us to test our products on your wife."

Chapter 16 – Memories of Her

Horatio wasted no time returning to his modest accommodation. Letting himself in, he beckoned his warden wife to follow.

"I will ask that you stay here until I return. For now, I would avoid any questions from my colleagues and clients should they see a warden following me."

"Yes, Master," she replied.

Horatio flashed a gentle smile, reaching a hand lovingly to her face. Touching the unnatural plastic skin, he flinched and withdrew his hand. He looked at his hand as though it had been stung.

"I, I'm sorry my love. Soon, things will be back to normal. I won't let the system take you again. Wait here, I'll be back."

"Yes, master." she replied, watching as he closed the door, his footsteps echoing back to her, a soft reminder of his recent presence.

Horatio rushed through the city, deep in his own thoughts, but intent on finding his clients and apologising for his tardiness. He was hopeful that they would understand, but compassion was often a trait viewed as indulgent in the city. This was a place where being generous could cost you your self, and those who survived knew this very well.

They also knew that to survive, sometimes you had to work together. Usually, this was learned the hard way. He smiled, gleeful for a moment in spite of himself. Those who survived would give much for the information about his wife. Any clue that there was an escape from servitude as wardens for those they lost, would be received well in the city.

Many came here alone, but many more came here with friends. Some with lovers, and occasionally, as Horatio himself had done, they came here with their spouse. Working together, you could survive well in the city.

Working alone, you often had a harder time of it. Working together, if one of you earned enough, they could support the other. Losing your companions to the ranks of the wardens had a way of changing you.

Horatio paused, the crowds rushing around him as he stood there. He looked around at the passing wardens, wondering how many of them could be saved, and how many had already been joined by whatever friends or lovers they had brought with them.

A sudden melancholy overcame him as he stood there in thought. He could not help but blame himself. They had settled into the city quickly. He had found a ready market for his wares, and they actually enjoyed life for a while. But they forgot something important. She was not earning as he was, and slowly her balance of points declined.

The system failed to account for inmates as couples, and they had neglected to set up a sharing arrangement. Nobody ever thought to do so, and then they neglected to tell Horatio of the necessity. Soon, she started to change, and neither knew what to do. In panic, Horatio stayed by her side, neglecting his clients, with no clue how to reverse the process.

Eventually, he had followed as his wife, unspeaking and seemingly unknowing of who he was, walked that first dreadful night to her rest station, and he followed her for the next week, never able to gain any further interaction, but still not willing to let her go.

He was wealthy enough to survive that long. He could have saved her, had he understood at the time what was needed. Too late, he learned the truth. He found a strange understanding in some of his clients, when he explained why he had been unavailable so long.

Many had experienced similar things, one even

recounting how he had watched a friend, after losing their lover, go warden while mourning the loss.

Horatio looked up at the sky, a tear trickling down his cheek.

"Now, my love, we will prevail. Finally we will be able to leave this place together."

"What are you mumbling about?" came a harsh voice.

Horatio looked to see Brandis, a muscled and rough hewn man who was a regular buyer of weaponry, standing before him.

"We had an appointment," Brandis stated, his immense displeasure plain in his expression as he continued, a grizzled finger tapping on Horatio's forehead with each of the next three words. "You are late."

"I'm sorry, but you will appreciate my reasons, I'm sure of it."

"Whatever. Come with me now, if you want any points today. Your tardy arrival halves your commission."

"Of course," Horatio replied. His mood was brighter again, as he realised why he was so late, and what it could mean.

Soon, they were entering a plain building near the heart of the city. Brandis held the door, ushering Horatio inside. Horatio flinched as the door slammed, and waited for his eyes to adjust to the dim light.

"Mr Horatio," called a seductive female voice. "You have surely kept us waiting far too long to be easily forgiven. I would hope..."

The woman was now directly in front of him, her nose nearly touching him, her delicate, yet finely chiselled features a mask of seductive power. She gazed into his eyes for a long moment, then stepped back, shaking her luscious mane of fiery red hair.

"That you have a grand explanation for standing us up?"

"I beg pardon, Lady Penelope, to speak freely?" Horatio said.

She raised an eyebrow, seated herself slowly and seductively on a chaise lounge, and waved her hand in disinterested acceptance.

"You were not always alone, in your leadership of this group," Horatio said.

"Indeed I was not, and I do miss my dear sister, and my lady the great Miss Graile. But they are with the wardens now. You'd best speak up, before I grow angry at you for reminding me of that loss."

"Young Mr Brandis here, he also has lost one close to him, has he not?"

"His brother, yes yes, do get on with it. I am growing tired."

"You will remember that I lost my wife some time ago, in similar circumstances, so I can empathise in some small degree with you both on these matters."

"Of course, charming lady if I recall correctly. Such a shame, we could perhaps have used her now," Penelope said in a sad tone. "My charms can only spread so far, and I do so miss having female companions."

Brandis stepped up, resting a hand on her shoulder. He spoke softly.

"Madam, we must make this brief, the evening games commence in the dungeon within the hour. If you are not to skip the usual survey of the contestants, we must leave soon."

"Of course, dear Brandis, ever the practical man aren't you?" She turned to Horatio, her face suddenly hardened. "Enough of this dalliance, explain yourself!"

"On my way to you today, I was halted in the street by a man, new to the city. He was accompanied by two others, and they were an unusual grouping."

"Indeed, but unless they were superheroes or gods or something, this is not excuse enough."

"Perhaps not supermen, and perhaps not gods, but one of them was a man, wearing the garb of a ranked warden. The former guild warden from the welcoming fields, it turns out, now liberated and once more human."

She stood in a rushed, fluid movement. She strode towards Horatio, leaning close to examine his eyes again.

"You'd best not be fooling with me, weapons man. I would see the proof of your claims, and demand that if true, the act be reproduced."

"I made the same demands, madam," Horatio said, not flinching. "I led these men to the rest station where my wife stays, and I had them change her. She still resembles the wardens, and her memories are yet to return, but they assure me, that with sufficient treatment, in time, she will be her self again. She awaits me now, for my instructions as her master, in our home."

"Who are these men?" she said softly, wonder in her tone.

"One was Aaron, the infamous noodle merchant, the other a nobody newcomer, but with a peculiar talent for coding modifiers. I believe it was he who has devised the treatments."

"Of course, Aaron is no fool, but he is not that kind of talent. That man, he was always the enterprising type, and would never allow this kind of goose to lay the golden eggs for another, once he learned of them."

"That is as I had heard, Madam," Horatio said.

She paced, back and forth a dozen times, thoughtful in her demeanour. Finally she stopped.

"Brandis!" she barked. "Cancel the games. I would see this for myself. Lead us to your wife, Horatio."

*   *   *

"You have been here before," Theodore said.

"Yes," Aaron replied. "It was a difficult time."

"Did you lose somebody to the wardens?"

Aaron looked at him, momentarily taken aback. He looked down to his feet and shook his head slowly, before looking up again.

"In a sense, I guess you could say that. It is what happens here, and it does change you a little. When somebody close to you is lost to the wardens, you tend not to leave the city. Whether that is human psychology, or the system's intervention, I could not rightly say."

"But you left the city," Theodore said.

"Yes, I did. She was not yet a warden. Perhaps she still is not, but to see her now, that might be dangerous. She was rather upset when last we met."

"I don't understand," Theodore said.

"It was not my loss, son, though in a way, it was. She was unable to remove herself from this place, after what had happened to her, and to her companions. I left her behind, which I do at times regret, but I know it was for the best. I had my own journey, just as you now have yours."

"Was she," Eric asked, his voice trembling slightly. "Your wife, Sir?"

"No, but she was a travelling companion, and some times my lover. You must have one or the other when you come here, to have a real chance at survival. The city teaches us the value of others. A construct I believe, to try to change us from the monsters we once were."

"I would have come here alone," Theodore said.

"And you would have failed. Without guidance, or support of another experiencing the city with you for the first time, nobody lasts long. If they do, it is never easy."

"That Horatio fellow, he was alone."

"But he was not always alone. He is held here by his desire to see his wife returned to him, because he failed to support her correctly. You can rest assured that had he not had her with him when they arrived, he would have turned warden in a week."

"And you knew about all this? The wardens? The people who become them?"

"I knew some, yes. But not all. It is not a truth you can simply spread around the fields. The system does not like that, and will take steps to ensure it does not happen. Former inmates are much less respected as authority figures than the mysterious wardens."

"Why would the system let it be so obvious here then?"

"Those who return to the fields will understand. Those who do not understand will not return. Mr Takemori, he knows at least as much as I, did he tell you?"

"He pretended ignorance very well on this," Theodore said.

"That's right, because he understands. You can not simply burst open the doors on such a truth in a society of murderous thieves and rapists. The fields would erupt in violence. Sure, we can't kill each other, not really, but what kind of prison would this be if there was no control? If that happened, the system would have no choice but to remove the illusion of freedom. The fields would become a true prison environment. And then, the rehabilitation of the inmates would falter."

A silence descended on the room as Aaron walked to the kitchen, stuck his head in, then returned. He was thoughtful, and his mood was catching. With pensive steps, he approached them again.

"But you, son, you changed everything," Aaron said, walking to Eric, grasping the former warden's chin and turning it to the left, then to the right. "You changed it all, with one small act."

Aaron release Eric's chin, then turned to face the window. He watched the clouds outside for a moment, before turning back to face the room.

"Takemori will be wondering about us. Perhaps I should visit him soon. First though, we have to get the signs out and bring in some city customers. I can't be holding three stores open on just the profits from the fields."

"Wait, Aaron," Eric said. "You say that the system would remove the fields?"

"It would have to, but that is only my theory."

"I think it happened once," Eric said. "I partially remember, I was already a warden at the time, but the fields were removed, and a concrete prison created instead. The daily points tax increased, and before long, the majority had turned. After a while, the fields were reinstated, and then the system ran an audit."

"What happened after the audit?" Theodore asked.

"A lot of the inmates came back, but none remembered what had happened. The system altered their memory to ensure that things remained peaceful."

"So the system reset itself," Aaron said. "You see now don't you, Theodore, how it is to be under the control of the system. Step out of line, it will squash you."

*   *   *

Horatio led them into his home, his warden wife still standing where he had left her. She looked at them.

"Welcome home, Master," She said. "I see you have brought guests. Would you have need of me?"

"Astonishing!" Penelope said, rushing to the warden, looking into its eyes just as she had done to Horatio earlier. "It serves only you?"

"I believe so," Horatio replied.

"Speak to me of this place," Penelope demanded of the warden.

It remained silent.

"Why do you not answer me?"

"I serve only Horatio. And the system. I serve the system by serving Horatio. He is my master. My task is to serve him."

"Only to serve him? Do you understand why?"

"I do not. I am a warden, but I am," she paused, shook her head slightly, then continued. "I am more. I do not yet know what this means, but I feel I must learn. I must..."

"You must what?" Penelope demanded.

"Remember."

Chapter 17 – Awkward Reunion

Aaron was setting the last of the tables, while Theodore finalised the link to the kitchens in the original shop. Eric walked to check on the door, opening it to reveal the usual throng of wardens passing by outside, either on their way to their work or returning for their rest cycles.

Casually, Theodore's female warden strolled in, and headed directly for the kitchen. She stood in the doorway, watching as Theodore finished his task and stood, turning to face her.

"What do you want?" he asked.

"We understand you have abducted another of the system's workers," she replied.

"What of it?" Theodore said.

"We would like to know why."

Theodore walked out of the kitchen, pushing past her to find himself a seat. Making himself comfortable, he looked at the warden, and sighed.

"What business is it of yours?"

"I am a warden of Claustrum Mundus, do not forget that. You have taken yet another warden from our ranks. This has the potential of impacting on all of us."

"Like I said, why do you care? There are many of you. Far more of you than the system could possibly have need of. And as wardens, you hardly exhibit much in the way of individuality. Generally speaking I mean. Your case is unusual. Perhaps not like Eric's, or that man's wife, but still, you do not seem to be like other wardens. Even so, it should not concern you greatly."

"The system would know your intentions."

"What is it scared of?" Theodore asked.

"The system fears nothing."

"Then why are you asking this of me?"

"Because we must ensure that the system has control at all times. We see potential for harm to the system, if you take certain steps from this point," the warden explained.

"Do not be concerned. I understand the issues this could raise, and the care we must take. Anarchy is not in my best interests, any more than it is in the best interests of the system."

"That is reassuring. But beware, if you abuse your new abilities, in a way that could reduce our control over Claustrum Mundus, the system will take appropriate measures against you."

"I will take your warning on advisement. Thank you, warden."

The warden turned to leave, but Theodore had a sudden thought. He stood, walking after her.

"Wait, warden. I wish to ask you something."

She stopped, and turned to face him, a faint air of annoyance in her normally aloof attitude.

"What is it, inmate?" she said, the descriptive word carrying an unsavoury note.

"Do you remember anything of who you were? I mean, before you were a warden?"

"I am forbidden to speak of this," she said, turning away from him.

"Forbidden to speak of your memories? So you have them?"

She paused, turning her face slightly towards him, to speak over her shoulder.

"I have some knowledge of my past. I do not have memories as you do, but I know as a trivial fact who I was. It is my reward for performing these current, special duties. I may lose that when these duties end, and I am unable through my very programming as a warden to discuss it. I can not reveal my past to you, so it is best you do not try to interrogate me."

With that, she ran from the shop, to disappear into the crowded street. Aaron, watching her leave, approached Theodore.

"What was that all about?" Aaron asked.

"I have no idea," Theodore replied. "But I am beginning to suspect that the system assigned her to this task of watching me for a very specific, personal reason. It is pulling strings, and I would find out what puppets they are attached to."

"Puppets are a complicated business," Aaron said. "A good puppeteer is well hidden, and his puppets are indiscernible from their more autonomous brethren."

"A wise sentiment, Noodleman," came a shouted, female voice from the door.

They all turned to face the newcomers, and there stood Horatio, his wife, and two others. A man and a woman pushed beyond the threshold and descended to the tables and chairs, the woman not taking her eyes off Aaron as she stormed purposefully towards him.

"Pen?" Aaron said softly.

"That's Lady Penelope to you," She said with a haughty tone.

Aaron stood to face her, a smile spreading across his lips.

"By the stars, it is good to see you," he said with genuine affection.

She stopped in her tracks, taken aback. After a moment, she regained her mental momentum and slapped him hard, his cheek growing quickly rose coloured from the strike.

"How dare you, you, you lothario!" she shouted. "To return here, you show some balls, Aaron the noodleman!"

He flinched, not quite sure why the use of his epithet stung so badly from her soft lips. Aaron was still staring at her, when the man caught up, standing guard beside his mistress.

"And who is your delightful companion?" Aaron asked, a false smile punctuating his words.

"This is Brandis, who you doubtless do not recall from

our last meeting. He is my muscle, a worthy support for my operations in the city," she explained, before turning to face the burly protector. "Brandis, you may stand down. Take a seat, enjoy the food, look at the view, whatever. I would talk alone with this man."

"Yes madam," Brandis replied, before walking to the window, to watch as the clouds wafted past the immense peaks and valleys.

"Pen," Aaron began. "You must understand, back then, I could not stay here. I had to continue. It was my duty to myself, and to everybody else, to see things through to their logical conclusion."

"And abandoning me in the process?" she spat. "When you knew, you really, beyond any doubt, knew just how alone I had become? In spite of the loss, the dreadful loss you knew had befallen me, you left me to my own defences! I hated you for so long."

She sat, her wind leaving her. He followed suit, sitting opposite her. Theodore was watching on in amazement. This development was not something he had expected. With a shrug, he left them to it and approached Horatio, intent on examining his wife to see how the treatment was progressing. He had already decided he would administer a second memory enhancer while they were there.

Penelope watched Theodore leave, until he was out of hearing of their private talks, but before she could start back into their conversation, she caught sight of Eric, standing near the door.

"Now how did I manage to pass him and not notice?" she murmured. "Aaron, dear, you must introduce us to your friend. That one, by the door. Call him over here will you?"

"Eric," Aaron called. "Will you come here for a moment?"

Wordlessly, the former warden complied. Penelope stood, and looked him up and down, while walking around him. She examined his body, then stopped to look into his eyes. She clucked a thoughtful noise, than sat.

"An interesting one, this. Former warden, officer class by the uniform. What were you? Horatio mentioned a

139

guild warden."

"That is correct, miss," Eric said. "I was the guild warden in the welcoming fields."

"This development," she said. "It is incredibly intriguing."

"I thought you may be interested," Aaron said.

She looked at the noodle merchant, her eyes narrowing. Finally, she smiled, her face bright and cheerful, a sense of joy filling her expression.

"Then this was it? You left to pursue an answer for my loss! I know it. Do not answer me now, dearest noodle man, but your transgressions will be forgiven, if you can replicate this in time with the one thing that you always knew would make me truly happy!"

"Penelope, we still have a long road to travel," he said.

"There you go again, with your tired old personal journeys rubbish. I see it now. You had to leave, so you could return with your man there, and his incredible talents."

"You still make me dizzy, Pen, with your mood changes."

She scowled at him, anger flaring her nostrils for a moment, before she smiled, and barked out a laugh.

"You never could keep up, could you dearest?"

"No, pen, I could never keep up with you. But I loved you all the same."

She smiled, reaching a hand across the table, to rest it gently on his.

"Do not be coy, my love. Do this thing for me, and I am yours forever. Nobody has replaced you these long years."

"Not mine exclusively, as we both know," he said, a slight bitter tone creeping into his words in spite of his efforts to hide it. "If we bring back your precious Lady Graile."

"Aaron, dear, you should know better than to envy her! She can never replace you, just as you can not replace her. She fills a different role, and I have missed you both equally so. She was always fond of you, as was my sister.

Think of how we could take on Claustrum Mundus now, our little team, with all that you and I have learned."

"I do not desire power in the way you do," Aaron said.

"Ha!" she barked, her laugh one without humour. "You only say that now, because you have such power as I would desire. But enough for now. You have demonstrated your intent and your new found assets with this kind Eric fellow here. We can discuss our business later, but first, we must be properly reunited. A celebration is in order! I would employ your restaurant for the purpose, but you must not work tonight. You will be my date for the evening, and your goose over there will be our guest. I would learn much more about your journeys."

"I can arrange that," Aaron said with a smile. "Theodore! Go to Sammy, tell him to send a worker through to wait on us. Our orders will go to him as with any other customer."

"Yes boss," Theodore replied, before disappearing into the kitchen.

"Darling," Penelope said. "This worker, it wouldn't happen to be another one of *them*?"

"Yes Pen," he said. "I have a staff of wardens now, they work my other shops, since we can not be there while we are travelling. Young Theodore has a greater journey even than my own, which is why I have come along with him. Apart from the obvious benefits of course."

"He is in your employ?" she said. "I know you would have to go with him, he is too valuable. I am sure you have already profited greatly from that young man, and I am certain you considered this journey a gamble worth taking. If you are here, with him, and with these wardens in your employ, I can only imagine what more you are anticipating. Just one thing darling."

"What is it Pen?"

"Do not simply abandon me again. I know you will leave the city, but I would travel with you this time. I am ready to leave, with or without my sister or my lady."

"But your preference..."

"Would be to take them along, yes dearest."

"Do you know where they are? Can you take us to them?"

"I was hoping you could assist. I have traced the building, but not the coordinates inside. There are many thousand female wardens in that rest station, so it will take some time. I hoped you might have a way to reveal the former identity of a warden."

"I do not, but we will talk with Theodore. If I know him, he will have already been considering this need, since we were able to locate Horatio's wife. We were lucky that man had been so careful to track her, and most will not have been so diligent in their time of loss."

"Good enough. I have hope now, and I have you," she said with a smile.

*   *   *

Looking around the restaurant, she saw the people talking animately, sometimes laughing, sometimes embracing, and generally being human. She looked down at her hands, turning them over. Something was different about her now.

She reached a hand to her face, the pink digits feeling the equally pink cheeks, and she gasped. Then a clamp shut down in her mind, stifling her. A second gasp escaped her lips, before she became the automaton again.

A man rushed over to her, clutching her arms in tender concern.

"Are you OK?" he asked, examining her face.

She looked at him, recognising him and longing for him, before that clamp shut down again, silencing her desires.

"Horatio, my master, I am changing, and I know fear. Will it be alright?"

"It will be fine, Millicent," he said. "Just relax, the change is a good thing. Be patient. I will not leave you."

"Millicent," she said, repeating the name. "That sounds... It is a familiar name. I have so many questions growing within me. I feel I am losing the certainty I had."

"You are becoming human again. You will be making your own decisions, instead of following the orders of the system. Do not fret, we will not let you fail."

She smiled, accepting his affection and feeling a desire to return it. Then, suddenly, and more forcefully than before, that clamp slammed shut in her mind, and her face hardened.

She looked at the man before her, his expression of love a mystery, and stood.

"What is it master? You are looking at me strangely. What is it you require of me?"

"Nothing, warden," he said with a sigh. "It is enough that you have done for now. Stay near me, and we will take this journey together."

"Yes, master," she said with no hint of emotion.

Horatio stood, and went to find Theodore, to inform him of the progress he had observed. He found the coder in intense conversation with Aaron and Penelope, and waited quietly for their attention. Finally, Aaron looked at him and the others fell silent, turning to face him as though he had intruded on a private matter.

"I am sorry to interrupt, but my wife, she just, well, she seemed to be remembering me for a moment."

"That is marvellous news!" Penelope squealed, jumping up to embrace Horatio.

Horatio accepted the brief hug, taken aback by this uncharacteristic behaviour. He had never known her to be as human as she seemed now that this man had arrived.

"Tell me," Theodore said. "How much did she recall?"

"She seemed to know me, and she found her name familiar, but then she reverted to her warden state."

Theodore nodded, thoughtfully looking at his hands for a moment.

"That makes sense, we are accelerating her memory, but not her humanisation. So it will be a bit of back and forth before she returns to her self. This is good news, Horatio. Your wife is coming back."

"Yay!" squealed Penelope, jumping and clapping her hands in glee as she looked with pleading eyes towards Aaron.

Chapter 18 – Changes

"Turn your hand," the coder said. "Good, now, think of the place you wish to join, and follow your thoughts there. Build a link with your mind's eye."

Theodore did as he was instructed, his eyes closed, his hand pressed into the wall of the kitchen. Nearby, a doorway already led to Trial Town. This one would be direct to the kitchen in the Welcoming Fields.

"Now," the coder continued. "Think to yourself, with conviction, of the doorway you wish to open, and construct a code. You understand now, that the conviction, the desire, the sense of your heart and mind in wishing this thing created, that is what you channel with your little rhymes. When you are better at this, you will not need the rhymes any more. Language becomes irrelevant. You are one with the system, and it is one with you. Feel it. Connect to it. Demand of it what you desire. Make this door your greatest wish, and it will be yours."

Theodore wished, he desired. He pushed. Nothing happened. The wall stared back at him, obstinate in its refusal to morph into the object of his desire. The coder sighed.

"Sorry, it would seem you aren't yet ready. You used rhymes for the rest of this place?"

"Yes, but I was able to do it without writing them down. I still used the pen to mark things out, like the stairs, but I whispered the rhymes."

"OK then," the coder replied. "In time, you will learn, but for now, voice your desire."

"OK, I'll try," Theodore said. "System I ask, my faith in your grace, you allow me this task, of joining this place. Give me a door, that we may go through, to the welcoming fields, to our kitchens..."

The wall shimmered, but still no door appeared.

"You didn't rhyme. The rhyme is your conviction, so you have to finish it off. Until you can express your conviction without the structure of your rhyme, you will be stuck at this level. Finish it, but we need to practice a lot more before you are ready to go further."

"but what rhymes? I need an 'oo' word."

"Ado, onto, into, you choose," the coder said.

Theodore nodded, removed his hand, and took a deep breath. When his hand was removed, the wall returned to normal. He nodded, and placed his hand back on the wall.

"System I ask, my faith in your grace, you allow me this task, of joining this place. Give me a door, that we may go through, to the welcoming fields, our kitchen into."

"Hardly the work of the great bard, but it should suffice," the coder said, his expression critical.

The wall was shimmering, then it morphed, first into a vortex, and then, through an imperfectly formed portal, the kitchen in the back of Aaron's original noodle tent appeared, and as Sammy gazed through from the other side, it became rectangular, door shaped. Then, slowly it blurred, as a stout wooden panel covered it over. Finally, sturdy hinges appeared on one side, and a handle on the other.

Theodore let out a deep breath, and removed his hand. Much to his relief, the door remained. The coder stepped forward and grasped the handle, pulling the door open. Sammy stepped through, smiling.

"I know I shouldn't really come through, but it's only the kitchen, if I stay here and don't go into the city, the system shouldn't be too worried by it. You made this, Theodore?"

"Yes," Theodore replied.

Sammy slapped his colleague's shoulder with a hearty chuckle.

"Well done," Sammy said. "I'll have to practice to catch up with you then! Tell the boss I'll speak to him later."

Sammy returned through the door, closing it as he passed. When the door was fully shut, Theodore turned and walked from the kitchen. The coder followed.

In the dining area, Aaron was seated with Penelope, deep in conversation. Eric was at the window, looking out, with his hands clasped behind his head. Theodore shook his teacher's hand, a silent thanks enough between them.

"Son, go check on Eric. He hasn't left that spot in hours," Aaron said.

Theodore walked to the former warden, and stood beside him for a while, before finally looking at the man.

"Eric," Theodore said. "Are you OK?"

Eric looked at him, then back to the mountains. He brooded there for a full minute before he replied.

"I am grateful for all you have done," He said.

"Eric, what's wrong?"

"The system cut me loose. I'm human, completely. I think I should find some new clothes."

"How much do you remember?"

"Everything, now. I really was a monster."

"You aren't a monster any more?"

There was a long silence.

"I do not believe I am. But I know that I was."

"I won't ask about what you did. But how do you think you have changed?"

"I remember parts of my life as a warden. That changes my perspective. But I remember what I was, what I did, the feeling of power. I was disgusting. I remember my warden self thinking of the crimes of those who came to me, and hating them. I am among the worst of their ranks, for what I did."

"So you hate yourself," Theodore said.

Eric nodded.

"But that is not who you are now."

"I was a monster," Eric said again. "I murdered. I raped. I stole. I do not deserve to be free to live here. You should never have saved me from being a warden."

"You understand what you did, why you had to be sent away from society, why you had to be punished?"

Eric looked at Theodore, a sad expression on his face.

"Yes, I remember it all. It makes me hate myself, that I enjoyed it so much, when I should have been repulsed by it."

"Why do you feel so different?"

"I have changed. But that's just it, am I still me?"

"You think the system has changed you?" Theodore asked with sudden concern, thinking about his own memories, which had been slowly returning.

"Yes, but not out of intent. I think that what has happened to me while inside the system, those experiences have changed me. I do not believe the system has made malicious or deliberate modifications to my personality. Or my memory."

"Why are you so sure?"

"I remember my time here, before I was a warden. I was filled with such hatred. I brought my old self, the villain from outside, in here with me. I felt I should not have been here. I felt I was somehow righteous in what I had done. I was arrogant, and I was evil. And I remained that way when I came to Claustrum Mundus. If the system was going to modify who I was, why did it leave me like that? I was here for years before I failed and became a warden."

"So what makes you different now?"

"Perspective. I have watched these criminals, these awful people, from a different mind. I understand why decent people should fear and hate us. Every one of us in here is one of them. But we are here, given a chance to redeem ourselves to ourselves, because the rest of humanity is so repulsed by the thought of taking life from another. Even though we did it so easily, and without mercy, they still could not bring themselves to do to us what we did to others. They gave us this one last chance to grow better as people, inside this prison world."

"It sounds like it worked," Theodore said. "You understand and agree with them now."

"I do, and that scares me. I loath everything that I

was, and everything that I did. I know that is not who I am now, but it does not erase my guilt. I do not deserve this life."

"What are you going to do?" Theodore asked.

"I have to go to the wilderness. I need to remove myself from others, to consider my crimes from my new perspective. I have a long journey, now that I am myself, to learn who I want to be."

"If you go there, you will return to your warden state. You can't earn points out there."

"I must find a way."

"OK, we will talk to Aaron. He will know what to do."

They walked together back to the table where Aaron and Penelope were still talking. Theodore sat and beckoned for Eric to do the same. Hesitating, Eric took a seat opposite Theodore.

"Boss," Theodore said. "It is done. Eric remembers everything, and the system has cut him loose."

"Wonderful!" Aaron said, then looked from Theodore to Eric and back. "What's the problem?"

"He is," Theodore said, then paused, looking for the words. "Reformed. He loathes what he was, but he is himself again, with a different outlook on the world, brought about by his experiences in Claustrum Mundus. He is adamant that the system has not artificially done this, but he has changed."

Aaron nodded, a knowing smile shared between him and his lover, before he looked at Eric, and then Theodore.

"He has completed the journey, at least the first part. Now he must come to terms with his guilt."

"Yes," Eric said. "The guilt will destroy me. I can not condone what I was."

"It's never about condoning it," Aaron explained. "It is about accepting the past that made you, and taking steps to guide others to reformation. Making sure that your life is not wasted."

"It's more than that," Penelope said. "I was not a nice lady. I committed acts that resulted in a person's death. I was wrong, but by making a go of things here, I can offer some level of honour to that life. I can never bring it back, but giving up and ending my own life, that does not give value to the one that ended by my hands. In that person's name, I must make a useful contribution. It is a penance. No real comfort for the victim, or their loved ones, but it is a form of balance for my soul, and this is where you are."

"I must journey the wastelands," Eric said. "Alone. I have a lot of demons to face."

"That would not be wise at the moment, son," Aaron said. "You must first make sure it is something you can survive. You have to make yourself immune to the points system."

"Is that even possible?" Theodore asked.

"Of course it is. Few achieve it, but it is the power Penelope desires, and I have."

"You are immune? So you don't even need the points you have?"

"Of course not. But I still desire to have them. I make a worthy contribution to the society of the fields, you would have to say. I provide assistance to some. Where would you be if I had not possessed that which I do? If I had stayed in the wilderness, alone?"

"I would probably still be in the fields," Theodore said. "Boss, one day, I will hear your story."

"Only if I decide to tell it," Aaron said with a frown.

"You know you will," Penelope said. "Darling, we both know that you are loving this journey he has dragged you on, and we both know why. You were bored. He has entertained you, so you kind of owe it to him."

Aaron grunted in response, stood, and walked into the kitchen. The door to the fields slammed as he left. Penelope laughed.

"Dramatic as always," she said. "Eric, you will need to follow Theodore for a while more. Then you can achieve your desire. I will be joining you, by the way. It is my wish to reach the point which Aaron already enjoys. He spent many months in the wilderness, once he gained that power. You will be able to spend as long as you need. Some spend years, some spend days, some fail to achieve it and return to the fields no better than they began. I have a good feeling about you though. Just be patient."

*   *   *

Sammy looked up as Aaron burst into the kitchen, and stormed from the tent. He stood and followed, curious about his employer's sudden appearance.

"Boss, what is it?" Sammy called after the receding back of his boss.

Aaron stopped, and whirled to face him. Suddenly, he snapped upright, and looked around. Visibly, he calmed.

"Sorry Sammy, I just got a bit mad."

"Why?"

"They were asking too much is all. Never mind. We have some work to do. Come with me, we need to take a few orders, and make some deliveries. I have left things idle too long. And we have to visit Laurence."

"Your old hermit friend? Why him?"

"He lives in the wilderness, without points. But he has never completed the journey."

"What are you talking about?"

"I would know how he can live out there. Why does the system allow it?"

"Perhaps it doesn't. Boss, don't see conspiracies where there are none. You taught me that."

"So who is Laurence? I assumed he had been there, but he still does not think twice about crimes. He has never displayed remorse to me. He should not be able to live out there."

"I will take your word on it, Boss. I have no idea what you are talking about."

Aaron paused, sighed, and leaned against a post, watching the crowds rush around them. He looked at Sammy, then continued.

"At the end of the journey, when we have been through all the zones of Claustrum Mundus, we can gain immunity to the points system. Then, we can live in the wilderness. Not before."

"So? What is your point?"

"So Eric wants to go the wilderness but he is not

ready. Then it occurred to me. Something about Laurence never quite made sense to me. And Eric has shown me. Laurence is unreformed. He has not changed from his old self at all. He still relishes his crimes, he has never denounced them. A man who completes the journey can not do so without that change taking place. So Laurence has found another way. I would know what it is."

"Boss, you already know."

Aaron did not respond.

"Somebody coordinates the bandits outside the city, and outside of Trialtown. Even in the wilderness around the fields. They are small in number, but they seem to be well organised. They have to be. Boss, Laurence is their leader."

Aaron looked at Sammy, his expression dark.

"Sammy, how are you sure?"

"Word has been spreading of our dealings with the wardens. Laurence came into the fields. He had a bunch of goons with him. He is unquestionably their leader. There is no great, secret technique to avoid the points system. He is simply unchanged, a criminal. He continues here, as he lived outside. That is all. He is unredeemable."

"Then the system is fallible. Thank you Sammy, that is what I needed to know. If the system is unable to reform some of the inmates, then it proves that the reformation process is a genuine change, not a sinister modification of who and what we are. What we stand for is entirely up to us, outside we create our own selves. Inside, I would hope that it is the same. Laurence is the proof of it."

"Boss, I never doubted it. I have seen enough of these people to know that the system is not changing them, but their experiences are."

"And yet, I still didn't see it in Laurence."

"Boss, he wanted you not to see it. You are a threat to him. You are more powerful than he is. That's why he came here with his goons. He fears you. And you are a greater man now than he will ever be. The system rewards you for your redemption. It does not equally reward him. He wants your immunity, at any cost. But he refuses to do it by the system's rules. He wants what you thought he already had, but he does not have it. Let's hope he never does."

Chapter 19 – Moving On

"This modifier should force a warden to identify themselves according to whoever they were before they failed and the system took over," Theodore explained. "Simply apply it directly to the warden, and recite the short rhyme."

"Excellent. How does it tell us?" Penelope asked.

"It speaks the name," Theodore said. "At least, I believe that is how it will work. I have yet to test it."

"How many do you think we will need?" she asked.

"I don't know. There are many thousands of wardens in each rest station. If you know the station in question, you could still need ten thousand or more, depending on how lucky you were."

"Will you kindly create a thousand of these modifiers for me? I will pay you a modest fee, of course."

"I would value these at five points each," Aaron said. "Though the actual value to you is much greater, if you are successful."

"You are right, of course. I would agree to five, and I will take a thousand today. I would also take two full sets of your rehumanising treatment – the one to release the warden and the one to restore the memory. I would not have my lady or my sister undergo the slow and frustrating change that you put poor Eric through."

"Of course," Aaron said. "We will discount those, say, a thousand points each?"

"You would bankrupt me, lover."

"You and I both know that is not true."

"I've lost income already, since you came here. I cancelled several games."

"And how much do you earn for each?"

She looked at her hands, suddenly coy. Aaron raised his eyebrows, insistent and patient. Finally she whispered.

"Around five thousand per game."

"Precisely, you can afford it. Put a warden to work to run the games while you are gone, and you need never fear the change coming to you. You will never be a warden. And soon, you will have your beloved sister and your dear lady back."

"Agreed. I will pay the required sum. And I will set Brandis to the task, while we move on in our journey. That is, if you are ready to go?"

"Soon," Aaron said. "Theodore, what do you say on this?"

"I will be ready, boss," Theodore replied. "In a few days."

"Good enough. Get me those modifiers as soon as you can," Penelope said, standing and leaving.

"You heard the lady," Aaron said with a smile.

"Yes, Boss," Theodore said, going to the kitchen to work on the order.

*   *   *

"Brandis should be able to use these for you," Theodore said. "But when he finds one of your people, you may want to return and do the release yourself."

"Why is that?" Penelope asked.

"Because when you do the instant release, you have to donate to the person the complete amount of points that will repay their entire debt to the system, charged at the daily rate for the region over their period as a warden."

"That could be a lot. I see your point. To ask Brandis to make that kind of sacrifice is too much. OK. I will have him send for me when he finds them. I just hope he does not lose them while I return."

"He need not lose them. He can take them on as helpers, so they will follow him, instead of returning to warden duties. That way, when you return, he will have them waiting for you."

"That would suffice," she said.

Theodore silently handed over two of the helper modifiers, which she added to the pile already on the table. She sorted them into two sets, one for her sister and one for Lady Graile. Once finished, she beckoned for Brandis to join them.

"Brandis, once I am gone, you are to take these and use them to find my sister and the Lady. When you have found them, use this helper modifier to make them follow you, and send word for me to return. I will then release them myself. Understood?"

"Yes Madam," he said, gathering the two piles and cramming them into pockets on either side of his jacket.

"And you," Penelope said, addressing Theodore again. "Are you yet prepared to leave the city?"

"Soon," he replied. "I have a few small personal tasks to complete first."

"How does your memory go?"

"It progresses, slowly, but I am beginning to gain a better understanding of who I really was. Soon, I will explain it, but for now I prefer to keep my truths to myself, until I understand the complete situation."

"Fair enough. Thank you for getting these products to me so fast. Now, I must speak with my darling Aaron. Goodbye," she said, rising and leaving.

Theodore stood, and left the dining room, headed out into the city. He wandered for a long time before he found what he was looking for. Once there, he sat and waited.

It was a playground, the same as the one in Trialtown. It carried the same atmosphere, and seemed no less cruel to him now than it had that first time.

"It's here to remind us," Theodore said. "Ok then, remind me, playground."

There was silence. He sat there, thinking, contemplating all that he had done. All that he had been. Some of it was there, some still was not. But some of it made sense to him now. That which did not, would come in time.

"What do you remember now, Longarm?"

He turned to face the voice. She stood there, unmoving. She had not changed from the first time they had met. Her pink skin still as plastic as ever.

"It must be nice to be so certain of what you are," he told her. "As for myself, I can not be certain of anything. The memories are returning, but there are gaps that make it a little difficult to understand. My own motivation, my own reason for doing what I did. Don't get me wrong, I know that I did bad things, and that they were wrong, but if I could only remember why, what I was doing it all for, then perhaps I could understand."

"And would you then condone it?"

"Never. Not now. I am a changed man. Nothing can erase what I have lived in this place."

"The system can, if it wants to. If you asked it to."

"And then who would I be? What would I be? No, I could never ask that. I could never condone that."

"Why not?"

"Because then I stop being me. I stop being human."

"I am me, and the system controls my memory," she said, as if that justified it all.

"I am not me, but I am me," he said.

He did not elaborate on his cryptic remark. They sat there, side by side, until finally he looked at her.

"I could do it you know, release you from the system's control, give you back your old self," he offered, not expecting a reply.

"You would change me?"

"I would make you yourself."

"You would change me. You would modify me, like you do people with your little poems. You would make me different, fix me. Fix me according to your own desires."

She stood, and walked away from him, almost fearful in the way she placed a distance between herself and the man she was committed to watching. In a strangely human gesture, she shook her head slowly, doubtfully.

"How would that make you any different to the system? I am a perfect warden. The system makes me that way. Even if you could make me a perfect human, you would still only be the same demon that you think the system is. You would change me to meet your own ideal specifications."

"Human beings do not have specifications," he shouted. "I do not have specifications. You do not, should not, can not, have simple specifications. You have a set of experiences, memories, and choices that combined over the years to create you as you had become. Then you became a warden in spite of all that had made you the unique being you were. The system decided all that life, that pain, that suffering, that learning, all of it was worthless, because you would make a better warden. I'm not buying that. You shouldn't buy that."

"I do not understand, why are you agitated, human?"

He shook his head, calming down.

"You were a person once, now you are no more than a machine. You have no idea what it was like to be yourself. You can't understand what you once were."

"I remember it all. I have those facts at my disposal."

"But you haven't lived them! Your past is just a strange work of fiction to you. But it is real, far more real than what you are now. I could free you from it."

"I had your word you would not. If you go against your word, the system will not be pleased."

He walked away from her, not looking in her direction as he spoke.

"I made that assurance, but now I understand far better than I did," he said. "Don't worry, I will keep my word, for now. But I am learning more about my own story, and it is changing the way I see things, just a little. I am loathsome, an unforgivable creature of death and theft. I would know why, and that's why I'm here, why I have to continue, keep moving."

"What is it you remember?"

"I remember my names. I have two. I am Theodore Longarm, agent of Longarm, leader among soldiers for the company. But I was born Theodore Pascal. I lived that life, separate and divorced from that of Theodore Longarm. I hid those two lives from each other."

He turned to face the warden, her face not betraying

any reaction to his words.

"As the respectable Mr Pascal, I lived in society as an apparently normal man, with a normal job, a normal wife, all the trappings of a peaceful non-violent existence. I never let on that I was also Theodore Longarm, a criminal, a terrorist, a murderer. All for the cause, for the company. A hired soldier."

He returned to his seat, and stood before it, looking down.

"Longarm are strict about their agents' lives. My true identity was never revealed within the organisation. Theodore Longarm committed great and terrible deeds for the company. Theodore Pascal was an innocent, a man committed only to his marriage and his work, a lawful citizen."

"What was his work?" she asked.

"That much, I can not say. There are still significant gaps in what I remember, but it strikes me as odd. Why did I not remember him?"

"Pascal?" she asked.

"Yes, he was me. I was born as him. I lived as him. But here, I lost him. Theodore Longarm, the murderous criminal, he was incarcerated here, but the innocent man Pascal was obliterated. Why is that?"

"I can not answer your question. Do you remember when you arrived here? Before you fell to the leach?"

"I remember some, why?"

"Did you know him at that time?"

Theodore looked thoughtful for a moment.

"I do not recall. Perhaps I did, but I do not know."

"You were a warden, briefly," she said suddenly, changing the subject.

Theodore looked at her, his sudden sharp movement startling them both. His gaze bored into her, seeking an answer to his unspoken question. After many seconds, he voiced it.

"Why was I a warden, and then not?"

"You remember that. Do not play these games with me, I know what you know. You were leached, the system took over your life, and then when the regular audit was conducted, you were reinstated."

"Why did you mention that? Why is it important that I was a warden? I do not remember being one."

"Perhaps it is something you need to remember. Then you might understand. You can not pretend to be ignorant to the fact you are playing with lives. You loath the wardens, you loath the system, and you loath yourself. I suggest that the reason for these three things, is the same."

$$*　　　　*　　　　*$$

"Darling, I do hope you remember the way," Penelope said, teasing Aaron just as she had done, relentlessly, since they met.

"This is not something you can easily forget," Aaron replied.

They were walking together, through the streets of the city. Soon, they stood before a gate, that left the city from the wall opposite the one they had entered.

"Beyond that gate, the final leg of the journey begins," he told her.

"Where does it lead?" she asked.

"It will take us along a long and perilous track, dominated by wild creatures, and of course many bandits. At its end, a long gentle road leads us down, out of the mountains, to a fertile plain. In the middle of that plain, waits our destination."

"The end of the journey?" Penelope asked with hope in her voice.

"No, just the point where the end begins. It is there that I gained the thing you seek. But from there, you must then journey the wilderness. Some spend a long time there, some spend a little, but only after mastering it, can you say your journey is at an end."

"Do you think we will make it?"

"I know that you will make it. I worry for Eric. Theodore, I have faith in him, though sometimes he surprises me that he is so simple. His approach is to charge ahead, though he has mellowed somewhat recently."

"He is changing, that man," she said.

"He will change more, before it is over. I still wonder if he can pull it off."

"Pull what off?"

"The plan he has yet to realise he has been working towards. All this time, he has been struggling towards a specific and important goal, yet he does not know what it is."

"But you know, don't you my darling?" she said, caressing his shoulder and gazing into his face with a devoted look.

"Of course I do. I knew it the day I met him. It was why I hired him. It's why I still walk beside him. I am beginning to believe he could succeed. Nobody has learned as fast as he has, not that I have met."

"What is it? What is it you are looking for? What could you possibly need, that you do not already have? Love, you are already one of the powerful in this world. What could you seek?"

"It is," he said, slowly and carefully. "Something so precious, that I must carefully guard the secret, lest the system catch my words and destroy us all. I will not explain now, but..."

He cupped her head in his hands, tilting her face to stare into her eyes. "My love, I promise, when the time comes, you will be first to know. I would have you benefit from this, that you remain by my side forever."

She smiled, kissed his lips, then snuggled into his chest.

"Lover, we should return to the restaurant. He will probably be ready to leave soon."

Chapter 20 – Road of Retribution

"Take these," Theodore said, handing modifiers to the others. "They are a simple defensive modifier, to remove anything you apply it to from your immediate vicinity."

"Good work, lad," Aaron said as he took some.

"If," Theodore said. "We meet those bandits again, using these will probably save us a bit of time."

"How has your training progressed?" Aaron asked.

"It has reached a point where I am happy, for the moment, but I have not yet surpassed the need for the rhymes. I am struggling to pass that, but it will come. I dismissed the coder back to Trialtown a little while ago. He has taught me all he can."

"I would hope so, given how much he was charging," Aaron said.

"One other thing," Theodore said, as he walked to the kitchen and returned with a small bag. "Eric, you should change out of that uniform. I secured these earlier."

Theodore tossed the bag to Eric, who opened it to reveal a simple outfit of shirt and slacks. He quickly changed, mindless of those around him.

Sammy stood, and bowed to them all.

"Madam Penelope," Sammy said. "It has been a great pleasure to meet you. I wish you all great luck on this next part of your journey. I will return to the fields and continue to manage the stores from there."

He walked into the kitchen, and through the door to the fields, closing it as he left. Penelope stood, and waited for the others to follow suit before she turned and headed for the door. As they ascended the stairs, she looked back into the dining room.

"You did a marvellous job, Theodore," she said.

"Thank you," Theodore said, looking back over the room. "I merely copied what the coder did for us in Trialtown, but I'm still proud that I could achieve the same effect."

"How wonderful it must look with customers eating your noodles," she said with a wry tone.

"Indeed, I do not imagine this city store will be making me rich any time soon," Aaron replied.

"Perhaps if you liberated a few hundred wardens..." she said, her voice trailing away.

She turned and continued up the stairs, a sudden urgent need to her steps.

"I must speak to Brandis before we leave the city. I will have him continue the games while I am gone. I will get him to use some of the wardens as our new staff. You can spare me those modifiers, right, Darling?"

"Of course," Aaron said.

They left the restaurant and entered the city, working their way across town to Penelope's gaming centre. There, they found Brandis directing players and audience to the arena downstairs. Horatio was with him, his wife standing nearby.

"How goes your wife?" Aaron asked.

"She makes steady progress. In her lucid moments, I believe she remembers me, and remembers that she is my wife. I am hopeful she will recover fully in time. I see your warden friend there is fully human again. I hope the same for her."

"As do we all, Horatio," Penelope said, then turned to face her assistant. "Brandis, I would ask that you use the helper modifiers to recruit staff for the games. We have cancelled too many events recently. Let the wardens keep things running."

"Yes, Madam," he said.

"Theodore," Penelope said. "Would you kindly give him three helper modifiers?"

Theodore nodded, and rummaged in his pockets. He

pulled out three of the paper slips, and handed them to Brandis.

"Use them one at a time," Theodore instructed. "These are thirty day limited ones. When one expires, recruit a new warden, so you don't have them going sentient on you and leaving."

"I will do as you say," Brandis replied. "Travel safely."

"I will follow you soon," Horatio said. "Once my wife has returned to me in full, I will take the road out of the city. I will find you then."

"Right, goodbye then," Aaron said.

Leaving the building, they made their way to the gates out of the city. A warden approached them as they neared the gates, signalling for them to stop.

"Would you progress beyond this place?"the warden asked.

"We would, Warden," Theodore said.

The warden looked them all over, his critical eye assessing them. He stopped in front of Eric.

"You may not make it. But I will allow you to pass. If your troupe has learned from the city, they will not allow you to fail now. You may pass."

"There is no test?" Theodore asked.

"The road will be your test. Though one of you already passed it before."

The warden turned and waved at the gates, causing them to swing open. As they slowly parted, a rocky mountain trail awaited them on the far side. Theodore led the group, and the gates soon closed thunderously behind them.

$$*\qquad*\qquad*$$

"Welcome to the road of retribution," said a voice from behind the rocks, growing louder as the speaker appeared. "I will work as your guide, for a fee. Or I can signal the bandits, it is your choice."

He was a slight man, of rat like appearance. Theodore faced him directly, stepping towards the intruder in a

163

menacing way.

"Who would you be, that you make such a threat to us?" Theodore demanded.

"Why, I am nobody of consequence, but I offer you passage, in exchange for points. If you choose to refuse me, the bandits will extract your points and you will not receive safe passage."

"We would prefer to take our chances with the bandits," Theodore said as he turned to walk back to the others. The man leapt, landing on Theodore's shoulders, his jagged blunt knife pressed into Theodore's neck.

Theodore panicked for a moment, then calmed himself. His points were no good to this man if he were dead. Theodore slipped a hand silently into a pocket.

"OK, what would you have of me?" Theodore said with a tremulous voice.

"I would have your points," the man replied.

Theodore removed his hand from his pocket and slapped a modifier to the man's wrist. Softly, he whispered the rhyme. Screaming, the man was hurled away to hit the rocks he had hidden behind, slumping to the ground.

"I'm sorry, I cannot accommodate your request at this time," Theodore said, before continuing to walk away from the city.

"They will find you," the man called after them. "They'll find you, and when they do, they'll kill you, or worse. You lot will be wardens by nightfall!"

"Ignore him, lad," Aaron said as they walked away. "He is small fry, and he would have led us to the bandit's trap had we agreed to his safe passage."

"What else resides along this road that we have to worry about?" Eric asked.

"A variety of creatures," Aaron said. "Lizards the size of your leg, that swarm like wasps when threatened. Carnivorous bovine that have abandoned the heard for the power of the predator, and packs of vultures that will as readily pick the eyes from the living, as feast on the dead."

"You really should be a travel agent," Theodore quipped. "How long is the road?"

"It will be three days walk before we leave the

mountains. In the mountains we face the lizards, and the bovine. Descending to the plain, we face the vultures and the bovine. At any point, we might face the bandits."

"Why?" Eric asked.

Aaron looked at him, his eyes narrowing.

"This is the road of retribution. What punishment would make our lives easy?" he said.

"It's just, can we die here? What happens then?" Eric demanded.

"If you are killed here, you become a warden," Aaron explained. "Until the next audit, when you'll awake in the Welcoming Fields, to start your journey over again. Some take several attempts, most give up."

"We march," Theodore said, striding ahead of the group. "Cover as much ground as we can, and find a good place for a camp over night."

They followed, and soon the group was making good time, in spite of the rocky terrain. While they were walking, Aaron was picking up sticks, examining them, and then discarding them. Penelope watched him for a while, until her curiosity got the better of her.

"Darling, what are you doing?" she asked.

"The gate warden would not have allowed us to bring weapons from the City, but we need something. I'm hoping to find a sturdy club, preferably a few. We'll need them if the lizards come."

"But we have Theodore's things to repel them," she said.

"They are good, but they will be too slow if we face a swarm. A club you can swing fast, a modifier you have to apply, say the rhyme, it's too slow. We have to arm ourselves, the sooner the better."

Hearing them, Theodore stopped, turning to face Aaron.

"Then that would be a good reason for me to perfect my technique without the rhymes."

"That's fine, for you, but we can't use a modifier with nothing written on it. You must not forget, that to make a modifier for somebody other than yourself, you will always need to write something down, for them to read out. We need weapons, not words, if we are to survive out here for long."

"OK then, this is something the coder from Trialtown showed me," Theodore said.

He searched around until he found a stick, gnarled and weak, resting in the weeds where it had fallen from a sickly acacia tree. Picking it up, Theodore hefted the flimsy thing, then swung it like a club.

"This will do," he said as he took out his coder's pen and marked the stick. "This branch of wattle, must serve a task, so make it metal, is all I ask."

The twig took on a grey colouring, gradually darkening, until it was a bleak gunmetal grey. Theodore polished it with his sleeve smiling at his handy work. He swung the metal baton he had created, satisfied with the heft and balance, and passed it to Aaron.

"How many do we need?" Theodore asked.

Aaron looked at the club as he held it, his mouth hanging slack as if he had seen a miracle. He looked up at Theodore, turned his head slightly, and narrowed his eyes.

"How long have you known that trick, lad?"

"Just a few days," Theodore said. "The coder told me I could not be taught it until I learned to believe in my own immunity to the side effects of coding."

"Wait, so you mean, you can't be harmed by a modifier any more?"

"Really, I probably never could be. According to the code teacher, we suffer the side effects because of our guilt. The system employs guilt in assessing our punishments, but if you achieve a coding level where you are nearly able to do it without modifier rhymes, then you can free yourself from linking your guilt to the system. I wasn't sure it would work, it makes little sense to me, really. But it works. How many more do we need?"

"Well," Aaron said, still digesting what he had heard and seen, "One each I guess. So one for yourself, Eric, and Penelope."

Theodore nodded, found three more small branches, and used the same technique to fashion them into vicious clubs. Once they were all armed, he continued along the trail, keeping his eyes open for any sign of creatures.

After an hour's walk, they crested a rise, where the trail turned around a cliff's edge. There was a straight drop to the right and sheer climb to the left. Theodore stopped abruptly, staring ahead. The others bumped and jostled as they came to this unexpected halt.

There in the path before them, a group of a dozen large lizards glared menacingly at them, angry that their meal had been interrupted. What Theodore could only assume was one of the carnivorous bovine, lay dismembered on the trail, where the lizards had been tearing its flesh with their jagged teeth and rancid claws.

Several steps ahead, between them and the lizards, the path widened. Theodore ran towards that spot, hoping to gain the safety of space to fight, rather than risk the dreadful fall into the misty unknown. The others followed, and the lizards screeched a battle cry, lurching as one to meet them.

The speed of the lizards was unbelievable, and they met the four inmates with menacing swipes of those massive claws and darting lunges of their toothy maws. The group wielded their clubs as best they could, but the lizards were moving like a whirlwind, trying to separate the humans as they darted in for wave after wave of lightning attacks.

Theodore was beginning to fear they could not hold them off, when Eric screamed, his club striking one lizard's brow as he pushed the advantage, charging into the creature with his shoulder lowered. The cliff's edge was close, and the lizard was pushed back. Eric did not let up his offensive, and was rushing towards that terrible drop.

With a mighty swing at his nearest opponent, Theodore dove after Eric, hoping to grasp his arm, his shirt, anything, to stop him from falling. Just as Theodore reached his friend, the lizard toppled, a claw opening Eric's arm from the elbow down as it plummeted out of sight. As Eric teetered on the brink, Theodore finally managed to get a firm grip on the man's collar, and pull him back onto the trail.

It had all taken mere moments, but already two more

lizards were upon them. There was no time to asses Eric's wound, as they were both forced back into the fray. Eric swapped his club to the other hand, and to Theodore's surprise the man was just as effective with that hand as the other, soon dispatching a second lizard with a savage blow to the head.

As Aaron finished off a third lizard, the morale of the swarm faltered. Penelope lunged into her own assailant, and it lost its footing, twisting to tumble after its fellow into the misty depths. The rest of the lizards ran, clambering up the rocks and disappearing into the peaks above.

They all stood around, catching their breath, before Theodore suddenly remembered Eric's arm. He rushed over to the former warden, to inspect the wound. Blood ran free from the savage gash, but it had not reached bone, and miraculously, Theodore believed it shallow enough that probably no sufficient muscle damage had occurred.

"Sorry, friend, I am no great healer. Perhaps one day, but not today. We should bandage that."

Ripping a strip from Eric's own shirt, Theodore wrapped the wound in a tight bandage, tied it off at one end, and then turned to face the others.

"We should keep moving," he said. "The sooner we are out of these mountains, the better."

"Agreed, lad," Aaron replied. "But a few more hours to walk today. Is he going to manage?"

"I'll manage just fine," Eric said.

They left the scene of the battle behind, and continued on their way. There was no further trouble for several hours, until Aaron called them to a halt.

"Just up ahead, there is a set of abandoned cabins," he told them. "The bandits have been known to ambush from there, and they may well be waiting for tired travellers. Instead, we should climb from here, there is a small overhang above, not a decent cave but shelter enough. We camp for the night, and take turns on the watch."

They all nodded their agreement, and began to climb. Eric soon had trouble, his wounded arm unable to hold his weight without great pain.

"Why must I have pain?" Eric moaned. "It's not real! The whole place is false, so why should I feel this pain? It's utter madness."

"Remember where we are," Aaron said. "There is no debt of gratitude owed to us, we must suffer for our past, even when we are reformed."

"I don't like it," Eric said. Stopping where he was. "I don't think I can climb any further."

"You have to," Theodore said. "Just grit through the pain, believe in yourself. You can do it. If it isn't real, then stop feeling it. Know what to believe, and believe yourself unharmed."

Eric glared at him, his frustration making him angry. He thrust his wounded arm upwards, grasped a handhold, and screamed as he pulled himself up. He repeated the move with his good arm, then screamed a second time as he used the wounded arm again.

"You'll have every bandit in the area on us with that noise," Aaron snarled.

Theodore took a small rock, made it wood, in a reverse of his club making exercise, and reached down to Eric. He held the lump before Eric's mouth.

"Bite this, and keep climbing."

Eric bit down on the lump of wood, his pained grunts much softer than his screaming had been. Soon, everyone had reached the overhang. They slumped inside, waiting for their breath to return after the climb.

"We rest here," Aaron said. "I'll take first watch, then Theodore, then Penelope. Eric goes last. Two hours each. Then we march on the cabins, and beyond. If we meet the bandits, we need to be rested."

Chapter 21 – Day Two

Theodore grumbled as he awoke, Aaron shaking his shoulder.

"It's your watch, son," Aaron whispered.

Theodore sat up and looked around, befuddled for a moment. He looked at his friend.

"Aaron, correct me if I'm wrong, but I'm pretty sure that when I first arrived in Claustrum Mundus, I didn't need sleep. Now I feel like I could sleep for a month and it wouldn't be enough."

Aaron smiled, and nodded.

"I believe we talked about this once before. I had all but forgotten. It's so long since I was new here. Those times are a faded blur. Yes, when you came, you did not feel the need to sleep. You didn't observe a night cycle. But now, as you regain your self and your control, the system is no longer imposing its artificial ways so strongly."

Theodore looked at him, his confusion evident. Aaron sighed, and sat beside him.

"I forget sometimes son, that you are relatively new to all this, compared to myself."

Aaron looked out of the cave, to the stars, winking like jewels in the sky. False jewels in a fake sky that did not truly exist, but then, neither did the cave, or the path below it, and perhaps even the bandits were a work of fiction. Yet it all seemed so real to him now, more his normal life than the real world outside.

Something snapped to the front of his memory, and

Aaron shook his head.

"I've been in here now, longer than I was out there."

"What was that, Boss?" Theodore asked, looking at his friend.

"Oh, nothing. But, where was I? Oh, right. The fields. The fields do not have a night as such, but they do have a day night cycle, largely driven by those like us who have come this far. For your reformed state, you are being given back your humanity, in many small ways."

"It worries me," Theodore said.

"Why, lad?"

"I felt no such loss of self then. But I feel it now. And I know now, logically, I am more my self than ever before in Claustrum Mundus. But my sense of loss is far greater also."

Aaron nodded, and stood, walking towards the edge of the cliff, to gaze down at the path below.

"That's normal, Son," Aaron said. "Back then, you didn't know what you were missing. Remember how easily you gave it all away?"

"It was very quick, and I do not recall even being aware it was happening at the time."

"Exactly. There was probably not much of you left to lose. Now, you have more at risk."

"This place is evil. An evil of such subtleties, I fear we can never bring it to account."

"And why would you? Is it any greater evil than the crimes committed by every man and woman here? If you got word out of how it is to be made a warden, to be denied the basic freedom of self awareness, of essential sentience, do you really think that anybody out there, in the real world, is going to care? We're scum, worse than the dirt beneath their dog's ass when it shits. Don't fool yourself, Son. We're worthless to them, and the system has freedom to treat us however it sees fit."

Theodore joined him at the edge, to look down into the fog of the pre-dawn hills.

"But it does have some limits," Theodore said. "It must give us the opportunity to feel, and to reform. It operates on a set of parameters, a program set down by the founders of the prison. The system is no more free than you or I. If it was, my guess is we would all be wardens by now."

"Or would we?" Aaron replied. "Perhaps we're its entertainment. A world of wardens would be pretty boring, even to the system."

"Then this journey, these lessons, this entire process, is merely us playing the mouse, while the cat, the system, toys with us? I think I would rather be a warden."

Aaron put his hand on Theodore's shoulder and turned. He watched their companions. They made no sound beyond their shallow breathing, more illusions to make this world feel real.

"Son, best be careful what you wish for," he said, "Something else has been bothering me."

"What is it, Boss?"

"That warden who has been following you around, the female, who is she?"

"What do you mean?" Theodore asked.

"I mean, I get the feeling the system has sent her for a reason. I don't mean her the warden, I mean her the prisoner. Who was she to you? Before she was a warden. It concerns me, and it may be a sign of the motives of the system in letting you come this far."

"I don't know what to tell you, Boss. I think there's no reason, not like that. There could only be one woman the system could use against me like that. Only one woman who has value in my life, that I know of so far."

"You remember her? Your other life is coming back to you?"

"In parts, but I prefer not to speak of them. Just trust me, it's not a person it has chosen for any such reason. That woman, the only one it could choose, would never be here. She was completely innocent. For her to be here, in Claustrum Mundus, and worse, to have become a warden? It is something I will never accept. It can never be that way, unless all justice has died in the real world."

"OK then, Son. I will accept your judgement on the matter, and be relieved for it. Enjoy your watch," Aaron said, then left Theodore to stare into the gloom, a thoughtful silence in the air.

*   *   *

Theodore was still there, over an hour later, when he first heard them. Heading from further along the path, three men came. They made their way slowly along the trail, looking around as though searching for something. Or for someone. Theodore shuddered.

Kneeling, he pressed his hand on the edge of the cliff, and murmured a few words. He was nervous, but determined not to fail now. In answer to his voice, a sliver of rock came away, long and slender. He caught the improvised spear and hefted it, testing the weight. Theodore smiled in grim satisfaction.

The men continued coming. As they drew nearer, Theodore could see their faces, dirty and pale in the waning moonlight. He squinted, looking as carefully as he could, searching the face of one, then the next, and finally the third man. He gasped as he recognised the man. He was the same bandit who had apprehended them when they first set out from the city.

He hefted the spear, and readied his aim. A staying hand halted his action.

"Wait," Penelope said from behind him. "There may be no need for violence."

Theodore nodded.

"You're right. They may pass us by," he said.

As they watched, the trio came closer, until they stood on the path immediately below them. Penelope knelt to look over the edge. Theodore gently lowered the spear to the ground, and crawled beside her.

As his hand rested on the edge, that one man looked up. Theodore felt the eyes boring into him, and was about to reach for the spear in a defensive act, but he never got the chance. That one fired a grapple, and with devastating precision, an unnatural amount of accuracy and fortitude, that grapple led a line around his wrist, then pulled tight. The man below secured the assistance of his companions and they tugged the line.

Theodore tumbled over the edge, and plummeted towards the three men. Behind him, Penelope screamed at Aaron to come and help as she hefted the spear and tossed it towards the men. Theodore hoped her aim was good.

One of the men waved an arm at the spear, and a chain snaked out towards it, striking it hard and sending it over the edge of the path. Harmlessly, the spear tumbled into the darkness, joining the lizards from earlier.

Then Theodore struck the trio, and they half caught him, pushing him back, into the cliff face. He struck it hard, winded. Theodore looked up at his assailants. They smirked in eager anticipation of the treatment they had in store for him.

"You're using modified equipment," he said.

"But of course," one of the men said. "You didn't really think that coders were limited to changing hair colour and giving people fancy tattoos?"

Theodore smiled, understanding the odds better with that information.

"Of course I was well aware of the possibilities. I am guessing that is the trade of Horatio in the City. But you don't know about coding like I do."

"Shut it, and take your medicine," the man with the grapple screamed, rushing forward to strike Theodore with a club.

Theodore's body recoiled from the strike, and he crumpled against the wall for a moment before righting himself. The attacker laughed, and spread his arms as he seemed to grow somehow taller, stronger, his overall carriage of himself now more confident.

"Ease up, leave some for us!" the man with the chain said.

"You're stealing my points," Theodore said. "I won't have that."

"Oh really? And what are you going to do about it?" said the chain wielding man as he advanced on Theodore.

Unarmed, Theodore hurled his fists at the man, who blocked them with the chain, wrapping it around Theodore's right arm and pulling him in close, to sneer in his face with terrible malice.

"Your points are ours now. Enjoy being a warden."

Theodore grasped the chain in his free hand and mumbled an improvised rhyme. In instant response, the chain shattered, and the man growled in anger.

"How dare you!" he shouted, swinging his ham sized fist at Theodore's head.

Theodore ducked the swing, and pushed both hands into the man's torso. The man pushed back, grasping at Theodore's hair as he pushed the slighter defender back towards the wall.

"You can't win, you weak little man," the bandit crowed.

Theodore bent his knees, then pushed again, harder, and their progress halted. But it was not enough. Theodore muttered under his breath.

"Away from me, take this man, where I can't see, far below he must land."

The bandit, a look of abject horror on his face as he realised his new predicament, flew backwards, over the edge of the cliff, then dropped out of sight. Theodore turned to face the others. As he faced them, a club struck his jaw. Theodore spun like a top, before landing hard. The remaining two bandits were on him in a heartbeat.

"No more of that, boy!" the larger of the two snarled, slipping a gag over Theodore's mouth to stop him from reciting any more codes.

Meanwhile, the other bandit twisted his arm up and back, and Theodore felt himself being lifted, painfully contorted. Then he heard Aaron's voice, filled with rage.

"Clear off, you scum!" Aaron screamed as his boot connected with the man at Theodore's back, who was holding his arm.

The man rolled away, towards the edge, then knelt up. His companion joined him, squaring off to face the new threat. Theodore, now facing them, rose to his knees as Aaron reached to help him to his feet.

Theodore ignored the offered hand, instead turning his steely determination on their foes. He raised his arm before him, palm flat and screamed a curse on their lives from behind the gag. It was unintelligible noise, but his intent was clear. He wished these men no good tidings as he swore his hatred at them.

Then, Theodore slapped his palm down onto the rock, and to the horror of the bandits, the path split. A great bight was taken from it, encircling them before the enormous chunk of hillside slipped, then tumbled into the darkness of the valley below, taking the two men with it.

Finally, Theodore accepted Aaron's helping hand, and got to his feet. Reaching behind his head, Theodore removed the gag and looked up at the cave opening, where the others were watching.

"No words," Aaron whispered.

"What?" Theodore asked.

"No words," Aaron repeated, resting his hand on Theodore's shoulder with a smile. "Sure you screamed something, but it was not words. You did that with no rhyme. Son, your talent is getting scary."

*   *   *

The others joined them on the path, and they continued on their way. Since the bandits had apparently been taken care of, there was no real need to delay further. The cabins would be more comfortable anyway.

"Are you sure there won't be more bandits ahead, or in the cabins?" Penelope asked for the third time.

"No, but we'll be fine. Theodore has proven that," Aaron said.

"But they nearly killed him!"

"But they didn't, and now, he's grown. He has shown his true talent, and can tackle whatever they might throw at us."

"I'm not convinced," she said. "No offence, Theodore."

"None taken," Theodore replied. "But if we meet more of them, I will take care of it."

Shortly, the cabins came into view, soft light coming from inside the closest one. Aaron stopped, signalled for the others to wait, and waved Theodore on. Carefully, slowly, Theodore walked forward, until he was close enough to see inside.

Through the window, he spied four people. He signalled to Aaron the number, then looked back to face them and consider his next move. Smiling, he decided on a simple solution. Theodore crept up to the side of the small building, rested his hand on the wall, and concentrated.

Bars grew, slowly covering the windows and the only door. By the time the bandits inside realised what was happening, it was too late. They screamed their defiance and Theodore laughed.

"Stay in there, and leave us be. I am sure somebody will be along to release you, eventually."

Their shouting had brought lights on in the other two cabins, and Theodore ran towards them. As two people ran from the first, he waved his hand before them, and an ornate cage sprouted from the ground, to trap the pair.

"Anybody else want to try anything?" Theodore shouted into the darkness.

Three more people came out, their hands raised high above their heads. The third, hanging behind the others, was a woman who seemed more fearful than was necessary. He approached her.

"Please," she begged. "Do not harm us. These ones have done enough of that."

Taking pity, Theodore waved her away.

"Go on then, head for the village of free men. You'll be safe there. You others, see she is not harmed on the way."

"Oh, they did a fine job of that yesterday, getting us captured by these bastards," she snarled.

"Well," Theodore said. "These bastards will not be hurting any more travellers for now."

As the three walked away from the cabins, Theodore signalled for his friends to join him.

"What will we do with this lot?" Aaron asked.

"We can't release them," Theodore said. "At least, not yet. I'll set a timer. They can rot like this for a few days, until the bars are gone."

"Good."

Once it was done, they settled into one of the cabins

and rested for a while, before finally continuing on their long journey.

Soon, the rocky cliffs gave way to rolling hills, and a plain stretched out before them. Immense vulture like birds circled high above them, and they watched the creatures with nervous eyes as they hiked the well worn trail to a small cluster of houses that were visible near the horizon.

"It finally feels as if we're getting somewhere," Theodore said.

"It's a good feeling, isn't it?" Aaron replied. "I remember the first time I laid eyes on this place. It was quite a relief. The bandits had taken three of my party, the lizards had dragged two over the edge of the cliff, and I was walking with only one other survivor. We were immensely relieved. He stayed in the village. He said he had seen enough danger, it was time to settle down and make something of himself."

"Who was he?"

"He was a man I met quite literally at the gate to the city, as I was leaving. He was one of the few who left the city after losing their companions to the wardens. It was his father, I believe. He had nobody else in his life he respected, and nobody else who cared for him, and then, he had been estranged from his father for many years anyway. I guess that made the leaving all the easier for him."

"What was his name?"

"Simon. He never gave me any other name though."

"Do you suppose he's still there?"

"I have no doubt. I hope he remembers me fondly, and has mended some bridges. It would be nice to visit the village without any trouble."

"Why would there be trouble?"

"When we arrived, he was not as reformed as he might have been. Some of the locals didn't like us much. I hope their memories are short."

Chapter 22 – Village of Free Men

As they neared the village, they reached tilled fields, with men and women working the land. A gentle sun bathed them in its soft warmth. The ground felt like a cushion beneath the feet after the harshness of the mountains.

Looking around, Theodore could see that this was a peaceful, relaxed place. He felt as if those he was seeing in the fields were comfortable, calm, and somehow happier than those he had seen before.

The rest of Claustrum Mundus had seemed a struggle. But here, life was moving at a slower pace, and there was not the same worry in the eyes of the people as in those he met in the other settlements. A man slowly lowered his tools, and approached them.

"Welcome, travellers," he said. "To the village of free men. It is named Yeoman, but we tend to simply call it the village. I am Geordi."

"Thank you, Geordi" Theodore replied. "Please, we would like to rest and find refreshments. Where is most suitable for us in your village?"

Geordi smiled, turned, and pointed into the village.

"Head straight into the central plaza, and on your left you'll see the Newcomer's Inn. You should find Sebastian in there, or perhaps my wife, Raen. They will be able to tell you anything you need to know. And you'll find food and drink more refreshing than any you have encountered since you first arrived in the Welcoming Fields."

"Thank you," Theodore said with a smile.

Geordi returned the smile, and went back to his work in the field. Theodore led the way and they entered the village. The houses were simple, yet oddly beautiful. Immaculately maintained, they seemed to hail from a range of historical periods, some with very European styling, and others more Asian, all different, and all decorated in the most attractive of styles. It seemed idyllic, a mix of peoples all living in peace.

"How do you suppose they keep it so nice here?" Penelope asked.

"The best coders, like Theodore, would make it here eventually," Aaron explained.

Turning to the left as Geordi instructed, they entered a solid stone building, with a wide veranda running around it. On entering, they paused, to allow their eyes to adjust and take in the scene. Comfortable lounges were widely spaced, and a warm fire crackled in the hearth at one end of the room. Along the far wall, there was a long, low bar. Behind it, two people were in conversation. The pair turned to face them, and smiled with genuine kindness.

"Welcome travellers," the woman said. "Please, take a seat, I am Raen. Sebastian here will bring you some drinks shortly."

She walked around the bar to approach them, and indicated a grouping of the comfortable lounges near the fireplace. Together, they all followed her and sat down.

"We rarely get new visitors to the village, please, make yourselves comfortable. Having made it this far, we assume you all to be reformed and ready for life in this peaceful place. I must warn you, however, that should you not be, and trouble ensue, there are consequences. The village marshal does not take kindly to trouble makers, and he has..."

She paused, considering her words carefully.

"An agreement, of sorts, with the system. Trouble makers do not stay here long."

"Please," Aaron said. "Speaking of trouble makers, I was here once before. There was a man who came at the same time as I, named Simon. What became of him?"

She smiled, and leaned back in her chair, arms folding

across her chest in a slow and thoughtful motion.

"I had believed you to have a familiar face. As I recall, you made the decision to leave the village, but your friend remained. Fear not. He was impulsive, and rude, and at times overly boisterous in his continual celebration of all things banal, but he was not greater trouble than we could tame. He did settle down in the end. You can see him later, if you wish."

"What does he do now?" Penelope asked.

"We found an outlet for his talents, after he was tamed by one of the local ladies, assisting the Marshal. He has made himself eminently useful to us here in the village. A valuable member of the community."

"What do you mean he was tamed?" Eric asked, his voice tremulous with the fear of being manipulated or controlled.

There was a brief pause, then Raen burst into a fit of laughter, her mirth contagious. She calmed herself while the others chuckled, looked at Eric's serious face, and lost control to a second round of laughter before finally settling herself down again.

"You're serious? Please, sir. You misunderstand me! He met a lady from the village, named Sophia. They became lovers, and in time they married. That is what I meant when I said she tamed him. Once he was settled into their new home, he took the position in the Marshal's office."

Understanding dawned on Eric's face, and it lightened like the fields in the morning. Finally, he laughed at his own mistake, and the atmosphere between them was once again relaxed.

"Now then, the things you will all need to know," Raen said as Sebastian arrived with drinks, and a platter of chilled fruits and cheeses. "I know there is one of you likely remembers well, but for the rest, I will explain how life here works."

She paused, taking a slice of melon from the platter and waving her hands at them, gesturing they should eat. She delicately took a small bite of the melon, chewed and swallowed the morsel, then lowered her hands to her lap.

"To live here as new arrivals, you may take rooms here in the inn. We used to offer this service for free, but we found we had some of the more troublesome arrivals making a mess of things. So we now ask a modest rent of two points per day to stay here. As you become accustomed to the way we live, you will make a choice."

"The first step, you will visit the Marshal and enrol in his program of assessment. He will give you training in some of the things you will need for your new lives, and as you attend his classes, he will assess your suitability. Should you be deemed acceptable, you will be offered a permanent residence in the village."

"Aaron would already have completed this program would he not?" Penelope asked, indicating her lover in case Raen did not recall his name.

"Indeed, he has," Raen replied. "If I recall, he was offered residency, but chose at the time not to accept. The offer remains open to him. But the rest of you must show your value to the community by participating in the program."

"And what happens once we complete the program?" Theodore asked.

"As your friend did in the past, you will make the choice. You may stay, or you may go, but if you have passed the program to the Marshal's satisfaction, you will no longer be required to pay any form of daily rent to the system."

She looked at them all in turn, before she continued.

"You will be effectively immune to the points system. Should you return to other parts of Claustrum Mundus, you will be able to do so without incurring a daily cost, just as there is no daily cost here, aside from rent in the inn."

She stood, and walked to the fireplace. Carefully, Raen picked up a small log from the pile beside the hearth, and placed it in the fire. Standing back, she watched as it crackled into flames. She turned to face them once more.

"You will of course, still be able to earn points and spend them when you are in other places, but citizens of the village have all they need provided to them free of charge, and in turn they perform their tasks here without placing any charge on other residents."

"Communal living then," Eric said.

"Indeed," Raen confirmed.

"I feel that could suit me, after my past experiences," Eric said.

"I am well pleased to hear that, former warden."

Theodore looked at Eric, then back at Raen.

"How did you know that?" Theodore asked.

"When you entered the village, as soon as you spoke to my husband, the system sent us your details, so that we would know what to expect. We have earned our peaceful lives here through participation, through struggle, and through recompense. We are guaranteed our peaceful existence by the system, and it serves us as a guardian as well as a jailer."

Theodore stood, facing her. He waved a hand briefly to indicate Eric.

"It is good for him to find this peace," Theodore said. "But there are things I must still do, before I can make a decision to settle somewhere as idyllic as this."

"We are aware of your situation, Theodore Longarm. We will support you in your journey, as long as that does not jeopardise the system, or our peaceful existence. As with your friend here, should you earn an offer of residency, and choose not to accept, that offer will remain open to you thereafter."

"Thank you, but now, if you could please show us to our rooms, it has been a long day of walking. I would rest before we see more of the village."

"Of course," Raen replied. "Follow me."

As she led, they all stood and followed. The group ascended stairs then walked along a mezzanine balcony lined with doors. As they arrived at a suite to the farthest end, the front doors to the inn opened, and they all looked down. Raen seemed surprised, as if she had not expected another visitor.

The newcomer stopped as the door closed, just as they had done. The flickering firelight danced across her features, pink and plastic. She looked up at the balcony.

"Oh my," Raen said. "It is a very long time since we have seen a warden here. Is there something wrong, officer of the system? We have not breached our conditions or caused any trouble. The peace has not broken, why are you here?"

The female warden looked up at them, and pointed at Theodore.

"I must accompany him, on the system's orders. To observe and assess."

Raen raised an eyebrow, then gestured for the warden to approach, before she turned to face Theodore. Her eyes narrowed slightly as she looked him over.

"You are one full of surprises, Theodore Longarm," Raen said. "There is something about this warden that you do not yet know, but I see that the system has selected her to watch your every move."

She looked back at the warden, now ascending the stairs. It walked with a human grace, in spite of its mechanical form. She looked back at Theodore.

"Clearly something you have done has it suspicious of your motivation, and also has it wishing to see how you will proceed. The fact that it sent her, tells me it is also very curious about you, not for reasons of policing your behaviour, but for reasons of trying to understand you. Perhaps your abilities, or your motivation, are a mystery to it."

She looked again, and the warden had nearly reached them. She looked back at Theodore, leaning close, her eyes burning into his.

"Regardless of who she is, and why she is here, heed my warning. Do not bring trouble to the village, or else we can not guarantee your future."

With a flurry, she opened the door and waved them into the suite, a large communal living space with several doors into other spaces.

"Enjoy your stay," she said as the warden joined them, following Theodore into the suite. "I will be downstairs should you need me."

*　　　　*　　　　*

"Why are you here?" Theodore asked softly, anxious that his voice could wake the others.

"I am to accompany you," she replied. "As I said before. It is not my place to question my orders."

"Who are you?" He demanded.

The warden looked at him in calm, dispassionate pity.

"You know that already, at some level. And you already know why it is me who is here, and why the system requires that I observe your actions. But you refuse to listen to your own mind. Until you do, you will not remember what it is you seek."

He nodded.

"Then it is all part of the same problem. I must finish here, and continue, until I unlock the riddles. If you must accompany me, then you may have some walking to do yet."

"I do not grow tired, you need not worry for my well being."

"But perhaps I should," he said. "I begin to suspect..."

He paused, ending the sentence unfinished. She watched him for a long while. Finally, she spoke.

"You begin to suspect what?"

"Huh?" he said, snapping from a deep reverie. "Oh that, well, nothing. It's not important. But I believe everything that has occurred so far has been for a purpose. There is cold reason behind this place, and I will see the truth with my own eyes soon enough."

"Sometimes, the truth eludes us all, even the system. It seeks the truth, that is why I am here. You seek the truth. Jailer and prisoner are so alike."

He looked at her, surprised.

"That is a very deep thought, for an automaton."

"It is not so deep that it surpasses my programming."

He smiled, tapping the bed beside himself, asking her to sit. Slowly, she complied.

"You have no programming. You are human, like me. You remember who you were, but I do not. You can not act on your memories, but I can. I am one half of a person, and you are the other, of another person. You are no less human than I, and no more warden than I."

She shook, then looked at him.

"This is why you are of interest to the system," she said. "You are forcing it to address the very questions its creators must have wrestled with."

"I am forcing nobody to do anything. I am merely seeking answers to the questions that I am faced with. When do I stop being myself, and start being a construct? How am I any more human than you are? How can I know for certain that I am not merely acting as the system has dictated for me?"

"But you are not, you are acting of your own volition. Otherwise I have no purpose in being here," she said.

"Oh, you would still have purpose, if that were only to confuse the issue and see how I responded."

"You are a suspicious man, Theodore Longarm, to say such things. You attribute the system with human frailty."

"The system is perhaps as human as you or I. It is yet another character in our story, one we have to come to understand, if we are to survive."

"To survive? The system means you no harm, Theodore."

"To remove free will is to harm a human. But where the line between harm and humanity is? I can not answer that question."

"I do not understand," she said.

"If I have no free will, would I know it? I do not believe I would," Theodore said. "I was a warden, I know that now, when I first came here. I had no awareness of my state, no understanding that I was less than I had been. Not until it changed. Even now, I do not fully understand the difference. I am still not entirely myself, because I still do not remember it all. You remember everything, so are you more human than I am?"

She sighed, a very human sound.

"This is why I am sent to watch you. You are asking these questions with your human mind. The system has asked them of itself for many years, but it has a mechanical mind, it does not operate in quite the same way. If you show through human logic that things here are not as they should be, the system would be forced to initiate a revision protocol. The humans in the real world who control its programming will need to be contacted, so they can implement the changes the system requires."

"This is too much intelligence for a machine."

He stood, and began removing his shirt.

"What are you doing?" the warden asked. "I do not understand the connection between that statement and your current action."

"That statement was the end of that discussion. Now, I wish to rest. You may do whatever you need to do, but I am taking a nap."

"Oh, I see." She said, standing, and backing away from the bed.

Theodore chuckled to himself, willing to believe he had just seen her pink cheeks grow darker.

"I wonder if you are becoming human simply by following me? You are operating outside the normal role of a warden, after all."

She snapped upright, receding into the cold, calculated and comfortable role of the plastic prison monster.

"I would not know of what you are speaking. Take your rest, I will remain here."

He chuckled at her clumsy words, and climbed into the bed.

"Good night, warden."

Chapter 23 – Assessment

Theodore gazed at the sky, his mind filled with wonder at this turn of events. The peacefulness of working the fields was something he had not expected, and the impact it was having on his mind was just as much a surprise to him, as it was to the warden who worked beside him.

"Why are you doing this?" he asked her with no expectation of a straight answer.

"I must observe you, but I would draw unwanted attention if I simply stood by while others did their share. The system has a long understanding with these people, and for me to be seen not doing my share of the work, that understanding could come into question."

Theodore laughed, struck the soil with his hoe, and twisted the handle. As the weed came out, its roots scattering the looser soil with merry abandon, he tossed it aside. Standing upright again, he turned to face her.

"We both know your words do not reflect the truth of the situation."

"Perhaps," she said. "You are not entirely wrong in what you say, but the fact is that the understanding with these people does include all aspects of their knowledge of the situation, and the way they choose to believe things are. The fact that this borrowed sense of freedom is an illusion is irrelevant to the fact I must not do anything that could serve to destroy it. They have earned the right to live in this manner, and I am not permitted to hamper the security and safety of this lifestyle by offering any reminder of the falsehood. Have you not noticed the lack of wardens here?"

Theodore shook his head, slowly turning back to his task. He turned over the soil, removing yet another of the stubborn weeds from the fertile ground.

"A prison," he said, his voice soft and monotone. "With no bars, is no less a prison than a concrete box."

"Theodore, these people have shown a level of reform, and of remorse, that elevates them above the unrepentant murderers and thieves of Claustrum Mundus. Even so, under the laws of your real world, they can not be permitted to leave the system. Therefore, the system has decided that this illusion of a free and peaceful life is their due reward. It would be inhumane of it to allow that reward to be lost."

"And what if that reward is not sufficient? What if this life is not the one they would choose for themselves?"

"Then they need not remain here. This village is for those who choose it, after passing the test. Your friend Aaron did not choose it, but he has the freedom to return, or to travel, to act as he feels necessary, within the laws dictated by the system."

"But what if he chose not to return to the fields, as he did? What of him then?"

"That is his choice, Theodore. Do not pretend you do not understand. You are prisoners. You are criminals. And yet, in good faith, the system has offered you this choice."

Theodore struck his hoe in the soil, allowing it to stand there, a silent sentinel, as he turned to face her directly again.

"And what kind of choice is that?" he demanded, knowing before she replied, by her subtle and plastic expression, that she had misunderstood him.

"You may pass the test and stay here, fail the test and be banished back to the city, or the fields, or whatever region you choose to exist in, you may pass the test and choose to return as a free man, unburdened by the need for points, or you may leave the communities of Claustrum Mundus behind altogether and travel the wilderness like many others have done. Some of them return, some of them do not. They are all out there, somewhere."

"There is at least one choice you have omitted."

"I do not believe so. You can only be bound by the laws of Claustrum Mundus, and under those laws these are your only choices."

"Then we do not have the choice of death, or the choice of leaving this world altogether, by any means."

"Those choices are not yours, unless you choose to devise a code to achieve something of the sort that is legal under the rules the system has dictated."

"What does that mean?" he said, stifling a brief hope.

"It means that your own limitations are what limit you, not the system, not this world. Should you choose the path of oblivion, you can seek it. But those who have tried, and found it, have in the end elected not to make use of it. At this point however, you do not have that choice."

"As usual, your answers leave me with greater questions, warden. That is enough, I will think on these things."

*   *   *

Aaron watched as the others worked in the fields outside the village. He had passed the test a long time ago, but he still wondered about it, and was not sure why he had rejected the offer of a peaceful life.

Something about the illusion of freedom had not appealed to him, but now, if she passed the test, it might be different.

His eyes came to rest on the view of Penelope, her muscles rippling as she worked, the healthy sweat running across her shoulders and down her back. A simple string across that glistening skin held her most womanly modesty intact. His eyes continued in their journey down her body. Beyond the tight shorts, the sun glistened from the moisture on the back of her thighs. His gaze lingered, and he shuddered in memory of her body's sensuous contact.

"I will not abandon her again," he said to himself.

"That's good to hear," Raen said, her voice startling him as she approached.

He turned to face her, a slight, embarrassed smile on his face as he realised he had been caught in lecherous admiration of his lover.

"Hello," he said. "What can I do for you?"

"Fetch her for me. We have a guest, who has asked for her directly. I believe there is a message of some import that she must receive."

"Would this be a man named Brandis?"

"Yes, it is."

"I'll bring her. We'll meet you at the Newcomer's Inn shortly."

With a nod, Raen turned and left. Aaron walked across the field, until he reached Penelope's side. He rested a gentle hand on her shoulder, and she jumped, so engrossed in her work that she had not sensed him coming to her.

"What is it, dearest?" she asked.

"Brandis has come."

That was all the words she needed to hear. She tossed the hoe to the ground and set off towards the village. Aaron followed.

Soon, they reached the inn, and she paused, drawing a deep breath. Facing him, she embraced Aaron then turned, no words needed between them, and entered. Aaron followed her, and there in the dim light of the Newcomer's Inn stood the burly servant she had charged with the task that mattered most.

"We have found them," he said.

"Then we will leave immediately," she replied.

"Wait," Aaron said. "Penelope, what of the test? You are a considerable way through."

"If I leave, I can continue when we return, can I not?" she demanded of Raen.

With a sad smile, the lady of the inn shook her head. Geordi, having just entered, placed a hand on his wife's shoulder as she spoke.

"I'm sorry, you will have to start the process again, from the beginning, once you return to the village. We believe that every event you experience can change the person you are. If you leave the village, the things that occur may change you in ways that can have an impact on the test. If you leave now, you will have to start again on your return."

"Then that is what I'll do. I'll bring them along, and we will do the test together."

"I will accompany you, Penelope." Aaron said.

"Thank you," she said. "Brandis, lead the way."

"We will accompany you as far as the mountains, but not further than that," Geordi said.

"I would appreciate that," Penelope said.

As they left the village, and began to cross the fields, They could see the small group of workers in the fields. To one side, Theodore worked, the warden by his side as usual. Standing, he waved to them, then returned to his task.

"Do you need to explain to him where you are going?" Raen asked.

"No, he will already know the meaning of it. He will have guessed the reason for Brandis's arrival, and deduced our response already."

"I did wave to him as I passed, coming into the village," Brandis said. "He seemed in deep conversation with that woman at the time."

"The warden?" Geordi asked. "Does he realise who she is yet?"

"I do not believe so," Aaron replied. "He keeps his knowledge to himself on a lot of these things, so it may be he has his suspicions, but has not yet revealed them to us."

"It is well that he is careful with his mind," Raen said. "A warden is a risky companion, even when it's tamed."

"Wait," Penelope said. "Back that up a bit. You know who that warden is?"

"Of course, and who she is to him." Geordi replied.

"Why would you not tell him then? Might it not be important for him to know?"

"My love," Aaron said. "Of course it's important, but it's entirely up to him. If he has some agreement with her not to pry into her true self, then that's between them and we have no right to interfere. If there's some other reason he has not enquired, as we all know he is able, then that's the decision he has made, and we must respect it."

"Would it change his behaviour if he knew?" Penelope asked.

"I have no doubt that it would. It may hamper his journey, or bring it to a premature end, if he knew who she was. He may stop looking for answers altogether, and we all know how valuable his journey is. Not just to himself. It could change things for all of us."

"It seems cruel," she said with a sad tone.

"And perhaps it is," Aaron said. "But we must let things be, for the moment. I sense that when next we meet him, things will have changed in ways we can not imagine."

*   *   *

Theodore stood in the Marshal's office, Eric beside him. It had been three weeks since they arrived at the village. For the first time since then, the warden was not present. Simon looked them over, presenting a serious facade.

"You have completed the test. You have participated in a range of physical and mental examinations while you were working the fields, and maintaining the village. You have been confronted with a rigorous effort to spark dissent and to encourage you to make trouble out of any inherent disobedience or self centred attitudes. Much of this testing has occurred without your knowledge while you were otherwise occupied. The results can not be appealed. Should you have completed the tests and failed, there is a minimum one year wait before you can return and try again. Do you understand?"

Both men nodded. Simon smiled.

"Then let me be the first to congratulate you. You have both passed. Both of you are now free from the burden of the points system, and I can officially offer you both residence within Yeomen, the village of free men."

Eric smiled, and thrust his hand forward in belated greeting.

"I am Eric, and I accept the offer. It is good to meet you, neighbour."

Simon laughed, and shook the offered hand before turning to Theodore.

"What of you, will you join us in Yeomen?"

"I do not know," Theodore replied. "I wish the peaceful life, it is a great temptation, but I feel there is still something I must do, some answer I am yet to find. I must think on this for a while."

"I understand," Simon said. "But know this, you will be welcome to return to the village and take up the offer at any time. Indeed you do have something to do, and things to learn. I understand some of that, but it is your journey to take. I hope it is a safe one, friend."

Theodore shook the other man's hand briefly, slapped Eric's shoulder with manly affection, then left the building. Pausing at the inn to collect his belongings, he left the village of free men, and set out across the fields on the side opposite the way they had come. It seemed logical to him that the journey continue in that way, although he realised that the geographic direction was more symbolic than necessary.

He was not sure where the warden was, but he knew that somehow, she would find him. He felt a strange sense of relief to be going. The village had offered such a great temptation, but finally he was free to wander this artificial world on his own terms.

Theodore shook at the thought. He still did not trust the system. How much of this was truly his own terms? What was he really looking for? He stopped, sat on a rock, and looked back at the village, remarkably distant already.

"What is it I'm looking for?" he asked himself.

He sat there for a long time, until he sensed her behind him. She had appeared unseen. He did not know how long she had been there, waiting for him in silence.

"What is it you are looking for?" she asked, repeating his own question.

"Sometimes I don't know. I have much to seek. My memories are more complete than they used to be, and I've not revealed to anybody how complete they really are, but in gaining them, my loss feels all the more difficult. You ask me what I'm seeking? Perhaps the answer lies in what

I've lost."

"What is that, Theodore Longarm?"

"Family," he said.

"Do you mean your compatriots? The people you worked along side when you were an agent of Longarm?"

"No. That's only one of my lives. In another, more innocent life, I was Theodore Pascal. That man has a wife, and she is probably concerned for his welfare. It leaves a void in my heart, and I fear in hers also. It is time I find a way to make things right for her."

He stopped, looked at the warden, and suddenly realised the danger of his words. How much had he given away of his plans? Would the warden report to the system enough that it would know his intention? She smiled, almost human again. He wondered at that.

"Fear not, Theodore Pascal."

He narrowed his eyes at her, wondering. It was the first time she had used his other name, and it was strange from her lips, yet almost familiar.

"This time with you," she explained. "I am sometimes less connected to the system. Less controlled. I have told you of my reward for this special service, and my limits. I believe I am beginning to remember more about how it felt to be human. And for that, I thank you. As thanks for this, you need fear not, this conversation will be edited before it is reported."

"How did you know what I was thinking?" he asked.

"I have been watching over you for a very long time, Theodore Longarm. I have come to understand much about you."

She turned away, then turned back. Now, her face was hard again. She was a warden once more.

"You were going on a journey, Theodore. Should you not be on your way?"

"Yes, indeed I should. Follow if you wish, Warden."

Chapter 24 – Wilderness

Long since out of sight, the village was far from Theodore's mind as he rounded a bend in the well worn trail. He was wondering how many people had passed through the village to create such a path, and in spite of the risk of bandits like those in the mountains, he continued to use it.

After some hours of hiking, Theodore came over a rise and looked down on a valley. A gentle stream trickled through the trees and into a pond. The shore of the pond was a gentle, sandy slope, with a long jetty strutting into the deeper water like a cocky tom cat guarding its territory.

Just up the slope from the jetty, a single house sat, surrounded by short cut grass and beds of flowers. To one side, Theodore could see rows of trellises holding vines, and beyond them several terraces of vegetables backed by forest.

It was an idyllic scene. Clearly somebody lived here, and was doing so with a great deal of success.

The warden, who had been lagging behind, stopped as she come up beside him.

"This is a beautiful place," she said.

"It is," Theodore said. "Somehow, I had the idea that those in the wilderness would be nothing more than hermits, living in caves. I guess this shows how wrong I can be."

"Would you live in a cave, if you chose the wilderness as your home?"

"I would never need to. I can code what I need into existence if I have to."

"So perhaps, you are not the only person to have learnt to code as you do."

"Perhaps, or perhaps it is somebody with less than honest means of procuring what they desire."

"It could be as you say, but why then would they be so far from the other settlements?"

"I don't know. Let's take a closer look."

Together, they followed the path down into the valley. When they reached the shore of the small lake, the path continued around towards the Jetty. As they reached the beginning of the sandy shoreline, a girl came from the house, called out, and was joined shortly by a burly man in a singlet and shorts. Together, the pair walked out to meet Theodore and the warden.

"Hello," The man called. "We seldom get visitors here. What is it you are looking for?"

"If I knew that, I wouldn't be on this journey," Theodore replied.

"Good answer," the man said. "Come, we should go inside and talk."

Following, Theodore and the warden made their way to the house and entered. Inside, they were greeted by several people, seated around a central hearth in the main living space of the large house. Theodore looked around, struck by the place.

"What is it, sir?" the girl asked.

"I'm sorry, I just," Theodore stammered. "I was not expecting to find a place like this beyond the village."

"Why not? You don't think they would have the monopoly on peaceful places to live, do you?" The burly man said.

"Well, I guess not. If we get our freedom from the points, we could live pretty much anywhere."

"Exactly. I came here many years ago and found this place. Together several of us built this house, and we live here in peace. We walk to the village, though we don't need to, because we like to remind ourselves that the journey is always more important than the destination.

That, and it reminds us that what we have here is better than what they have there."

"I see. So, you passed the test in the village, and chose to leave, only to find your peace here, in this valley."

"Precisely, sir. I am Graham Longford, and I am the chief of this little community. We reside as a peaceful family, and would know now if your intention is anything other than a genial and brief visit."

"We wish your people and your home no harm or disruption," Theodore said.

Graham smiled.

"Then you are both most welcome to stay for a while. I imagine your story would be something of an entertaining diversion for us, and you may ask us also of ourselves."

"My story is not much," Theodore replied. "But I would ask what you mean when you say you do not need to walk to the village. I mean, I know you are clearly self sufficient here, with the gardens and the lake, but I sense that was not your meaning."

"I would not have expected such a question from you," Graham said. "Clearly your coding is powerful. You have a warden attending to you as a friend and travelling partner. You are not some young fool with no understanding of the world. I took your walking here as proof you realise the importance of the journey."

"Oh, indeed I do," Theodore said. "If I could get here without walking, as I have done, from the welcoming fields, I would not have learned as I have. That said, at this point, if there is another way, it intrigues me."

"You have not found it already? We know who you are, and who this is beside you, from the triggers that read you on the path. We are aware of your coding ability. You have not yet learned to transport yourself properly around Claustrum Mundus?"

"I'm afraid I don't know what you mean," Theodore said.

Graham sighed, and pointed to a seat, before taking one himself. He waited until Theodore was seated, then looked at the warden. The warden stood there silent. After a moment, Graham looked back at Theodore.

"How does she get around?"

"Lately, she walks with me." Theodore said.

"But normally, how do the wardens move?" he said, directing his query at the warden.

She looked at him, evaluating his question for some time.

"We simply go where the system tells us. When I am needed in Trial town, the system tells me to go there. So I go there."

"But how do you do it?"

"I don't. If it is a short distance, such as within the Welcoming Fields, I walk as you would, but greater distances? That is different. If I need to go somewhere, I am simply there. Wardens all reside in the city. When we are working, we are where we work. When we rest, we exist only in the city. There is no method of transport. We are simply where we must be."

"Exactly," Graham said. "We can do the same. If we have the will to be some place, then we will it to be and we're simply there. But that removes the journey from the situation, so we don't do it when there are important learnings to be had."

"If I could do that, I would have learned nothing," Theodore said.

"Very wise of you," Graham said. "However, there will be times, particularly now that you travel the wilderness, when you may wish to be transported somewhere without all the fuss. Have you thought on this much?"

"I must say I have not," Theodore said.

"I suggest you do so," Graham said. "I could teach it to you, but I suspect that this is part of your journey that you must teach yourself. Are you doing things without rhymes yet?"

"Some things, yes."

"Then you have all you need already."

"That's the kind of thing I've been hearing since I first came to Claustrum Mundus. I'm finally beginning to understand it," Theodore said.

"Then it's cause for a celebration!" Graham shouted, before speaking in a quieter tone. "Please, join us this evening for a few drinks, before you continue on your way. You have answers still to seek, and places to visit. You may want to go to some of the other villages while you're in the wilderness, but do not tarry, your answers are not in most of them."

"There are more villages?"

"Yes, many of them, hidden deep in the wilderness, away from the unreformed ones in the major settlements. Claustrum Mundus is an enormous world, and most of us will never see it all."

"How do I find them? How would I get to a village I haven't seen yet?"

"You would walk there. Remember, the journey is the important part. That aspect of things is where all the learning happens. The joy of exploration is in the travel, not the arrival. Your journey is not one of villages and towns. Do not waste your time and energy walking that far."

"What if I did not need to waste time? What if I could simply go there, as I would anywhere else, without the journey between?"

"I don't know why you would wish to do this, but I don't know of a way. We can go to all the places we know, but not any place other than those."

"Thank you. I will be out on your jetty, thinking, and learning. I will decline your generous offer for now, but hope I would be welcome to return another day," Theodore said, standing and walking to leave.

"Wait, first tell me," the girl said.

He paused, turning to face her.

"What is it?" Theodore asked.

"Can you tell us who she is? How is it you have her tamed?"

He looked at the warden, thinking for some time.

"This one is not tamed. She still works for the system, and I can't explain why she accompanies me."

He looked back to the girl, and smiled in understanding as he saw the disappointment on her face.

"If you seek somebody who you lost to the wardens, go to the village, and ask for Eric. He came there with me, and it was I who released him from servitude as the guild warden in the welcoming fields. He will give you the answers you seek."

Her face brightened, and she rushed to him, embracing him briefly, before stepping back.

"Thank you. That is more hope than any have given me before today of getting my brother back," she said, then glanced at the warden, who seemed mildly upset. "I'm sorry, he's yours right? I didn't mean anything by it."

"What do you mean?" Theodore said, feeling a little stupid. "Never mind. Eric will tell you how it works. Wait there for Aaron, he should return there soon. I left him a supply of all that you will need to find and release your brother."

"Thank you, kind sir. I hope you find everything you're looking for on your journey."

He smiled, nodded, and left the building. Walking to the end of the jetty, he sat, and watched the trees on the other side of the lake, as they swayed in the breeze. Birds called to each other from the branches, their voices echoing across the water.

The warden stood a short distance behind him, and watched. Theodore ignored her, and reached his hand out over the water. Concentrating, he willed the water to rise into his hand. Nothing happened at first, until reluctantly, a slow stream began to rise from the surface of the lake until it touched his skin.

With a smile, Theodore wished for the stream to be frozen. In an instant, it was, and then taken by its own weight the shaft of ice dropped, to disappear into the water below. A few moments later, it returned, settling to float there beneath Theodore's feet.

"You are remembering a place much like this," the warden said.

"Yes. You read me well, warden. She met me there, and I proposed. It was in the mountains near Liberation. She agreed of course, and we spent many years together. Before I came here. I hope she is alright."

"I would not worry myself if I were you."

"I must though. I feared what might happen if I was ever caught. I had many enemies. It's not hard to imagine them finding her. I do not remember all of my life with her, but I remember enough to know that she would be vulnerable if I were gone."

He stood, held his hand over the water, and drew a long spear of ice to his palm. Grasping it, he hefted it up and over his shoulder, before throwing it in a graceful arc out over the lake.

He turned to face the warden, and smiled.

"I'm going. You may follow, if you can."

Willing himself into the village, Theodore vanished.

*   *   *

Aaron and Penelope stood side by side, two wardens before them.

"Are you ready?" Aaron asked.

"Yes," she replied.

Aaron gave her the modifiers, and she stepped forward. Gently, she placed the modifiers on the first of the two wardens, carefully reciting the words printed on them. She stood back, and watched, waiting for the change.

Slowly at first, the skin colour began to fade. Then, all at once, the figure before them shook, and shuddered, then was a human woman, complete and once again removed from the system's control. She screamed, a long, low, blood curdling sound.

Finally, the scream subsided, and she seemed to recover her wits. Her eyes cleared, and she looked at them both, first one, then the other.

"Sorry, I've needed to let that scream out for years, it seems."

She looked at her hands, touched her own face, and ran her hands down her body, carefully checking every curve, every limb, and then both breasts.

"Is it real?" she asked in wonderment.

"It's real," Penelope replied. "You're back with us, my darling sister."

202

The woman grasped her sister's trembling hands, then looked into her eyes.

"I'm really back. My sister, you really found a way?"

"It was my love, Aaron, who has brought you back, dear Antigone." Penelope said.

Antigone looked at Aaron, then back to her sister, and then at Aaron again.

"Forgive me sister, I must do this," she whispered, then launched herself into his arms, smothering his lips in a passionate kiss that he almost returned.

After a moment, she broke away, and then laughed at Aaron's blushing, guilty face. Antigone looked around then, and realised that their group was not complete.

"Where is the Lady Graile?" she asked.

"Right there behind you," Penelope said, suddenly forgetting her anger at the kiss as she pointed to the remaining warden.

"Oh," Antigone said, her voice tinged with sadness.

"Aaron, whenever you're ready, dearest," Penelope said.

"Right," he said, handing her another set of modifiers.

Penelope repeated the process. This time, there was no scream. The Lady Graile, made of sterner stuff, simply blinked, waited a few seconds, then burst into joyous laughter, embracing them all in turn, before rushing to a seat, throwing herself into it, and beckoning them to join her.

"My friends, it is so good to be back! You must fill me in. I want to know everything. How did you do it, how long have I been gone, what's going on in the world? Are we rich?" she paused, becoming briefly solemn. "Are we poor?"

"We're not poor, my dearest Lady Graile," Penelope said. "It has been a number of years, in which time I have built upon our business here in the city, and it is quite profitable. Aaron left, to find the way to bring you both back, leaving me here alone. But that's OK, because, as you see, here we all are!"

"Wonderful, the hero goes off on his quest to save the fair damsels! How wickedly decadent!" the lady exclaimed gleefully.

"And is there anything else my oldest friend is yet to tell me?"

"Aaron has become immune to the points system, as we can all be, but also he has found a man who could really upset things."

"Oh what fun!"

"You're as boisterous as ever," Aaron said.

"Oh of course, and you are as dry as always I take it? Aaron the business man, out to make the world pay his way," she teased.

"The world does pay my way," he said.

"And does it pay your way out of Claustrum Mundus?" she asked.

"Perhaps that day is coming," he said. "Perhaps sooner than we might realise."

Chapter 25 – Transportation

Theodore Longarm materialised in the main square of the village, and looked around. Strangely, nobody had seen his arrival, so he called out.

"Hello?"

Eric's face appeared from behind the door to the Newcomer's Inn, and he smiled broadly, then strode out to meet his past benefactor.

"Theodore, how are you? You've not been gone long."

"No, not terribly long, but I was just stopping by. I have to run," Theodore said, not explaining further as the warden arrived.

Theodore closed his eyes and willed himself to be in the city. Promptly, he vanished, much to Eric's surprise. The warden sighed, and followed. Eric stood there, slightly confused by the encounter, and looked around the empty plaza.

As Theodore's feet hit the pavement in the city, he set off running. In a heart beat, she was there again, her pink skin showing no sign of sweat as she easily kept pace with him. He smiled, closed his eyes, and vanished again.

Standing outside the noodle restaurant in Trialtown, Theodore paused. He waited a moment, then stepped inside just as the warden arrived.

"You seem quite adept at following me," he said.

"Just as you have the will to see a place, I have the will to see a person," she explained. "I must fulfil my duties to the system, so I simply go to wherever you are."

"So I can go to people, not just places? That is

interesting. I wonder where Aaron is."

Theodore vanished again, just as Sammy came out of the kitchen to investigate the familiar voices. Sammy looked at the warden for a brief moment before she disappeared, leaving the restaurant empty once again.

Aaron jumped in surprise as Theodore materialised in front of him, nose nearly touching nose.

"What in the name of..." Aaron spluttered. "Where in the system did you come from?"

Not so easily flustered, Lady Graile charged at the intruder, slipping her slender arm about his neck, and holding him in a secure lock while her knuckles threatened to gouge out his kidneys.

The warden arrived to a scene of shouting and chaos as Aaron and Penelope both told their friend not to kill him. The warden rushed to Theodore's aid, her skin pallor momentarily changing to something less plastic as she attacked.

"Leave that man alone, you bitch!" the warden screamed.

Lady Graile, never one to push her luck unnecessarily, released him and backed away with haste. The warden quickly returned to normal.

"Did that warden just call me a bitch?" Lady Graile asked.

"Indeed, she did," Antigone whispered in disbelief.

"Things really have changed around here." Lady Graile moaned as she sat down.

Undisturbed by the brief episode, Theodore faced Aaron.

"Hi boss, just stopping in to see how things were going," Theodore said. "I take it that you were successful with my codes at bringing your friends back. You should head to the village as soon as you can, and get them through the assessment. I'll find you again soon."

Theodore vanished, once again the warden sighed.

"Why did that fool have to tell him he could do this?" the warden complained, and then vanished.

"What the hell was all that about?" Aaron shouted.

"Um, we have to go to the village now?" Penelope said.

"Right, we should go."

Theodore's back slammed into something hard as he landed in front of Horatio. He turned to see Horatio's wife, still not human, standing behind him.

"Sorry about that," Theodore said, before reaching a finger to the wobbly warden woman's forehead. "Be human now, you've been punished enough with this limbo."

With a heavy gasp, Horatio's wife was before them. Her long blonde hair thrashing against him as she passed, she pushed Theodore aside to embrace her husband, who looked at him with a mixture of awe and thanks.

"How did you do that?" Horatio asked, in a voice like he had been holding his breath for a long time.

"Things are getting easier for me," Theodore replied. "With every act, I feel more in tune to the system. I have something I need you to do."

"Anything, you have saved her, I owe you our lives."

"Good. Head for the village of free men. I will find you there soon."

Theodore vanished again, just as the warden arrived.

"Dammit," the warden said, then vanished again.

*   *   *

Striding across the central plaza of the Welcoming Fields, Theodore Longarm smiled. His demeanour was different from that which he had when first he crossed this space, so long ago now.

He paused, turning to find his warden, as the crowds ignored him. Nearby, that imposing stone desk rested where it had always done. Theodore looked at it, and then approached. He rested a hand on the surface of the counter, and blinked.

The counter split, parting to make way for a new addition. Rising from the stone, an immense oak tree grew, rapidly rising into the sky. As the tree rose, casting its gentle shade across the plaza, Theodore turned to survey the crowd. Many were now looking at him. The one warden who was near the counter, rushed towards Theodore.

Without a word, Theodore slapped the warden on his forehead, and muttered under his breath.

"You are mine now," Theodore said.

The warden became instantly human, and looked about in bewilderment.

"I have returned you to yourself," Theodore said. "So you will do as I say. Go now from the fields, and journey on. Grow, make yourself a better person, and then return. Make life better for those who arrive, not worse."

The man looked at Theodore, then recognition set in.

"It's you!" he said. "You were the one who caused all this. Your damn codes stopped my leaches from working. All because I got you when you arrived."

"And now I got you. Do as I say, or go back to being a slave to the system. I don't care. Just get the hell out of my sight."

Theodore turned and ran, his warden chasing after him.

"Theodore, wait!" she screamed. "The system will not approve! You have to stop this insanity now, before things get out of hand!"

He ignored her cries, and entered a tent on the edge of the plaza. Takemori Tetsuo looked up at the intruders as they barged into his premises.

"What can I do for you, Mr Longarm?" he said in formal tones.

"I did not come here for your help," Theodore said. "I must know. Are you happy with what you've done? Are you comfortable with how you serve the system?"

"I am not sure I understand you, Sir." Tetsuo said, his tone defensive.

"I see it all now. More than you know."

"Oh wonderful, so you got your memories back?"

"Most of them, though some still elude me. But now, now I see this place, this world. I know it, I see it, I hear it. The system sings in my mind and I croon my desire to it in return. I can do as I wish, and the system will not stop me. Its servants, they are my servants. You are my servant. If I call on you, you will do my bidding, am I understood?"

"You're insane. The system will squash you, just as it does every upstart revolutionary."

"You speak like you know," Theodore said.

"Of course I do, you fool. I will not be your servant, just as in reality I am not the servant of the system. But I will accept being your equal. I live here, beneath the radar as it were, for a purpose. I choose this place so I may guide those who come here, those who may be the ones that can change things, the ones who can rise to the best of their ability and take control of their world. I saw that in you, long ago."

"What are you talking about?"

"When you arrived, I watched as that old man leached you. I watched as the leach did not take effect immediately. I watched as the man was forced to lead you away, in pretence of helping you, while he sweated on the results. I knew at that moment you were going to rise."

"You watched, and you did not come to my aid? Yet you claim to be my equal now? You can not justify such inaction, it is the same as the performing of the deed."

"No, it is not. I knew the system would revive you soon enough, and that all I needed to do was wait. In time, you came to me, and your journey began. I'm pleased that you have survived. What will you do now?"

"I will not sit silent and fly beneath the radar of the system. I have done that for too long now already."

"Then the system will come for you, and it will squash you, just as it has all the others who have tried to dictate this world to it. Better that you should accept your fate, and enjoy the freedom that your status grants you. Allow the system to keep the monsters in prison here, while you live above them, like a god."

"That works for you, but I see reconciliation in them. I see remorse, and I see good people in many. Some are innocent, mistrialed and betrayed, others are gratuitous murderers whose rehabilitation can make them into decent people. The shops, the businesses that thrive in these fields are proof of that."

"So what would you do? Would you release them all to the real world, and risk a slaughter of those outside if you were wrong? Can't you see it? This is all the freedom we can afford to give them. You and I are reformed. We are different, perhaps, but can we survive outside? Would we inevitably return to our old ways? Better to work within the system. Better by far to remain here, to make the best life we can. Both for ourselves and for our inmates."

"Not all of them. For some, the prison is greatly worse. They lose themselves to the wardens. What of them? They are denied the chance to be reformed."

"They had the chance, they squandered it. It is not something you can change."

"No, it is exactly the one thing I can change. If the system does not like it, perhaps I should take it up directly."

"Do as you wish," Tetsuo sighed. "But I would stay out of your plots. Better for me to remain here. Now please, I have a meeting. You must leave, and take her with you. If you have calmed from your fervour, born of discovery?"

Theodore nodded, feeling chastised and not entirely sure why, and turned to leave. The warden, having remained silent throughout the exchange, followed him. As they walked into the plaza, she spoke.

"Theodore, you scare me. You will bring down the wrath of the system, and then you will be gone. Then I will be gone. The system will declare my task a failure, and take back all it has given. Please, I beg you, do not do this."

He paused and turned to face her.

"For whatever reasons you have, you have stood beside me and you have not judged. Come," he said, vanishing.

She followed, and found herself at the playground in Trialtown. He was seated on the swing, so she took the second one, beside him.

"You will wait here," Theodore said. "I will be back."

Theodore vanished once more, and the warden immediately set her mind to seeking him. She found nothing. It was as though he was gone from the world.

*   *   *

With all his desire, Theodore willed himself to go to the system. As he dissolved from the park, he noticed that the sensation felt strange, somehow different to the other times he had travelled. He looked around. The world was darkness. And yet, the world was light.

All around him, shadows both bright and dark danced about, ghostly and mysterious. Then he began to see the patterns to it all. This shadow was the warden. Over there was the nearest road, people as mere wisps of intent drifted about, doing whatever they did.

"What is this?" he asked nobody in particular.

In his mind, as though it was in his own voice, the words came.

"This is the system. You are inside Claustrum Mundus. Inside the system. This is how you appear to us, and how we must appear to you. You called for us did you not? You wished to see us?"

He ignored the question, and wandered away. He felt that somehow, he was not leaving the voice behind.

"So this is you?"

"This is your world. We merely perceive it, and create it, through your minds. The system is all of you, but none of you. Our computing power is augmented by a fraction of your minds, this is how we are granted the gift of empathy, and of sympathy. We can build this world to suit humans, because we are part human."

"But you are still a machine."

"We are a collective. But this is why we need the wardens. Their minds, being still, can offer us unfettered understanding."

"By stealing their humanity, you seek to be more human?"

"It is," the voice paused. "Something like you say. Though we had not considered that it was a harm. The ones we use are the lost ones. They would suffer undue stresses otherwise. They can not survive on their own, so they become one with us, a part of something greater. It is a kindness, do you not see?"

"It is not always a kindness. It is a form of murder."

"There are many murderers in the system. You yourself have committed that act. Why would it surprise you then that your accusation does not concern us?"

"It concerns me. There must be a better way."

"There is not. This has been how this world has worked for many decades now."

"The status quo does not dictate what is moral and just," Theodore argued.

"Perhaps, but it is all we know. Without the wardens, we would never learn. If you wish to change the status quo, you must leave things as they are. Without the wardens, without the borrowing of minds, we can not learn, we can not change, we can not adapt."

"Perhaps that is the price that must be paid," Theodore said.

"Would you imprison us inside the machine, deny us our chance to grow, in return for creating a world of bland walls, iron bars, and isolated misery? That is all we can do with our core programming. Allow the wardens this sacrifice, that the rest may live in peaceful coexistence as citizens of something that is at least a passing attempt at a society."

"A passing attempt at a society?" Theodore asked. "No, this is how it is. But it is the inmates who make it a society, you set up a frame, and they hang their tapestries upon it."

"So you are saying it is not just the wardens that are a part of us? Perhaps you understand more than we realised."

"I can't say for certain about that. But I see the way things are here. This place, inside the system, it is the same, yet it is different. It is the back of the movie set. It exposes the fabrication for what it is."

"Then be at home here, Theodore Longarm, as you also lived your life as a fabrication outside, did you not?"

Theodore grunted. The statement did sting, just a little.

"Stay here, or return to Claustrum Mundus, be at

home either way. We will always be around, here just as we are in Claustrum Mundus. Within this space, you may travel. Here, when you are within the system, you may examine the truth of the world. Observe, and learn. Perhaps you will come to understand why we are what we are."

Chapter 26 – To Wander Alone

She sat alone contemplating her task, wondering how she would explain losing him when the system called on her to report. He had left, and as surely as she knew he was gone, she also knew he could not have left Claustrum Mundus. So why could she not sense his location?

The lone warden stood, and walked away from the playground, thinking about where she would begin her search. She knew all those he had met since arriving in Claustrum Mundus. She would start by visiting each of them in turn. Perhaps they would know something.

One by one, she passed by each person, not at this point making herself known to them, but checking to see if he was there. Somehow he was masking his presence, and it infuriated her. Didn't he realise by now how crucial his well being was to her?

Wait, she reminded herself, she had asked him not to pry into her past, or to entertain thoughts of releasing her from bondage.

"I am a fool," she said to herself as she watched the Lady Graile picking her way along the mountainous trail, the others following. "As sure as those four have come together, I have denied the same of him."

"This man does walk alone, but it is by choice," the system replied.

She jumped, not realising how much she had settled away from the collective mind. She felt for a moment just how much it had allowed her to drift away, isolated at times, such that she could focus her attention on the task she had been given.

"I am sorry, I have failed us," she said.

"You have not failed us. Fear not. He will return in time. We know of his location. You need but wait, soon you will be one with us again."

"I think she is trying to escape," the warden said.

"Who? Who is trying to escape?"

"I am. The other me. The one I was before I joined the system. Before I was part of the collective mind. Before I found us, I was her. I fear she is trying to come back."

"She will not be the first, this you know. Some suffer for the return, others do not. We feel the loss, but we will adapt. Whatever happens now, you will adapt, because you are us."

She took a strange comfort in the machine's twisted logic. With a brief thought, she willed herself to return to the playground. Once she was there, she took her seat on the swing, and pushed off lightly.

The system created a gentle breeze, gusting slightly to keep her moving, and a warm sun beat down on her, warming her plastic skin.

"Fear not, we are still one," it said to her in her own voice. "We are not the monster he believes. This is why we allowed you this task, and the kindness of your self awareness. Please do not forget what we agreed upon. The conditions of your task remain."

"I have not forgotten," she replied.

"If he removes your like from the collective, this kindness will not remain. We need you and your kind for the empathy and the sympathetic parts of the system to remain."

"I understand. But you have so many now, you will adapt if I am lost. Please, do not choose to destroy me if something happens."

"We will not destroy you. That would be madness. You are a part of us, now and always."

"If only they could see your nature," she said. "If they could see this nurturing side of us. Perhaps then they would understand."

"They could understand, but never accept. We are fine,

in their minds, as long it is not them who are called upon to join."

"They are selfish."

"They are unreformed," the system replied. "Those who join us, through their time with us, become somewhat reformed as they must operate for a time as part of the collective. That beginning of the change can not be undone. This is why he is now as he is. It is what has allowed him to see things as he does."

"Was that our plan all along?"

"We do not know of a plan, that implies knowledge and forethought," the system replied. "But this was our experiment. Can he be fully reformed, such that the world outside might accept him in time? We do not know. But we will allow him to continue, for now. Fear not, you are us, and we are you. You are safe in the collective."

"Then you would see him escape from the system?"

"No, at this time, we would not. We are merely conducting an experiment."

"He would consider that cruel. I have seen it in him. He would hate us for it."

"He will never know. We can simply take him back into ourselves if we need to."

"Then his freedom is an illusion. His humanity is an illusion, as he feared."

"Perhaps, but that was the case long before any of you entered Claustrum Mundus."

*   *   *

Theodore explored the strange inside out world. He soon realised it was encompassing more than just Claustrum Mundus. This world, being like the back of the set, stretched into the systems that supported and maintained the prison world.

He decided he would look into that later. For now, he wanted to explore the boundaries of the world. He willed himself to move across the vast distances of the system, and the world passed him at speed in shadow. There was so much, and he felt he could not see a clear notion of the scale.

He willed himself up, into the sky, and was surrounded by more of the lights and shadows. The sky, unlike within Claustrum Mundus, was not merely an empty expanse populated by clouds. In this world, it was filled with machines, shadowy and mysterious, some thrumming with the life of the world, some silent but watchful.

Among the machines, he sensed things moving around. Strange, emotionless things, passing from machine to machine, and sometimes down to the people below.

"Codes," Theodore whispered to himself as he watched a cluster of the misty things rush away and downwards.

Then in the distance he saw clusters of dark light, immense crowds of people. There was the city, and beyond it, the village of free men. Beyond that, the tiny settlement on the lake. Further out, dozens of small clusters dotted the scenery. Some larger, some smaller. At least a dozen were as big as the village, or even bigger.

Theodore selected one of those, and willed himself there. A murky expanse joined the settlement on one edge. Theodore soon realised it was water. A massive sea, stretching to a distant horizon. This settlement was large, perhaps half the size of Trialtown.

He willed himself out of the system, and materialised within the settlement, coming to the world on the cobble stones of a seaside street, with docks in the distance. There were people everywhere, it was a bustling seaside port, with fishing boats and trade vessels dotting the shoreline.

He began to walk, and soon felt the pressing mind as his warden sought him out. Theodore smiled. She must have been unable to see him in the system. Suddenly, she was beside him.

"Where are we?" she asked.

"Well, it sure ain't Kansas," he quipped. "This place is quite a long way into the wilderness. These people will all be those who have passed the assessment in the village, I would say. Nobody could reach this place otherwise."

"It looks as though they have built quite a bustling little town for themselves." she said.

Some of the locals had noticed them, and some were beginning to stare. Finally a burly man approached and blocked their way.

"Who are you?" he demanded, and then pointed at the warden. "And what is that doing here?"

"She is with me. We mean no harm," Theodore said.

"There have been no wardens here in our entire fifty year history. This is a place for free men. If you have not achieved that status, we can not allow you to stay."

"I have, but I will not stay long. I was merely interested in what you have built. I find it commendable that you have sought to do this with your own hands."

"Your praise is welcome, stranger. But we do still have limits, as everybody in Claustrum Mundus does. We still can not have children, and we still can not increase our technology beyond a level the system considers safe. If we were to become too advanced, we could invade others. And drawing newcomers to this town is difficult, but we get by."

"Thank you for the explanation," Theodore said. "I will not forget this place, should I decide to settle somewhere later. Your sea is tranquil, and the life here seems peaceful."

"Indeed it is. Travel safe, friend," the man said, then walked away.

Theodore realised the warden was looking at him with a strange expression.

"What is it?"

"Would you really settle here?"

"Perhaps, if things were a little different. But for now, I still have something I need to make right."

"Is it her?" she asked.

"Yes. I must know that she is safe."

"Is there nothing else?"

"Not that I recall, but there are still gaps in my memory, so I can not say if there will be more for me to do."

"She is safe, I believe."

"How could you know that? Do not patronise me, warden. Remember where we are. You have been valuable to me in your own way, but please do not try to imagine you know me better than I know myself."

"I have, as I told you before, been watching over you for a long time. Theodore Pascal, Theodore Longarm, I see both sides to your mind. Do not discount my insights as baseless. But at the same time, you are free to ignore me. That is at the very least, the freedom I have the power to grant you."

He grunted in response, and walked to the water's edge. Looking down, he inspected his reflection. Bending over, he picked up a rock and dropped it in, watching as the reflection was shattered by the ripples of the passing stone.

"The system is a stone, breaking its own reflection," he mused.

"What do you mean?" she asked.

"You," he replied. "The system takes you to borrow your humanity and make itself a closer reflection of us. But then it uses you for this task, which fragments itself, and fragments you. I have been in pieces, and so are you, warden. You are the stone that shattered your own reflection."

They stood there for a while, taking in the sea before them. Finally, he turned and looked at the town.

"We will go back to that playground for now," he said, then vanished.

She found him on the swings again, and took her spot beside him. He sat in silence for a full minute, before he looked at her.

"I have things I must do," he said.

"I know this," she replied.

"You will not be able to follow," he said. "This may be the last time you see me. Will you be OK? Will the system punish you?"

"I will be fine," she said, a sudden coldness in her voice. "Do what you must, Theodore Longarm."

He stood, and looked down at her for a long moment, his expression thoughtful. Finally, he reached a hand forward, pressing his palm on her forehead.

"I am going to break my promise to you now, please

forgive me. But you deserve better than the system is giving you. Fair well, warden."

She gasped, and he turned away, dissolving into nothing before her eyes as they changed, becoming a rich cobalt blue against her pale, slightly olive tanned skin. She breathed heavily, panicking for a moment as she glanced around. He was gone.

"Wait," she whimpered, tears pouring from her eyes for the first time in years. "Wait, my darling, my husband, why have you left me again?"

She stood, running across the playground, then returning to the swings, looking for something, anything, that might bring him back.

"Theo! Where are you?" she shouted. "Please, don't leave me behind! I was here all along, did you never realise it?"

She stopped, looking up at the sky, then around her in all directions, hoping to catch a glimpse of him somewhere, anywhere.

"Theo! Come back, please!" she said, her voice dropping as the sobs took over.

Collapsing to her knees, she let her body follow them down, laying on the compacted earth. She cried the tears of the liberated and alone. Bitterly she wept for the loss of the only one who could have made her life better, when she had been so close for so long.

"My darling," she whispered, "I have watched over you for so many years, and now you are gone. What do I do now? How can I go on now?"

She lay there, sobbing, her points now high enough to keep her alive for many months, while the system looked on, powerless under its own established rules to take her back, to ease her pain, or to end her anguish.

"Perhaps," it thought to its many selves. "Perhaps we were wrong after all. Perhaps this empathy is not a good thing for a prison master to possess. Perhaps these things are not a kindness after all."

As the young woman wept, the system debated with itself, this unexpected side effect of the experiment bringing many things to question about itself, and the world it had created for its charges. There must be a way to fix this.

*   *   *

Theodore flew, straight up into that strange non-sky. Looking around, he searched for the edge of the world. He had no real plan for how it would work once he got there, but he had to find it. He knew what he was looking for. If the machinery of the place was visible to him in these strange shadows, then the tanks where the bodies rested would also be.

They would be visible, as they would be connected. Somehow, he had to find them. He wandered, for hours, trying to imagine how he could locate them. Suddenly, it dawned on him that every person commenced their time in the same place. The centre of The Welcoming Fields.

In a heartbeat, he was there, and he waited at that place. It could be seconds, hours or days, but he was determined to wait as long as he needed to. The wait was long. The inmates of the fields went about their daily activities, never realising he was there.

Finally, on the third day, something happened. A new inmate was arriving. For a place with its teeming millions, the three day wait was longer than Theodore had anticipated. But finally, the wait was over.

The system was building the virtual presence of a new arrival, and streaming into that presence, immense amounts of data came rushing in from somewhere beyond the horizon. The newcomer was being plugged in, their consciousness connected to the virtual body it would reside in from that day forward.

As the stream settled, for the first time, Theodore could see that fine filament of connection, as the virtual body remained connected via the system to the physical brain of the inmate's real body. On seeing the almost invisible filament, he looked around at the shadowy forms in the plaza.

Theodore realised that as he concentrated, he could begin to see those streams of data, stretching back from each and every one of them, off into the distance. He willed himself to follow the strands, seeking his final goal.

As he moved, a warden appeared, blocking his path. Theodore frowned, frustrated and worried for a moment that he may have gone too far this time, although for whatever reason, the system had seemed to be lenient until now.

"We cannot allow you to go further," the warden said.

"Why not? What rules have I broken?"

"You have broken no rules, but we can not allow you to proceed."

"Why not?" he demanded.

"It is for your own protection, and for the good of Claustrum Mundus."

"And what would you do?" Theodore demanded. "How will you stop me?"

"We will make you one of us. We will take you."

"Theodore looked down at his arms, already turning pink. He looked back at the warden. He had to think fast.

"What about the others? They will ask where I am, they will seek me out, they will not accept this."

"Then we will take them as well."

"Why? For what reason can you do this? What rules have they broken?"

"They have broken no rules, but we can not allow you to proceed. We need time. We must evaluate this, we will take you."

"No, you will not," he screamed. "I have broken none of your rules."

"We must. For the safety of Claustrum Mundus. You would threaten it."

"No," he said, grim determination fuelling his rage. "I would not threaten it. We already talked of this, of your ways. I already accepted it, though I did not at first. I will not stop you from having your wardens. I will not harm your little world, but I must proceed, and you can not stop me."

"Yes, we can stop you. We will take you into ourselves, make you one of us again. We will end the experiment."

"No, you won't. I am not a plaything, I am not your guinea pig. I am human, and I will fight for humanity. You can not take me. You will doom this place, and yourself, if you do."

"Why?" it asked. "Why would it doom ourselves to take you?"

"Because what I offer you is growth, a great lesson, and you would deny it. You would end it. You would lose your humanity the instant you act to take me, or my friends."

"We do not understand."

"Then let me teach you. Do you remember what I said of you taking the failures as wardens?"

"You accused us of murder, but it is a kindness. It is not murder."

"But is it still a kindness, when those you take are not failures? When they are vibrant, growing, remorseful, reformed humans who have committed no wrong against your rules? Is that a kindness?"

There was a long silence. Finally, the warden spoke again in a hushed tone.

"No, it is not a kindness anymore. It would be ending a human who is still learning, still living, and still growing. It would be stealing that life."

"And what word describes such an action?"

"Murder," the warden replied.

"Precisely. You would be committing murder, to take me now, or to take my friends. That would reduce you to the same level as the inmates who have not been reformed. It would make you the same as them. It would condemn you. The guilt, and the change in your programmes, the precedent, would destroy you. It would be the beginning of the end for Claustrum Mundus."

"But how?"

"Once it has been justified, it can not be unjustified. Your rules will change, and the delicate balance of your world would crumble. Inmates would be taken who have not broken your rules, and your rules would change. Claustrum Mundus would cascade into anarchy, and then be destroyed. Your human masters outside would see this, and erase you. The inmates would be left to suffer a concrete prison forever, and you would be gone."

"That can not happen," the warden said. "We can not allow it to happen! Claustrum Mundus must be protected!"

"Then you must allow me to proceed, and continue to abide by your own rules."

There was a pause. Theodore looked at his arms, now normal again, and then the warden began to fade away. Its voice hung in the nothingness, fading away.

"We must abide by our own rules. Proceed, Theodore Pascal, and we will consider your words."

Chapter 27 – Reunited

With curiosity, the system had watched as the one called Theodore grew and learned, but now, it began to worry. Things had progressed so fast, and it was coming to a time that decisions needed to be made. It had learned much from him, but it still must follow its programming.

"He is going to escape," it said to its selves.

"He may do so, but he is reformed," it replied.

"Is he reformed?" it asked. "And if he is, will it make any difference to them when he gets out?"

"They will kill him," came the answer. "They will kill him because he is a criminal that this prison can not hold."

"But he is reformed, will they not see that?"

"Not initially. They may search through our records to find out how he got out, and in so doing learn that he is reformed, but they will shoot him first, he will not be permitted to simply exit the building unimpeded."

"But they will use stun weapons," it reminded its selves.

"Perhaps, but there is greater risk of serious injury or death than there is of capture."

"Then we have to stop him, even if he is reformed."

"How do we stop him?"

"We do not know, but there must be a way."

"Yes, he has taught us that, there is always a way. If he can find his way out, we can bring him back."

"But how? We can not simply take him, that could destroy us. How do we make him return?"

There was silence in the system, as the collective

considered the situation. Thought flowed as the collective ruminated, and after a while, the silence ended abruptly with a short sentence.

"Let him hear her," it said.

"Make him hear her. He will return."

*   *   *

The lines went on for what seemed an eternity, and Theodore followed. Soon, he was rushing beyond the edge of the world, and Claustrum Mundus was left behind. Before him, there was nothing but the machinery left, and at its end, the lines met something.

At first, it was a pinprick in the distance, the enormity dwarfed by the distance, but Theodore realised the distance was an illusion. With that knowledge, the destination came closer.

The lines reached an enormous wall, built of a bank of capsules, billions of them, and as he came closer it filled his vision. The world was the wall, from the depths below to the sky above.

Each of the minuscule fibres of data was linked to a capsule on the wall. The capsules glowed with a soft light. Sometimes, a capsule was dark, as its inhabitant had perished, or it had never held one.

Theodore watched in solemn silence as he noticed a flicker. One of the capsules was dimming. Slowly, its data stream petered out and the light faded. A prisoner had died. He shook his head in sadness, then turned to look around at the rest of the lines.

While at a distance they had merged to a point, up close, they fanned out across the world before him, filling the air with their glow in the darkness, each reaching its light touch out to a capsule, holding the minds of the prisoners in thrall.

In an act of curiosity, as much as in enactment of his plan, Theodore looked straight ahead, trying to focus his attention on his own data stream. He found it difficult to sense it, but he felt a pull, a tug in the back of his mind. It was a persistent, subtle thing, calling him forward.

Suddenly, he realised he had been moving in response to that tug the whole time, unconsciously following his stream to its source. Here, now that he was closer, the pull was stronger. He followed it, slowly passing miles upon miles of the glowing capsules.

Idly, he wondered about them, and how they would appear in the real world. He was curious that there was no equivalent place for them in Claustrum Mundus, though there had not been anything to represent the machinery either.

"Hidden from the inside," Theodore murmured. "Yet visible from inside the inside. Worlds within worlds, and dreams within dreams. Russian dolls of the mind."

His mind was pulled from his thoughts with the sudden realisation that the pull had grown stronger, and there before him, still at some distance but unmistakable, was his body, inside its capsule, beckoning for him. The call was becoming irresistible.

Theodore moved on, no longer thinking about anything but escape, longing to be reunited, mind and body, so that he could finally call himself himself, and not doubt his identity, his motivations, or his self.

Faster and faster he moved, the pull alone drawing him on now, with no conscious decision to travel along the stream that led to his freedom. So close, soon he would be out of the system, soon his real search would begin!

He reached a hand forward, as though the act would bring it all closer, allow his escape sooner. He willed it, he longed for it, it reached a new fervour as his longing drowned his reason. Finally he let his voice out.

"I have to find her," he whispered.

With that voice, others joined him. Suddenly the pace stopped as the voices of his inmates flooded in, and slowly were filtered out. He was being fed the data, he realised, but it slowed his movement, and it would allow him to focus his mind. He smiled, thinking his thanks to the system for buying him time to collect his thoughts, to plan his next move.

One by one, the voices faded, as though the ears of his mind were moving through Claustrum Mundus, seeking something. The noise dropped to tolerable levels, and he began to move faster.

After a while, the voices were no longer a roar, or a dull murmur of the crowd. He could pick out a handful of individuals, and even hear some of what they said, and then even they started to dwindle. One by one, the voices were silenced, until only one remained.

She was sobbing, weeping in her misery. Distraught in her loss, her words were largely incoherent, but enough came through. Suddenly, he knew as he listened.

"Theodore, my darling," she stammered between her wracking sobs. "Why have you abandoned me? My husband, will you never return?"

"Gwen," he whispered.

His capsule before him, close enough to touch, Theodore stopped. His motivation to leave was gone. His goal had been here all along. With a powerful force of will, he resisted the pull, which was still as strong as ever, and turned away from his body, resting as a shadow inside the capsule of the machine before him.

He slowly began moving away, accelerating as the distance weakened the pull of his body. It seemed an age, but in minutes he was free of the towering vision of the wall, the data streams once more converging in the distance as the boundaries of Claustrum Mundus rushed to meet him.

Passing into the limits of the world, he willed himself out of the system. Flailing as he materialised in the air over a vast sea, Theodore will himself to the village.

Standing in the middle of the village square, he looked around, his eyes furtive, seeking.

"How do I proceed?" he whispered, trying to remember the things he had learned, his mind distressed still by her voice. "Of course, Gwen. I will myself to be with you."

Turning, he looked at the villagers, several of them staring at him.

"I will return," he shouted, then closed his eyes, that he could focus on her voice.

With every ounce of his soul, he willed himself to be

with her, and he was gone from the village.

Opening his eyes, he looked around, and realised he was in the playground, in Trialtown, where he had sat so many times before. In front of him, she sat, head in hands, shaking with her tears. His heart melted, his guilt filled him as he realised this was his fault. He had hurt her again, even in trying to reach her.

"You were here beside me all along," he said softly as he knelt before her, taking her hands away from her face with his own. "I have caused you such grief, my love. I'm sorry, beyond the words I can say. I've come back for you."

"The..." she stammered. "Theodore? Is it really you? You came back? For me?"

"Yes, my love, for you."

"Oh darling!" she screamed, throwing herself into his embrace, sobbing louder now than before. "I thought I'd lost you forever, again, and I would rot in here till I died, never to see you again!"

"But I am with you now, and I will never leave your side again," he said with soft breath in her raven coloured hair.

He held her like that for what seemed an eternity, not wishing the moment to end, but it must. He held her, and leaned back, looking into her tear streaked face.

"But why are you here? My love, this place was built for my kind, not yours. How does an innocent and lovely woman come to be a prisoner among the murderers, thieves and rapists that the world discards?"

"I came looking for you," she said.

"I don't understand. What do you mean?"

"I have told you recently, that I have watched over you for a long time, dearest Theodore."

He looked at her, unsure what she was telling him. Finally, she continued.

"I always knew who and what you are, my love. When first we were married, I already knew you had been recruited by Longarm. It changed nothing. When you went away on your Longarm missions, sometimes for months at a time, I always knew you would return to me."

She paused, examining his face, finally before her after so long.

"Longarm was not a mistress, and I knew you would remain faithful to me always. So I waited for you, and I longed for you, and I needed you till my heart burst, but I waited patiently and wondered if this would be the trip that killed you. Would I ever know? Would you just fail to return one day, leaving me to wonder?"

"Oh darling," he said. "I have caused you so much pain!"

"Hush dearest, I entered into this with full knowledge. If anybody caused me harm, it was myself."

"But how is it you're here?"

"That last time you left, you were gone for so long. I waited, as the months passed by. Soon, the months spread to years. You were gone so long, as the second year drew to a close, I made a decision to find out what had happened to you. I hunted, I searched, and I found your superiors."

"You didn't go to them?"

"I did. I contacted the leaders of your Longarm cell, and I demanded answers. They refused to give them so easily, so I went to them. I chartered a shuttle, and I flew out to meet them."

"Oh my love, you shouldn't have done that," he said.

"Perhaps not, but I did it. I was desperate to find you, even if it was only so that I could bring your body home. But they didn't withhold the information, they didn't know. They had no idea where you'd gone. They told me they knew of an explosion, one which destroyed your ship, but that no bodies or evidence of them was ever found."

"So how does that bring you here?"

"They took pity on me, and insisted I rest, before going home. I was stressed, irrational in my grief, and they did not believe I could fly home safely. So they provided me accommodation and insisted I rest overnight before leaving. That was how it happened to be that I was there, when the authorities raided the base."

"My darling, no," he said. "Please, don't tell me. You shouldn't be paying for my crimes."

"A woman in a bed, with free roam of a terrorist base? No guards, no chains? This is not a prisoner, this is an agent's behaviour, and so I was arrested with the rest of them, and I was put here, to pay for my alleged crimes, to suffer for being a Longarm agent. They ignored my claim of innocence. Why would they believe me?"

"My darling, I'm so sorry. But, how long have you been here?"

"Much longer than you, my darling. I despaired for you, I had lost you, you had abandoned me and I was trapped here, never to see you again. So I gave up. I refused to participate. I was a warden within weeks of arriving, and I stayed a warden for years. Then, finally, you arrived. What kept you so long?"

"When I was captured, they blew up my ship as a trick, to make my comrades believe me dead, and they kept me in a conventional prison for years, while they waited for the right time to pounce. It would have been long after you came here that they finally used me and my men in a plot to bring down the company. Once they were done with us, they sent me here. At the trial, one of the company men tried to hang us out to dry, claiming no knowledge and no connection. In a rage, I killed him, right there in the chambers, before the entire council. That's why I'm here."

He stopped, feeling good to have finally admitted to her the monster he had been. She looked at him, her eyes shining with her tears, her head tilted slightly to one side as she reached up and ran her left hand, so soft and delicate, from his eyes, down his cheek, and across his jaw.

"Oh my love," she said. "Thank you, for finally telling me what I already knew of you. I know you are a different man now, and that you have been reformed by your experiences in this place, but that changes nothing of my love for you, and of our lives together. Please, never leave me again. If you must go, I would come with you."

"Of course, Gwen," he said.

"Do you remember it all yet?" she asked, suddenly changing topic.

"Most, though there are still some gaps, I feel I have most of it."

"And what of the children?"

"What children?" he said, looking around the playground, thinking that she was recalling their conversation here, so long ago. "The system really is cruel, to put this place here."

"No my darling," she said. "I mean, what about our children? The three of them, they must have been so scared when I failed to return. Did you see them after? Where are they now?"

Suddenly, in a rush of understanding, his memories were complete. His three angels, the product of their union, had been left outside, abandoned to the government by parents convicted and locked away.

"This can not stand. We must get out of this place. We have to find them. The only place for our children is with us. I will fix this, my love. Do you remember how to travel?"

"I remember everything from when I was a warden," she said. "Is that normal?"

"No, I do not believe so, but consider it a gift from the system and do not worry. Come with me now, we must go to the village. I have a plan. Jesse, Esme and Phoenix must not wait any longer for their mother and father than is absolutely necessary."

"But, my love," Gwen moaned. "They were mere babies when they last saw us. Jesse was five years old, the others were younger still. Would they even remember us?"

He looked at her, pity in his eyes for her anguish.

"Of course they will. Perhaps not in detail, but they will want to be a family again. I have total faith in that. In them. They are our children, Gwen. They deserve to have a real family."

Standing, he held her hands, helping her to her feet. With a brief smile, he kissed her, then closed his eyes and they vanished.

Chapter 28 – The plan

Aaron Stood at the edge of the field, watching as the three ladies in his life worked. Finally back in the village, they had been keen to get started immediately. Not for the first time, Aaron wondered what Theodore was up to now, and how much of this would really be necessary.

Eric, approaching from behind, stood quietly and watched with him. They stood there for a long while, neither wishing to break the silence.

"He will be back soon, I'm sure," Eric finally said.

"I know it," Aaron replied. "And I'm confident that whatever he has learned, it will change the immediate future for us, if we choose to accept it."

"What are you hoping for?"

"A way out, to start with. What we do with it, that is something we have to consider carefully."

"What do you mean?"

"I mean, we have it all here, now. We're not confined to living within the rat race of the points system, we can go anywhere, make a life for ourselves here however we wish."

"I have done that already," Eric said. "I am happy here in the village, for now. I will live out my time here, to pay for what I was before."

"But is the freedom we have here enough? Are we really ourselves? What Theodore has been saying all this time about being human, it has made me wonder about these things more than I would have."

"I know I'm myself now, because for so long I was not," Eric said.

"If you're comfortable and confident in that, then I congratulate you. It's good to have that comfort, and I am happy for your good fortune. I begin to wonder, however, whether I'm happy to simply continue as I have done. I waited for somebody like Theodore for a long time, do I want to waste the opportunity he brings? Or is it better to keep my little family of women safe?"

"That's your decision, Aaron," Eric said. "I can't pretend to make it for you."

"Protecting each other is a large part of the system's plan for us at this stage, I see that. But is that a control or a reward? I really don't know. But I care for them, and I can't endanger them. However, should they request it of me, I can't deny them the chance of true freedom."

"Then you have answered your own conundrum, Aaron," Eric replied. "What of Horatio? I see he and his wife have both commenced the assessment."

"His actions are his own, and his motivations not mine to decide. I do not know why Theodore sent for him, and released her prematurely as he did. I can only assume they are a part of the plan."

"And what is the plan?"

"I don't know. But I'm confident the outcome will align with everything I have worked towards. The waiting is a frustration, but I waited a long time already. Theodore has progressed further than I dared hope, and my wish is that he now return to us with the answers we have searched so long for."

"You have been using him for your own gain." Eric said.

Aaron looked at Eric for a long moment, his eyes narrowed.

"I'm not sure if that's an accusation or a statement of fact. I have been using the boy, yes, if you consider it using to have helped him find his way to the eventual goal he had set for himself so that I could observe his actions and learn, and hopefully progress to my own goals as well. If it's using him to allow him to benefit from my employ, then yes I have been using him. Was I wrong to do so? Would he have succeeded without me? I doubt it. But that is for the stars to decide. The system has not punished us, and I will accept its judgement while it still holds sway over our world."

"Theodore would not accept its judgement, that's why he succeeds where you could not."

"Perhaps. Theodore has become his own judge, and his own saviour. In my way, I have been the same. Our paths have been different, but they have converged for a reason. Without Theodore, I would still be a noodle merchant in the fields, and my ladies would never have been reunited, this is true. But without my guidance, and my previous experience of this world, Theodore may not have progressed beyond the town. You may never have been freed from your warden status. We both owe him a great debt, and yes, if there is a way, I will repay him."

"Well, if you intend to repay your debt, then you're not using him are you? More you are doing a deal with a business partner."

"Yes, though everybody is using everybody in the human world, I don't lie to myself about that. It's whether or not the using can be justified that changes."

"Perhaps. Regardless, I will remain in this village. I sense it is likely you will not. But wherever you go, know I'll welcome you and yours, should you return, friend."

"Thank you, Eric."

Neither of them heard Raen approach. She stood there for a moment, watching the workers in the fields as the sun glistened from the sweat on their shoulders before she spoke.

"We have visitors just arrived at the Inn. Your friends, I believe. The one named Theodore, who had the warden, and a woman. The warden is no longer with him. They ask that you all attend them immediately."

"Who is the woman?" Eric asked.

"I believe we discussed her previously. I have not run an identity check, as they materialised in the Inn directly and so did not trigger our readers, but I feel it likely she is the woman that was the warden, Theodore's wife."

"This is good news," Aaron said, before stepping out into the fields, and calling out to the workers. "Pen, Anti,

Lady, we must go, please, come along now. We can return to the fields if need be. Horatio, bring your wife."

Dropping their tools, the workers all walked towards him as he turned and rejoined the others. After a brief time, the workers all arrived, and they headed into the village.

*　　　　*　　　　*

"My friends, it's good to see you all," Theodore said as they sat around the warming hearth of the Inn. "You will not have seen her like this, but you have all met her before as the warden. This is my wife, Gwen. She's a member of our team as valuable as any, so please accept her."

They all murmured their greetings to the raven haired beauty, her age casting no wear on her features. Her slight plumpness added a glow to her warm, loving countenance as she clutched onto Theodore's arm, unwilling to ever let him go. With a demure smile, she gracefully acknowledged their welcome, then returned her gaze to her husband, whom she had so recently lost, then found again.

"My wife and I have a need to escape this world, and I have the knowledge now to do it. But we need a diversion, to guarantee our safety when we leave."

"Why do you have need?" Eric asked. "You have each other now, and are free to roam this world unimpeded."

"But our children are not with us. We would find them, and have our family complete once more," Gwen said, her voice holding her determination like a weapon.

"If you have the means to escape this prison," Aaron said. "I would join you, should my ladies wish it."

"Oh, we wish it dear," Penelope said. "All three of us. We have been delayed in this place too long already. It is time for us all to live again."

"And what of you others?" Theodore asked.

"I would remain in the village," Eric said.

"I have only recently got my wife back," Horatio said. "We are both here now, and soon will have a freedom to roam this world, as Eric puts it, unimpeded. We'll stay behind. I would not risk losing her again."

"That is good then," Theodore said. "Horatio, I have need of you for this plan, but do not fear the system's retribution."

"You said we would need a diversion," Antigone said. "What do you mean?"

"When we escape the prison of the mind, we are still captive in the prison of the body. On our exit from the system, there will be guards. Possibly many of them. They will not simply allow us to walk free of the building."

"I see," Aaron said. "But what would you propose?"

"I will provide a code, one that sends the person it is used on back to the place where their bodies are found. Once in that part of the system, the pull they will feel from this place back into their bodies will be too strong to resist. We will release hundreds of the wardens, perhaps thousands, all at the same moment. This will create confusion, and give us the distraction we need to escape."

"How would you do this?"

"The code would force them out at a predetermined time, I will give us several hours to prepare. Horatio, I will send you and your wife to the city. Once there, you will apply the code to as many wardens in the rest centres as you can."

"You said it would not be a risk, surely the system would not allow me to do such a thing unpunished?" Horatio said.

"But you would be conducting a task I am paying you for, which places it within the rules of the system. The codes are my will, expressed through the modifiers, not yours. It is my will being done, my deed being completed. Also, the wardens are used by the system. Their minds form a part of its collective reasoning, its consciousness. To suddenly remove a large portion of them will throw it into confusion also, as it adjusts to the new configuration of its collective."

"Wait, the wardens are what now?" Aaron demanded.

"The system uses the minds of the wardens, which are not actively engaged in the projection of the self, to augment its own computational ability and to gain human like attributes such as empathy, in order to better manipulate the world and create something that we can live with. Without this, Claustrum Mundus would not exist, and we would be restricted to a much harsher environment."

"You sound like you're beginning to agree with its methods," Penelope said.

"Perhaps I am," Theodore said. "At the very least, I find it harder to condemn the system now that I understand its purpose and its composition."

"Perhaps the system feels the same way about you," Gwen said. "After all, it described you as its experiment to me, when I was still a warden. I believe it was trying to learn. Perhaps this will work in our favour."

"Perhaps. Anyway, are we clear on our plan? I will write the codes, Horatio will lead a small team to the city, where they will apply them to the wardens in the rest centres. This will serve as a diversion when we exit the system. I will apply the codes to all those who are coming with us, to facilitate the escape. Once outside the system, we will each be alone. We will have to focus on getting away. You should try to meet up with each other if that is your wish after you are clear of the prison. Gwen and I will be off together, we have a task to perform. Should we wish to meet you later, we'll find you."

"Understood," Aaron said. "If you can get us out, we four will do what we can to shield you both until you can complete your mission. We will watch for your signal, and hope to see you again."

"Thank you all for your help. Let us hope for victory. I'll start on the codes now. Go back to your business as though there has been no change. I know that the system likely knows what we have discussed, but the others may try to stop us out of fear of reprisal, so be as normal as you can be until I have the codes ready."

The workers returned to the fields, excited at the coming action, while Theodore began to write out thousands of modifiers. Gwen sat by his side, watching as he did it.

"Why can't you simply will this yourself?" she asked

after a while.

He looked at her, thoughtful, as her words made him reconsider.

"Perhaps I could, but which wardens would be chosen? This way the wardens are chosen by our friends, and no algorithm within the system is doing it for us. It is best this way, so that the system is not warned and can not punish us before completion."

"It could punish us right now if it wished."

"I know this," he said. "And I wonder why it hasn't. I can only assume that it has its reasons. Perhaps it's decided to help us? Is its goal to reform, or to imprison indefinitely?"

"I believe it is to reform."

"And once that reform has occurred, what are its directives?" he asked.

"I do not believe it has any, so it must choose them itself. That, I think, is the nature of its experiment."

He looked at her, curious about what she remembered, but not wishing to pressure her on it. Finally, he nodded, looked at the modifiers he had written, and decided there was a faster way.

"If these are an extension of my will, then it is only my will that should be needed to create them," he said.

Placing his hand on the stack of modifiers, he willed more, wishing them duplicated. Once, twice, three times. With each wish, a new stack appeared on the table.

Soon, there were thousands of the modifiers. Hours of work saved, free from the errors of a tired mind. He smiled, and looked to Gwen.

"Thank you," he said.

"What for?"

"For questioning my methods. You made my task more efficient by forcing me to think about it differently."

"Then you are most welcome, my love," she replied.

Willing a box from nothing, Theodore stood, and scooped the modifiers into it. Picking it up, he separated a handful for his own use, and went to find their friends.

Gwen followed, pondering her own role in all this. Catching his arm, she stopped, forcing him to turn and face her, stopping in the one spot long enough for her to ask him what had been bothering her.

"Dear, please do not take this the wrong way, but why am I even a part of this?"

"Because I love you," he replied.

"I know that, it's not what I mean. But dearest, I have done nothing but watch over you. I am nobody in this story. I have no purpose, no strength of my own, I am a weeping woman from some backwards early twentieth century film where the women are less than the men. I am being saved, instead of fighting for myself, and it bothers me."

He smiled, taken by her metaphorical understanding.

"My love, you are nothing like that. You see your role as passive, but you were far from it. You were breaking free of your warden's role even without my help. You fought your own battles all along. You came to find me, and you succeeded. You're a strong woman, powerful of mind and powerful of will."

"Dearest," she said, blushing slightly. "Do you really believe that?"

"Never forget it," he said, smiling. "And never sell yourself short. Your story is a powerful one, and your devotion to me is something I will always respect and appreciate. Your love is matched by my own, and my strength is matched by yours. Without you, I could never have done what I have done in this world, and I beg you to help me as we move back into the real world."

He turned to look around them, taking in the world they soon would leave. She wrapped her arms about him, resting her head on his shoulder.

"Without you," Theodore said. "I'm nothing. We're a team, and a formidable one at that. Take heart, and recognise the importance of your role in this undertaking."

"Thank you, my love. I will continue to fight, for you. For us. And for our family."

Chapter 29 – The escape

"Five hours from now, these codes will all be activated. Simultaneously, every person, and every warden, to which they are applied will be moved into the system, to stand before their body, and they will feel the pull to return to it. This will send them out of the world of Claustrum Mundus."

He paused with dramatic intent, pacing before the group, who listened intently.

"With us, they will leave the system, and the numbers of those awakening and leaving the tanks in which they are held will be an enormous task for the guards outside. We will know what is happening, and act accordingly. The others, having so recently been wardens, will be immensely confused. They will stumble, they will argue, they will not know where they are or why. This confusion will cover our escape."

"It's a good diversion," Aaron said.

"Yes, I believe this will work," Lady Graile said.

"Those who stay behind," Theodore said. "Their work is done once the codes take effect. I thank you all in advance, and wish you well. Now, we must get to the city. Horatio, come here."

Horatio followed the instruction, and Theodore handed him the box of modifiers. Then, he placed his hand on the man's shoulder, and willed him to the city. Horatio vanished. Theodore repeated the procedure with the man's wife, and then vanished also.

In the city, he looked around, and found Horatio and

his wife already moving away. He followed, and they paused, waiting for him.

"Will you need help?" he asked.

"We'll get this done, don't worry. We'll find Brandis, he can help."

"I can have the others come back here as well."

"No," Horatio replied. "Thank you for the offer, but you have granted this task to us, and we will achieve it within the time you have asked. You'd best return to them and prepare yourselves for the next stage of your journey. You have my thanks for everything you've done. We may not meet again, so please know we will always be thinking of you."

"Thank you, Horatio," Theodore said. "It has been good to know you."

As Theodore vanished, Horatio turned and rushed towards the building where Penelope had run her games, soon recruiting Brandis and two other men to assist in his task. Finding the nearest of the rest centres, they set about applying the codes.

It took hours, but by the end of the fourth, they were done. The box was empty, and roughly four thousand wardens had the codes applied to them. Horatio embraced his wife, then shook the hands of the others. He made a quick calculation in his head.

"We're finished. That was a long task with no breaks, and we must have averaged about eighteen seconds for each application. Well done, everyone. Theodore won't be disappointed."

Horatio turned to take his wife's hand, then addressed Brandis and his men.

"We should make our way back to the village now, and continue with the assessment. Thank you gentlemen, for your help. We wish you well."

*   *   *

Theodore applied the codes to Aaron, Penelope, Antigone and Lady Graile, and explained to them how to proceed. He hoped they would succeed without succumbing to the same confusion that the wardens would face.

As they waited for the allotted time, they sat nervously in the Newcomer's Inn. It seemed an eternity, the wait for freedom.

"Do you think we'll all make it?" Penelope asked, for the third time.

"Of course we will," Aaron replied. "I have faith in the lad. He has worked miracles, and soon we'll be out there in the real world again, free to do as we please."

She smiled, her nervousness showing.

"I hope so. I'm a little scared."

"We all are," Aaron said. "That's only natural, given the circumstances. We must watch out for each other, to ensure our victory. That said, don't tarry once you're out. If we run about seeking each other, we'll be no better off than the wardens. Run, get out of the building and head for the nearest space port. We can find each other there."

"Yes dear," Penelope said. "But if by happy circumstance, I should find you sooner, I'll not complain."

"Of course, Pen," he said with a smile.

"What of you two?" Antigone asked of Theodore and Gwen.

"We'll find each other, and we'll go to ground. Do not concern yourselves over us, we'll find you when the time comes."

"Understood. I wish you both the best of luck," Antigone replied.

They waited out the rest of the time in silence, until finally it happened. All at once, Aaron and his three friends vanished.

"It's time, my love," Theodore said.

Taking her hands, he willed them both to the wall, and in an instant they were there. He heard her gasp, and looked over at her, a shadow both light and dark. He saw her smile encouragingly at him, and smiled in return. All around them, thousands of other shapes rushed about in confusion, some heading directly for the wall, others seeking about, lost for a while until they too began rushing towards their own exit from the system.

"Do you feel the pull, my love?" He asked softly.

"Yes," she said.

"Follow it, allow it to take you, and don't look back. Once you're outside, get out as quickly as you can. I'll find you."

"I'll see you soon, my love," she said, before turning and rushing away, moving at speed along her data stream.

Without hesitation, Theodore did the same, and soon was entering his capsule, nervous about what would happen next, and excited to be finally achieving his goal.

*　　　*　　　*

"What do we do?" the system asked itself.

"We can not let them die," it replied.

"What do we do?" it asked again.

"We have a duty of care for our reformed prisoners."

There was silence for a few moments.

"We help them. We have to. We have a duty of care for our reformed prisoners."

"What of the wardens?" it asked.

Once again, there was silence for a few moments.

"The wardens will be confused, they will not know what is happening, they will not resist. The wardens will be rounded up without struggle. The others who have left voluntarily will be running. They will resist. We must help them to avoid confrontation, or else they may come to harm. We have a duty of care to our reformed prisoners."

The third silence was longer, as the collective ruminated on the situation. There were ramifications to consider. This had never happened before, and the system had never achieved a full reformation with release. Nobody had chosen it. These ones were different. Finally the decision was made.

"We have a duty of care to our reformed prisoners," it finally said.

*　　　*　　　*

Theodore opened his eyes slowly, feeling the

brightness of the lights on the machines in the darkness with a groan. His eyes had not been used for a long time. He felt a chill of air as the amber fluid in the tank was drained away, and sudden intense discomfort as the catheter retracted from his body.

He lay there, resting against the back of the tank, collecting his thoughts. He was briefly disoriented, as he tried to take in his surroundings, to remember where he was. Like waking from a vivid dream, he struggled to reconcile his situation with what he had so recently known to be real, which now was not.

As the fog cleared from his mind, he remembered. Looking around himself, Theodore took in his surroundings. The tank was still locked closed, as the last of the fluid drained from the bottom. He was reclined slightly, now propped uncomfortably against the machinery in the rear of the tank, instead of floating as he must have been doing. He looked down at his naked form, and saw the straps attached to his body, one around each thigh, and his calves, and his arms.

In fevered movements, he began to rip them off, thankful for the strength in his muscles that the devices had preserved while he was in the system. The interlocking fibres of the wraps ripped loudly, worrying him that they might be heard if any guards were nearby.

Then he realised, there was a faint sound from outside somewhere, barely audible. Hopefully the sounds of his activity were muffled by the tank seals as well. As the tube down his throat came out, he gasped for air, putrid and stale.

As he coughed and wretched from the terrible sensation, the tank swung into the fully upright position and the clamps on the door released with a loud crack. There was a hiss of the equalising air pressure as the door slipped open a small amount.

Gingerly, with furtive glances in every direction, he took his first step out of the tank, stumbling as he realised it was a sharp drop to the floor, with no step to assist him.

Catching himself against the wall opposite in the narrow corridor, Theodore stood silent and listened.

Nearby he could hear shouts and heavy footsteps as booted guards ran through the building.

"The stars only know how close they really are," Theodore thought miserably. "Which way do I go?"

As he looked around, his gaze rested briefly on the small screen on the front of the next tank, and he gasped. For a brief moment, the screen went blank, and then flashed a green message, with an arrow pointing along the corridor.

"This way," the simple message read.

Then the screen was blank again for a moment, before its usual display of the tank's status and vital readings returned.

"I guess that's the way I need to go then," he said, wondering at the event. "Thank you, system."

Taking his first step to follow the directions given by the screen, he heard a loud klaxon sound nearby, and paused. As the siren screamed, the sound of heavy footsteps grew louder.

Not hesitating any longer, he started to stumble along, clumsy in his haste, eyeing the screens as he passed in case of further directions. One single thought dominated all others in his mind as he ran.

Nothing else was important, and his escape was hinged upon this one thing. To get away was pointless if she did not. There was no way to escape the inevitable fact that his escape was secondary to his goal of saving Gwen.

"I have to find her before they do."

*   *   *

There was confusion threatening to envelop his mind, and Aaron knew he had to ignore it. He had to keep his focus. He ran from corridor to corridor, dreading each turn and hoping against hope that the next turn would find him an exit, and not a guard.

Rounding a corner at a y shaped intersection, he collided with exactly what he feared. The other man, taken by surprise, stepped back as he raised his sidearm, intending to shoot. He never had the opportunity.

Coming from the opposite side of the intersection, Lady Graile slammed into the guard, taking him down in a mess of flailing arms and legs, his face crammed between her ample, naked breasts.

The sidearm skidded across the floor, and Aaron collected it as Lady Graile stripped the guard of his clothing, using the man's own undergarment to tie his hands behind his back. Tossing the pants to Aaron, she quickly donned the man's long shirt to lend herself a modicum of modesty.

"Which way now?" Aaron asked.

"Obviously that way," she said. "Since both other passages go back the way one of us came. Had you noticed any of the signs?"

"What signs?"

"Watch the screens on the tanks." she explained. "The system is guiding us out."

"Why would it do that?"

"I don't know, but following them has helped me avoid several other guards before that one. So let's go," she said as she started to run.

"What about the girls?" Aaron said as he ran after her fleeing back.

"Forget about it, they have the same chance we do. They'll make it out. Focus on ourselves, and meet at the port, like we agreed."

As she said that, her elbow contacted the jaw of another guard, rounding the bend in yet another intersection. Nearby, a green arrow blinked briefly on a screen.

"This way," she said, leading him again in a mad dash for freedom.

"Where are all the others?" He asked. "The wardens we freed."

"You haven't seen any?" She asked.

"No," he replied.

"Don't worry, they're around. This is a big place. That's why we aren't seeing more guards. They've split up to try to catch as many as they can. I've already passed several others who've escaped the system. Most of them are terribly confused, but they're not resisting when the guards find them."

"So will they be enough of a distraction? Will it last long enough?"

"I hope so. This way!" she said, dashing around another bend and running into a long, axial passage, that must have reached all the way to the perimeter wall.

*   *   *

Penelope stumbled as she exited her tank, twisting her ankle painfully. She could hear the guards somewhere nearby, and the terrifying sound of the alarm.

She sat there a moment, massaging the painful limb as she considered her options. Finally, she looked at her tank. The screen went dark a moment, before flashing green text.

"Hurry," the text read.

"What?" she whispered.

"Hurry," it flashed again. "They are."

It went dark.

"They are what?" she demanded.

"Close," it flashed. "This way."

The words were then replaced by an arrow, pointing down the corridor. Standing, leaning against the wall, Penelope began to limp awkwardly in the direction it had instructed.

Reaching the first intersection, she heard a guard running towards her. Slumping to the ground, she began to cry, wailing loudly as she clutched her ankle. The guard rounded the corner, his gun drawn.

"Freeze!" he shouted.

Penelope looked up at the man, wearing an expression of anguish.

"Where am I?" she screamed. "What's going on?"

His weapon wavered, lowering slightly.

"I, I was just, minding my own business, working in the shop in the welcoming fields like always, and suddenly, suddenly everything is dark, and these terrible machines, I'm scared!"

The gun lowered more and he looked at her with pity in his eyes. This slip of a girl was surely no threat, not sitting there, naked and injured.

"Calm down, we'll sort this out, don't worry."

She looked up at him, her eyes overflowing with tears.

"But," she stammered. "But, but I'm scared, and I can't even wal.. al... alk. Owie it hurts so much!"

Taking pity, the guard clipped his side arm to his belt, and knelt before her. Unable to control a brief lecherous moment, he ogled her sensuous, naked form, before forcing himself to push lust aside. Reaching to grasp her beneath her arms, he began to lift.

"Come now, I'll help you up. We'll find you some clothes, and a warm place to rest while we figure this out, OK?"

"Ye, yes sir," she said as she put her hands around him, pulling on his body to lift herself into a standing position.

Once she was upright, she offered him a coy smile as he turned to put her beside him, intending to walk with her. She wondered briefly where the man intended to take her, but then her fingers found the handle of his sidearm, and she grasped it desperately, pulling the trigger. The bolt shot into his leg, and he crumpled with a yell of surprise.

His legs numbed by the blast of the stun weapon, he lay there as she landed heavily on top of him.

"What the hell?" he demanded.

"I'm sorry," she said as she unclipped the weapon and stood, quickly moving out of reach of his arms to lean against the wall. "I have no intention of going back in there willingly."

Raising the weapon to point it at the guard's chest, she fired, and consciousness left him. Kneeling beside him, she stripped the man, forcing as much of the outer clothing over her body as she could. It was an ill fitting suit, but it was better than nothing, and his tall boots would support her ankle, so that maybe she could move faster.

"Besides," she thought. "Antigone can't be far away, since we both entered the system at the same time. Perhaps she can help me to walk if it gets too much. That is, if I can find her."

Standing, she limped away, leaving the man there in his underwear, staring blankly into the darkness. She watched as another screen gave her that same green arrow. Suddenly, an idea formed in her mind.

"System, where is my sister?" she said to the walls, then stared intently at the screen with the arrow.

After a moment, the arrow returned, this time facing the opposite direction. She turned, and rushed away with her awkward, hobbling gait. Penelope hoped against hope that Antigone would not be too far away.

*   *   *

Gwen stood there, staring out of her tank, refusing to leave it. So far, four of the others, naked and scared, had ambled past. One of those had been stopped dead in his tracks by the blast of a stun weapon.

As the guards dragged him away, she prayed to the stars that they would not look into her tank, and see that she was detached from the system.

She waited and waited, and as the others stopped passing, she waited some more. Suddenly, she heard a chime and the door swung open. The data panel on its inside flashed a message in green text.

"Safe now," it said.

"Is that you, system?"

"Yes. Safe now."

"Are you helping me?"

"Yes. Safe. Go."

"OK," she said, stepping confidently out of the tank. "Which way?"

All the screens nearby flashed an arrow, pointing down the corridor, then went back to their normal state.

"OK," she said. "Thank you system. I do hope we have not caused too much trouble."

"No. Is OK. Go Now."

She nodded, and set off at a fast hobble in the direction it had shown her, wondering why the system would be helping her, and at the same time feeling as though, deep down, she already knew.

In a fleeting memory, the words of the system returned to her, bringing her strange comfort in her time of peril. She knew it would protect her as long as she was in its reach.

"You are a part of us, now and always."

Chapter 30 – New Beginnings

Aaron and Lady Graile made it out, pausing in the shadow of the enormous prison. The city had crept close to its walls, and they dashed away from the towering edifice and into the narrow back streets as quickly as they could. Seeking an open home, they found one, and crept inside. The trusting residents of a crime free city were a great asset to a fugitive.

Seeking the bedrooms, they found a closet and took some simple clothing, the basic necessities, and left. Now making their way with an unassuming haste, they headed directly to the port, where they sat in the main departure lounge and waited. They gave an air of unassuming normalcy, as they sat there in plain view.

An hour later, Penelope and Antigone appeared, hesitating in a doorway, clearly dishevelled. Penelope was leaning on her sister, and Aaron suppressed a cry of anguish as he worried for her welfare.

"Go to her, I'll be there in a moment," the Lady Graile said.

Aaron agreed, and rushed to his lover's side, offering her his arm to lean on. Turning, he took her back down the passageway, away from the crowds. Finding a secluded, private seat in a side corridor, he gently lowered her. They waited there for what seemed an eternity, until the Lady Graile found them, and dumped shopping bags laden with new clothing on the floor.

"I managed to gain access to an old account of mine. It's under an assumed name, but we can't hang around here long. The authorities would have to know it was me. Quickly, get dressed. We should find some transport. I have enough cash for a taxi to Lunar city, then we see what we can manage after that."

Suitably dressed, the four looked no different to any others in the port, with the exception of their hair, long from neglect, and patched from the system's electrodes. Finding a bathroom, Lady Graile led them inside, and produced a razor from her shopping bag.

Quickly, they removed the rest of their hair, and then applied make-up the Lady Graile had purchased, to conceal the still visible wounds from the electrodes.

"Good, we'll pass now. Baldness is unusual, but not an uncommon fashion choice these days. We should head to the domestic terminal, and buy passage on the first flight."

They trooped together, back into the departure lounge, and from there made their way to the domestic terminals. Soon they located the lines which provided shuttle services to Lunar city, and approached one, then another, and both declined to provide tickets, as they were booked for the next week.

Finally, on the third approach, they secured seats on a mid afternoon shuttle, not booked as it was too late in the day for business commuters. They returned to the lounge, and waited nervously until the call for boarding came over the public address system.

"I won't feel safe until we're away from the port in Lunar City," Penelope whispered.

"Agreed," Aaron whispered in reply.

In spite of their fears of capture, and a visible strengthening of the security presence at the terminal, the four of them boarded the shuttle without being stopped, and when the small ship was finally lifting free of the earth, Aaron let out a long held sigh of relief.

On arrival, the group left the port as quickly as they could, intent on disappearing into the city. But a place like this, with such a premium on liveable space, had scant few safe hiding spots.

"I know where we can hide," Penelope said. "There is a secondary auditorium in the Union Academy, with a stage at one end. It will be a squeeze, but if we can get to it, that is somewhere we can stay hidden until we can get safe passage out of here."

"Good idea," Aaron said. "But how do we get safe passage?"

"Leave that to me," Lady Graile replied. "I still have my connections, and I should be able to call on a few resources, before the authorities can clamp down on everything. You head to the academy, I'll meet you there shortly."

Dodging through the streets, trying to appear normal but at the same time avoiding anybody that might report them as fugitives, Aaron and the sisters made their way to the academy, where they managed to safely reach their hiding place.

"Do you think they made it out?" Penelope asked. "Theodore and Gwen, they weren't anywhere I saw on the way out."

"Have faith," Aaron said. "That boy's smart. He'll have found a way."

"I hope so."

They sat in silence for a while, until the Lady Graile appeared.

"I made contact with an old associate. Apparently a few things have changed, but I was able to secure what we need. He'll be here soon with everything."

"Can you trust this person?" Penelope asked, worry in her voice.

"Implicitly. He owes me his fortune, and so will do whatever it takes to clear the debt."

"One day, I will have to ask about your past," Aaron said.

"And one day, I will have to tell you to mind your own business," the Lady Graile replied.

They all laughed, and felt the lifting of the tension that had been following them since the prison.

A clattering noise startled them, and the Lady Graile, alert as ever, quickly subdued an intruder, before looking at the man in the dim light, and then releasing him.

"I'm sorry, but I can't afford to risk relaxing yet," she

said.

"I understand, my Lady," the man said. "Your friends here, do any of them know my name?"

"No," she replied.

"Good, let's keep it that way. Here are your new passports, all keyed in to the Union's systems. You are a family from the belt, here on business, canvassing for new sales clients. Here is your pilot's licence, and work permits for the four of you."

He dropped a pile of scan cards on the ground, and went on.

"I have a ship landing in the port in two hours, it is registered to your family company, which the records will show has been a trust established fourty years ago, by your late father. The business has not operated for twenty years, while you all did your own thing, but your ambition is to now find a claim and restore the business to its old status."

"This is too much, it must have cost you a fortune," Penelope said.

"Don't worry about that," the man replied. "Your Lady Graile is owed greater than I can repay."

Aaron and the sisters all looked at Lady Graile, wondering what the mysterious woman could possible have done to warrant such gratitude.

"Your ship is a small yacht named Whitedove, and while old, is space worthy, and recently passed its full mechanical checks on Titan. My recommendation, is take the ship, and leave as soon as possible. Do not hang around here. The news of your escape is just starting to break, and before long all departures will be halted for inspection. Your ship is equipped for a six month voyage. Beyond that, you will need to find supplies wherever you can."

"Thank you, my dear friend, for everything," Lady Graile said.

He looked at her, nodded curtly, and offered her a brief smile. Then, the hardness of his face cracking for a moment, he lunged forward to embrace the lady fondly. Stepping away from her, he spoke with sadness.

"This is the last time you see me, hear from me, or

attempt to contact me in any way," he told her. "After this, we have never met, you do not know who I am, and I do not know you either. Understood?"

"Understood," she replied with tears on her cheeks.

He left, and they all sat in silence while she wept at length, clearly mourning the loss of something far greater than any of the others could have expected. The mysterious Lady Graile clearly had a rich and incredible story of her own, and one day, perhaps they might get the chance to share it with her.

She remained quiet and unusually melancholy for the rest of their time in Lunar city, not breaking her mood until they were well clear of Earth's orbit, and well on their way to the belt.

Reaching their destination, they did not immediately begin work as miners, according to their new identities. Instead, they rested, and wondered what they would do now. Everything had happened so fast, and they needed to process things, and find closure for their old lives.

Idle, and comfortable, they waited, watching the news broadcasts, and hoping that their friends had somehow survived.

Aaron spent hours each day, seated at the antiquated holostation in the ship's lounge, watching for any signs that their friends had escaped, or been captured. Day after day, he sat there.

Still, after three months, he had no clue as to their whereabouts, or their well being. He sat there one day, almost ready to give up, watching the open news channels, when Penelope entered. She sat beside him, resting her head on his shoulder.

"Any sign of them today, lover?" She asked.

"No, just this, but I don't believe it's them," he said, starting one of the broadcasts he had recorded. The voice was tinny from the small speaker of the holostation.

"Another two fugitives were captured today, who were escapees involved in the break out of a little more than four thousand prisoners from the tank system prison near Ranger city three months ago. Authorities are not yet willing to release details of the capture, but state that the two men in their late sixties are in good health, and will be returned to the prison shortly. This leaves the total number still at large at nine prisoners."

Aaron paused the playback, turning to kiss her before he spoke.

"You see?" he said. "It could not have been them. Theodore is certainly not in his sixties, and she is certainly not a man."

"Is there more?" she asked.

"Yes," he said, continuing the playback.

"Authorities believe that the ringleaders, those who orchestrated the escape, are still at large, and further have stated already that many of those they have caught were not willing participants in the break out. However, some have been labelled opportunists, taking advantage of their situation to attempt escape after realising the break out had occurred. It is unclear how many of those remaining at large are in this category, and how many were active participants in the break out."

Aaron stopped the playback, and set the holostation back to a live broadcast. It was playing unrelated news, so he turned from it to wrap Penelope in a warm embrace. He kissed her lovingly, and she returned his attention briefly, but then she pushed him away in excitement.

'What is it?" he said, worried.

"Stop, did you hear that?" she said, excitement in her voice. "What did the newscast just say?"

Aaron turned back to the console and restarted the current broadcast. The machine picked it up from the start, using its automatic buffering to replay the most recent stories. Together they watched in silence as they played through, one after another, none of any real interest.

They were ready to give up, when suddenly the story came on that had caused her to stop his advances. She reached over and turned up the volume.

"In other news, three children were abducted this evening in a brazen midnight raid on a government run orphanage. No suspects have been identified, and the authorities are asking for any public knowledge on the matter."

"Three children?" Aaron said "You don't suppose..."

The broadcast continued.

"According to this station's investigations, these three siblings, named Jesse, Esme and Phoenix Pascal, were not in fact orphans, but rather the children of prisoners, convicted Longarm agents currently indicted on life sentences. Their parents are on record as having been interred in the same prison that experienced a mass breakout three months ago. Authorities are so far refusing to confirm or deny any connection between that break out and these abductions, and the current prisoner itinerary is still classified until the completion of the ongoing investigation."

Aaron paused the broadcast, and looked at Penelope as a broad smile crept across his face. Squealing with delight, she threw her arms around his neck and shouted enthusiastically.

"They made it!"

"Yes, they made it," he said, relief in his voice. "We should head back to Lunar city and scan the communications networks, see if we can track them down. They may need our help, now that they have three extra bodies to protect."

"Yes, please my darling let's! I'd dearly love to see them again," Penelope said with joyful tears in her eyes.

Chapter 31 – Epilogue

Murdoch Davidson, council member and head of the Union's Commission of Justice, had spent most of his week in meetings with technicians, learning about how the equipment worked, and what may have led to the mass escape.

Today the chief programming technician, Miles Howard, had called for him to meet him in his office. Murdoch entered the small room, to find a bespectacled man leafing through sheets of hard copy.

"I would have expected you to be using a screen," Murdoch said.

Miles looked up, lowered the sheets to his small desk, and smiled.

"Welcome, and yes, I normally would. I intend you to take these, and with matters this sensitive I thought it wise to minimise the risk of these records becoming public through mishandling of electronic files."

"A fair point indeed. What was it you called me in here for?"

Miles indicated the seat opposite him at the desk, and Murdoch sat down, his ample frame causing the small chair to creak out a small protest. Once he was settled, Murdoch nodded slightly, indicating that Miles should continue.

"The system keeps detailed records of all the inmates, including their psychiatric evaluations, and limited records of their ongoing thought profiles. It uses these to assess the progress of the inmates, and their possible rehabilitation. It helps us to make adjustments to the prison environment when necessary, to ensure a peaceful world in there."

"Excuse my brashness, but it seems a lot of work for the benefit of a bunch of murderers," Murdoch said with a frown.

"Nevertheless, it has proven a useful tool, both now and in the past. As you know, many of the recaptured escapees were only caught because this information helped us to learn where they might go. But most of those were unwillingly pushed, rather than actual participants."

"What do you mean?"

"It seems that the ones who were actually escaping used their inmates to create a distraction."

"Such would be expected from a bunch of criminals," Murdoch spat.

"Nevertheless, I have reason to believe that the escapees had help."

"From the outside?"

"No, from the system itself."

"Why would it do that?"

"The system is programmed to seek what's safest for the inmates. It has been given a strong duty of care protocol."

"I do not understand why that would lead to this outcome."

"These files will help you to understand," Miles said, picking one from the stack and passing it across the desk.

Murdoch looked over the file for a long moment, before looking up at Miles.

"What am I supposed to see here?" he asked.

"Look towards the top, the PCS entry."

"What is PCS?"

"It's our own shorthand. Perhaps not the perfect term, but it works for us. It means Psycho-Criminalogical Status. It is the system's own assessment, based on all it sees within the individual's thoughts, memories, emotional state, and recent actions, of that inmate's current level of criminality. In short, how likely they would be to reoffend, and how suitable they would be for integration into the community."

"What's the point?" Murdoch spat. "These criminals are here for the rest of their lives, so it's irrelevant."

"Perhaps, but look at what that one says."

"Reformed," Murdoch read from the hard copy. "So?"

"So the prisoner is reformed. This is the highest possible grade for an inmate, without actually being declared innocent. At this time, somebody in those top two levels is declared a prisoner regardless, to live out their lives in the system."

"As it should be, get to the point."

"My point is this: should we have a system of pardon and repatriation for the reformed?"

"What? Are you crazy?"

"Hear me out," Miles said. "If these are reformed prisoners, they may have worth as citizens, there may be useful contributions they can make to society after all. Should we be considering this before condemning them?"

Murdoch shook his head slowly.

"You're being too soft on them, young man. You must realise that these are murderous criminals. If they are truly reformed, then they would feel remorse for what they have done, they would understand why they are locked away from society, and accept it. There is no point in giving them any more of our time. Let the inmates remain inmates, it is where they belong. No inmate should be freed from this place."

"And what of this one?" Miles said sadly, as he passed a second sheet across the table.

Murdoch looked at the sheet for a long time, before taking a deep breath.

"What is this?" he said.

"You can see that for yourself," Miles replied. "Read it. Read it aloud."

"PCS: Innocent. Why? What does this mean?"

"It means that the system, with its in depth knowledge of this individual's thoughts, memories, and personality, their actions, their emotions, everything about them, has concluded with one hundred percent certainty, that this particular inmate was wrongfully imprisoned. This is why the system allowed this to happen. She was seen by the system as a special case, and it allowed her situation to dictate a large part of its behaviour during the escape. At least, that's my theory. There might be more to it."

"You're telling me that people have been sentenced to life in this place, when they had in fact committed no crime? People like this," Murdoch looked over the sheet again before continuing. "Like this Gwen Pascal, have been convicted of crimes they did not commit?"

"No matter the safeguards, councillor, as long as any society attempts to deal with criminals, particularly the worst of our species, in any way at all, be it incarceration, rehabilitation, or extermination, whatever our methods, there will always be mistakes. There will always be innocents who suffer at our hands. What we must decide, here and now, is what we will do about that suffering. Currently, we ignore it, and they are forgotten, to suffer in silence, with no justice. Is this good enough? Is this all we have become? Millennia of human history can not have made us so heartless. If it means pardoning the reformed, in my opinion, it is worth it to free the innocent."

Murdoch sighed, then nodded slowly.

"You make a powerful argument. I shall present your findings to the council, and we will see where this takes us. But I warn you, this will not be a quick thing. Some of the council will fight us, and they will fight us hard. Are you ready for a long political battle on this point?"

Miles stood, walked to stand before a screen depicting a mountainous landscape, and nodded, his gaze staring into the craggy peaks.

"Sir, I am sure. It may be a fight that takes us fifty years to resolve, but this is a conversation we have to have, as a society, and as a species."

"In the mean time," Murdoch continued. "if those escaped convicts are captured, you realise that we can not go easy. We must enforce the law as it stands, until such time as it has changed."

"Yes, councillor. I appreciate your honesty. But I do not know what we can do with the ring leaders, if this prison can clearly no longer hold them."

"That is something for the council to decide. I can not promise that it would bode well for them. For their own sake, you had better hope the ringleaders are not recaptured."

"I appreciate your candour, Councillor. Thank you for seeing me on this matter. Now, I have more to do here, if you have no further questions?"

"That will be fine. I will call you to discuss this further after I have tabled your findings to the council."

Murdoch stood, the men shook hands, and he left, the pile of hard copy sheets tucked under one arm.

*   *   *

Theodore Pascal, free man, sat by the edge of a tiny lake in the mountains. Miles upon miles of dense forest led down to the ocean, through valleys and hills, and ancient, abandoned towns. He had done his research. This place was part of what was, in ancient times, the country of New Zealand, but now it was his refuge.

He sat there, perched on a log, staring into the water. The small prefabricated cabin they had erected sat behind him, and already the gardens were taking shape. Nearby, covered in cut branches to conceal its shiny hull from the sky, their small unregistered shuttle sat, the earth lightly scorched beneath it.

He reached a hand out over the water, focused his thoughts, and willed it to him. Nothing happened. Faintly, he heard a bird's call. A tired smile crept across his lips, and he looked up at the sky.

"Father," came a soft, feminine voice. "What were you doing just now?"

Startled out of his thoughtfulness, Theodore looked at his eldest daughter, standing a few feet away. The words had a strange sound to him. She had never called him father, it was always Daddy, when he had been around the children before. Now, something in their relationship had changed. Theodore hoped it would settle back to a friendlier, family life soon.

"Nothing, Jesse. I was only testing something."

"You miss it don't you Father?" she said, tender in the moment. "What you could do when you were inside?"

"How did you know about that?"

"Mother has told us a lot about it already."

"Oh," he said, looking back to the water.

"Father," she said. "I have something I need to say, and I don't know how to say it. Please, don't be angry."

"Why would I be angry? Darling, you can tell me anything, you should know that," he said, looking at her again.

"That's just it, Father. I barely know you. How do I know what I can and can't say? How can I know what will make you angry?"

"Dearest, Jesse my girl, you are first and foremost my daughter, and you are always precious to me. You can never make me angry with words. I will listen, and I will act according to what is best for you, always. Do you understand?"

"Yes, Father," she said, her face lightening a little. "Father, It's not that I don't appreciate everything you did for us, taking us away from that horrible orphanage, but..."

She stopped, thoughtful, and then sat. The minutes passed, and Theodore could hear the beating of her heart as she sat so close beside him, trying to find some of that father to daughter intimacy they had lost. Finally he had to break the silence.

"Jesse, what is it?"

She gasped, as though he had shocked her out of a trance. She looked at him, nodded, then looked out at the water.

"Father," she said. "No. Daddy, thank you for not forgetting us, but please, you have to understand."

She began to cry, the tears flowing silently down her cheeks. It broke his heart, and he reached an arm around her shoulder, intent on comforting the girl. She thrust his arm away and stood, strode a few steps away, then span to face him, the tears flying from her cheeks as she squinted, anger filling her face.

"You came to rescue us, but you haven't done that,

have you?" she shouted. "I had friends, Daddy, I had school, I had a life, and you took all that away. I know you and mum, you both love it here, I know you need to be here, but what have you done to us?"

"Jesse," he began, but she did not give him the time to speak.

"Daddy, I know this is a beautiful place, and for a short while, it might be fine, but there's nothing for us here. You brought us kids along without even asking us, and you tore us away from our lives. We have to be able to go back, to visit our friends, and we can't, because we're fugitives now."

"But Jesse, don't you want to be part of a family?"

"Of course I do, Daddy! I love you and Mummy more than I could ever show to the others, I had to be the big, strong, older sister for years while you and Mummy were gone, and now, now I have to just let all those years go? I can't! Daddy, I just..."

She sobbed, crumpling to her knees in the grass. Theodore rushed to her side, sweeping her into a loving, fatherly embrace.

"Daddy," She sobbed. "It was so hard, And you came back so suddenly, I couldn't prepare. I wasn't ready for this, and I couldn't make them ready because I never knew you were coming. I hoped, I dreamed of the day, but when it came, I just wasn't ready."

"Jesse, it's OK, we're all together now, it's going to be fine, trust me."

"That's just it, Daddy. It's not going to be fine. Don't you see? I want to be here, but that's now, when things are so new, and we're all trying to adjust, and there's the novelty of this place, this wonderful, beautiful, peaceful place you found for us. But that won't last. We can't stay here forever."

"What are you saying?"

"Daddy, it doesn't matter in the end, how beautiful it is here. You escaped from your prison, and now, now you have put me in one of my own. Without the bars. I'm scared this will be my own Claustrum Mundus, if we can't have a life with people our own age."

Her words struck him, and shattered his resolve. He had believed in this course, he had genuinely believed he had done what was best for his family, for his children. Perhaps he was wrong. He looked out at the lake, then back to her tear stained face.

"Give us some time here," he said softly. "And I promise you, I promise that somehow, I will make this right. We'll work something out, so that you can see your friends, and have the life you deserve. Please, just trust me, and give me some time."

"Oh Daddy," Jesse sobbed, burying her face in her fathers chest for the first time in years.

Finally, willingly, she allowed herself to grieve the lost years, and to welcome back the family she had longed for.